Moonlit

Jadie Jones

WiDō Publishing • Salt Lake City

WiDō Publishing
Salt Lake City, Utah
www.widopublishing.com

Cover Design by Steven Novak
Book Design by Marny K. Parkin

Library of Congress Control Number: 2013932905

Print ISBN: 978-1-937178-33-8
Printed in the United States of America

For my husband
the reason this book came to fruition,
and the reason I believe in soul mates

Contents

Prologue

THE FIRST ANNIVERSARY OF MY FATHER'S DEATH WAS even harder on my mother. Back then, I thought she was haunted most by what she didn't know. I refused to blame her when she raged above me on our staircase that night, drunk and sad and angry. When she made me promise I'd never ride again. When she hurled a half-full bottle of vodka at my face and it exploded on the wooden stairs at my feet. I hadn't tried to get out of the way. She had just missed.

I wanted to tell her that knowledge was no solace, that what you know can burn inside you until there's nothing left but guilt and ash. I also wanted to protect her from losing the only piece of him she had left. So I didn't say a word.

1
Wildwood

VIRGINIA'S TREES LOOK LIKE THEY'RE BURNING. MOST of them blaze crimson or gold, but some still have a chokehold on their green. I wish they'd give it up already. Leaves are more beautiful when they're dying.

I've watched these trees turn through the windshield of my father's truck ten times. They are the only thing that seems to change around here. Unless you count the driveway. I swear there's a new crack in it each morning. This crumbling asphalt is the final stretch to Wildwood Farm—a place I'd consider home. A place I'd consider hell.

We moved here when I was eight. My father landed a job running Wildwood, a competitive horse farm in the Shenandoah Valley. That first morning we ate breakfast on top of an overturned cardboard box and he promised he'd show me how to put on a saddle. By the end of the day, I was tacking other people's horses for two dollars apiece. Travis Hightower was the kind of man that always kept his word.

"Tanzy, you're going be in heaven here," my dad said. If I close my eyes I can remember exactly the way his unshaven face looked when he said it. His sideways glance over his shoulder. The blue-gray plaid of his worn shirt. I'd never seen him so excited before.

I squeeze the cracked leather under my hands to distract myself from the sudden prick of tears. *There's no place for that this morning.* The truck's old steering wheel still has a groove at the top where he always rested his calloused hand. Sometimes it hurts to notice that spot. Other times it hurts worse not to.

Aromas of cedar and earth drift through the failing heater as I pull into the parking lot. Dana McDaniel's gloved hand raises over her shoulder in greeting as she spots my arrival. Her red quilted jacket doubles the size of her lean frame. A customary hoof-pick sticks out of her worn back pocket, and a utility knife that you can't see is tucked into the waist of her jeans. She runs Wildwood now. Days are better when she's here. She knows horses. Really knows them. Like I know them. *Like Dad knew them.* The thought makes my insides warm and then clench as thawing grief trickles a drop at a time into my veins. *It's just another day, Tanzy. Get on with it.*

Wildwood Farm is a symphony of motion. Boots and hooves march down the concrete aisle. A working horse tattoos a path on the dirt floor of the indoor arena, his steady trot like a heartbeat. Most of the time I fit here, I'm a note in this melody. But some days the song is too loud. Other days I don't hear it at all. Especially since—well, especially since…

"Happy birthday," Dana greets as I step inside her office door.

My mind bats her words away. It might be November 1st, but we both know there's no room for celebration anymore. She hands me coffee in a plastic cup. It hurts. I hold it tighter.

Only after a hard swallow can I speak. "First frost."

"There's a front coming through," she says, following my lead to a subject I can handle.

I guard my mouth with the cup and train my eyes straight ahead. She steals a couple of sideways glances at my face as we walk the rest of the way down the aisle in silence and pass through the open doorway at the other end of the barn. Wildwood's rolling pasture stretches out in front of us, still gray in the morning sun as the light reflects off the coating of frost.

"How's your mom?" Dana asks.

"She's fine."

We lean against the black rails, which are faded in places. *Dad would be out here with a brush and a can of paint as soon as he was done with the morning chores.* I don't say anything to Dana. She's doing the best she can.

I watch her over the rim of my cup. Dana's elfin features and bare skin make her appear ten years younger than other thirty-somethings I know. The red tints in her maple hair gleam in the bright sun. I envy its straightness. My fingers immediately tangle in my own shoulder-length chaos of brown hair that has once again escaped the ball cap I shove it under each morning.

"Hopewell could use a tune-up ride later on if you're free. He needs to be in top shape before we send him to Florida for the winter show season," she says.

My father purchased Hopewell six years ago as a gangly three year old and named him for my mother, Hope. Dad always knew talent when he saw it. Hopewell is nearly impossible to beat.

That's because he never showed against Moonlit. The sudden swell of pride is short lived because I can't think of Moonlit, my old show horse, without thinking about the day I walked to her stall and found it completely stripped down. My mother had sold Moonlit to a stranger for one dollar before the smell of her vodka had left my boots.

For weeks I didn't ride at all, determined to keep the promise I'd made my mother as I cleaned up the mess on the stairs. Then one night, a note left on my windshield read: *"Tee— Hopewell needs a ride before you go. —Dana."*

As soon as the barn was empty, I slid on to Hopewell's bare back and found the somewhere else I'd been searching for. So I ride at night now, under the cloak of darkness once everyone else leaves. Dana stays sometimes though. "You're wasting your talent," she's said more than once. I never answer.

"Hi y'all!" Kate Morris's chipper voice is a needle-stick to the comfortable quiet.

"Hey, Kate," Dana returns.

I offer a hollow smile. It's not that I don't like Kate. She's okay. But every time I'm around her my hands instinctively shove themselves into the pockets of my jeans so they don't instead leap to her blue eyes and claw them out.

"Your life can change any day," she says to me at least once a week. She likes to hand out sayings like they're free candy, but that one hits too close to home. My father said that once, too. I watched him die an hour later.

A high-pitched shriek emanates from the woods across the pasture. The eerie tones bleed together into a single, razor sharp sound. Almost like a whistle. It pulls at the deepest corner of my heart like metal to a magnet. I lean harder into the chill of the wooden fence.

"What is that?" Kate's voice is a whisper and her fingers guard her throat.

The cry fills the pasture and then fades into the gray morning. I ache to hear it again.

"Coyotes, maybe. It's about that time of year," Dana says, her face taut.

That didn't sound like any coyote I've ever heard. But Dana's been doing this a lot longer than me. She knows what she's talking about.

"Let's all be on the lookout. If you use the outdoor arena for lessons, walk with the students the whole way. Just to be safe. I need to make some calls." Dana turns on her heels for the barn.

I wouldn't want to be in her boots. Coyotes spell trouble for any farm, especially ones with potential food sitting in locked boxes like an all-night buffet. They hadn't been a problem here in years. Three years. *It's just a coincidence.* I push the thought down as quickly as it surfaced.

"Well, remember to seize the day," Kate chirps.

"Yeah. You too," I respond, somehow managing not to snarl. But I can't help glaring at her back as she hurries to catch up with Dana.

Once they disappear through the barn door my eyes move back to the pasture. The sun has begun to burn the frost off the grass in places, and the dark spots look like holes you could step into and never have to come back out of. Without a second thought, I pour out the rest of my coffee. The hot liquid sizzles in protest as it smashes against the frigid ground. But the hole it leaves is not big enough for me. Three years ago today.

The quiet solitude feels like it might swallow me whole. The skin on the back of my neck prickles with a familiar alarm; dread leaves a sour taste in my mouth. *There's nothing in those woods.* Before I can prove myself wrong, I retreat to the safety of the crowded barn.

"Tanzy! Phone for you," Dana calls from down the barn aisle.

"Who is it?" I ask as I approach her.

She shrugs. "He didn't say. Just that it was important."

He? What he would be calling me? The last man that called for me was a police officer who'd found my mother babbling incoherently by a water fountain in town a few months back. I hope she didn't try to drive somewhere again. I thought I hid her keys pretty well this time.

"You got a boyfriend you need to tell me about?" Dana teases before she hands me the phone.

"Right. When have I ever had time for one of those?" She gives me a playful swat before moving back to the center of the riding ring. "This is Tanzy," I say into the receiver. No one answers, but I can tell that someone is still on the other end. "Hello?"

"Be careful today," a man's voice whispers. The gravelly sound makes my ears hot and stirs at something under my ribs.

"What's that supposed to mean? Who is this?"

"Just please be careful. It's an important day," he repeats. His deep voice is thick with urgency. "I need you to be careful. I need you…"

"Who is this?" *Is this some kind of joke?* The restraint it takes to keep myself from yelling makes my words come out like a growl. Immediately, the line goes dead. I glare at the beeping receiver and then hang it up.

"Who was it, Tanzy?" Dana calls from the arena.

"Wrong number. Is Molly coming for her nine o'clock lesson?" I ask, changing the subject before she can tell that I'm lying.

"I just saw her mom pull up," Dana answers as she watches a student trot by.

"All right. I'll go get Winchester ready."

"Sounds good. Kate's first lesson cancelled so she's setting up a new jump course in the outdoor arena. I don't think there are any changes to your schedule today. I'll come find you between lessons if something comes up."

I nod a response and head for Winchester's stall, grateful for the time to clear my head. The caller's voice circles my brain like a shark. Every word echoes in my memory, the urgency in his voice even more clear than his short message: *Be careful today. It's an important day.*

Who else would remember the anniversary of Dad's death? And then the last thing the caller said: *I need you.* Needed me for what? Something about the word "need" in his voice sends a shiver down my spine and leaves me with a feeling I don't recognize at all.

The questions follow me into Winchester's stall. The big horse noses my pockets for mints as I knock off the grime with a stiff bristle brush and pick out his hooves. Our routine makes it easier to forget whoever was on the other end of the phone, and the prickly warmth finally leaves my skin. I quickly slide the saddle in place, fasten the bridle, and lead him out of his stall.

"Hi, Tanzy. Hi, Winchester," Molly Beck's mother greets us as we amble into the waiting area.

I always worry that her pastel sweater set or pearl earrings won't make it through a Saturday morning at the barn, but each week she leaves as prim and spotless as she came. Over time I've learned that she's much warmer than she looks. The way she watches Molly ride almost makes me believe in mother-daughter relationships again.

"Hi guys!" I call to them.

Molly grins, and skips toward me and her favorite horse. Mrs. Beck always outfits her daughter in perfect equestrian attire, down to her polished tall boots. And today is no exception. Her tan riding pants are crisp and clean, and her white fitted jacket is finished off with a pink, hand-sewn monogram. The only uncooperative feature is Molly's curly red hair, which pulls free from its tight braid in countless places.

"Do you want to lead Winchester to the outdoor arena?" I ask.

Her entire face lights up as she breaks into a big smile. "Can I?"

"Helmet first."

Molly dutifully slides it in place and snaps the buckle.

"All right, he's all yours," I say.

Winchester stands perfectly still as Molly sorts the reins in her hands and adjusts herself next to him.

"Have fun, sweetie. I need to go pay Dana for this month. I'll be down in just a few minutes," Mrs. Beck says.

"Okay, Mom." Molly gives her a little wave and then clucks to Winchester.

I start ahead of them down the barn aisle and steal a glance over my shoulder. The thousand pound horse dutifully follows his six-year-old charge. *That horse is worth his weight in gold.* We head for the lesson ring, nestled in the heart of the open pasture. I unlock the weathered metal gate. Molly and Winchester amble ahead of me and into the field.

"All is quiet," I whisper to myself, scanning the tree line for any signs of movement.

A low growl stops me in my tracks. I screen the width of the field, but the pasture is empty. *Get a grip. It's just in your head.* But the dizzying fear won't leave me. I can't shake the feeling that I'm being watched from the woods. I steal a reluctant glance at the first row of trees and my blood goes cold. A shadowed figure slides from behind a tall oak tree and steps into the light. Its frenzied form blurs as the empty black mass quivers like an angry sky before a lightning strike.

Just keep walking. My hands tremble. I shove them in my pockets. *It's not real. It will go away. Just like last time.*

But it doesn't disappear, and try as I might I can't look away as it slinks closer. The living darkness solidifies and takes shape. I can't breathe. My pulse pounds in my ears. A face emerges in sporadic flashes from the pulsating void. Its eyes glow brilliant white against the shuddering black.

Go away. Go away. Go away.

"Ms. Tanzy?" A faraway voice calls my name. "Ms. Tanzy!"

The second cry breaks through my daze. *Molly.* Everything moves in slow motion as I turn to face her. Winchester stands stone still. His brown eyes roll in their sockets. Molly glares down at his planted hooves. Winchester shifts his weight into his back legs.

"Molly, let go!" I yell. My feet feel magnetically connected to the ground as I take a heavy step forward. "Let him go!"

Both of her hands spring open. Winchester rears the instant he senses her release. His huge body rises over her small frame. All I can think to do is scream her name. I motion her to me with flailing arms.

Winchester reaches the crest of his climb and strikes at the air. His eyes never leave the oak tree. I focus all of my senses on Molly, who is a blur of pumping hands and stumbling feet as she closes the short distance between us.

I let out the breath I'd been holding as she flings her arms around my waist and buries her face in my jacket. Winchester lands, his hooves stabbing the ground still fresh with the imprint of Molly's boots. He spins and gallops back toward the closed gate, which is the lone barrier between him and the safety of the barn.

My stomach drops into my boots. "No!" The crack of my voice hangs in the air as he gathers and launches himself skyward.

2
Be careful what you wish for

FROM THE MOMENT WINCHESTER TAKES OFF I KNOW HE won't clear the top rail. The clang of his tucked knees against the rusty bar brings bile to the back of my tongue. His back legs catch in a sickening thud. I can't bear to watch, but I can't turn away.

Steel groans as his body tumbles sideways. The wood posts splinter as the hinges are stripped from their mounts. My heart stills in my chest as his body goes limp. The silence that follows is the worst sound by far. Half of me wills him to stand up, the other half steels myself for the chance that he never will.

I hold Molly tighter. *She can't see this. She's too young to see something like this.* Her heart thumps against my hip like a hummingbird. I focus on the racing beat to keep myself from falling apart on the spot.

Kate's hand is light as a feather on my shoulder. I hadn't heard her approach. We stand together in silence, forcing ourselves to wait because we both know that interfering too soon might do more harm than good. The two or three seconds it takes before Winchester begins to thrash his legs feel like hours.

He's alive!

"I need to get closer. I might be able to help him," I say quickly to Kate, who nods. "Molly, look at me," I whisper. Her eyes seek refuge in mine. Her cheeks shine where they are wet. "I need to go check on Winchester. Will you give Kate a hug for me? She's scared, too."

"Is he going to be okay?" Molly cries.

"I hope so," Kate says as she crouches down and reaches out for her. "Tanzy is going to go help him." Molly steps quickly into her open arms.

As I race back up the hill to Winchester, I have to fight the urge to glance over my shoulder and see if the shapeless creature still lingers in the trees.

I don't know what you are and I don't care. Just leave me alone!

I shove everything else from my mind as Winchester begins an unsteady climb to his feet. I move quietly to his side. He stands still as I strip the battered saddle from his trembling body. Out of the corner of my eye I see Kate and Molly carefully approach.

"I don't think he did any real damage." I can't help but worry that if I say it too loud it won't be true. The sound of racing footsteps makes Winchester spook, which is a good sign. Dana and Mrs. Beck rush through the open doorway.

"Is everyone okay? What happened?" Dana asks, not slowing until she puts a hand on her favorite horse.

Molly catches sight of her mother and runs for her open arms. Mrs. Beck drops to her knees. Her cream-colored pants meet the dirt without hesitation as she cradles Molly's head to her chest. For the first time in years, I wish my own mother was here. I wish she still hugged me like that. I can't remember the last time we touched each other at all.

I busy my shaking hands, running them along Winchester's sweaty shoulder. "Molly's fine, Mrs. Beck. Really scared, but she did great," I say. "She was a good listener and did exactly the right thing."

"What in the world happened?" Dana asks again, failing to keep the panic out of her voice.

"There was something moving in the woods." I risk a glance back into the field, but it's not there anymore. A sudden surge of anger collides with the cool sensation of relief and leaves me feeling ragged. "I couldn't really see what it was, but it was dark and moving toward us, kind of stalking us. Winchester saw it first."

"Coyotes?"

"No. I'm not sure. Maybe? I mean I guess it's the only explanation." *The only explanation you'll believe, anyway.*

Dana and Mrs. Beck respond in agreement. I say, "Mrs. Beck, I can't imagine how scary this is for you, but he really did try to take care of her in his own way. Horses have a flight-or-fight instinct that's almost impossible to control when they feel threatened."

"I know, Tanzy." She smiles weakly as she takes Molly's hand and climbs to her feet. The knees of her pants are soiled but she doesn't move to wipe them. She'd have to let go of Molly to do that. "Will he be okay?"

I can tell she doesn't really care, but I don't blame her. I still don't know where they buried my father's horse. "I think so. He'll probably need a little vacation." Winchester props one of his back legs and I make a mental note to run cold water on it.

"I'm going to call the vet just to be sure," Dana says, her cell phone already beside her ashen face.

As Dana talks to the veterinarian, my eyes move from Winchester's battered body to the twisted gate. Something had been out there, but it wasn't a coyote. That much I know for sure.

"What was Winchester scared of?" Molly's little voice braves from the sanctuary of her mother's arms.

"We're not sure. But he feels really bad about scaring us. I hope you can forgive him," I say earnestly as I crouch down to her level. She nods solemnly. "You handled a scary situation like a real pro."

"Molly, can you go pick out a wash stall for Winchester? I need to talk to Miss Tanzy and Miss Kate for a minute," Dana asks.

"Sure!" she exclaims and skips through the barn door. Mrs. Beck finally makes a couple of quick swipes at her pants and then hurries after her daughter.

"I can't believe that just happened," Dana starts once we're alone. She pulls her weathered hand out of her glove and presses too hard against her eyes. "Dr. Barrow is coming first thing in the morning to check Winchester over. We got really lucky here, girls. Let me know if you see anything else out of the ordinary."

She heads into the barn without waiting for us to respond. I stall to give Kate time to follow after her, but she doesn't. She absently chews on her lip as she toes at the dirt with boots that are too clean for my taste, no doubt searching her mental Rolodex for one of her quotes. I brace myself, willing my pulse to stay the same no matter what comes out of her mouth next. But nothing does.

"You okay?" I venture.

"Yeah," she says, but the shine in her eyes says otherwise. "You?"

"I'm glad he's okay." I avoid the real question altogether. I've finally started breathing normally again, and being honest with her or myself isn't going to help that.

We watch him nibble at the sparse grass for a minute longer and then make our way to the barn door. Winchester's hooves shuffle unevenly on the pavement.

"That was horrible," Kate whispers.

"Dana's right. We got lucky. That could've been a lot worse."

"I know. I think that's what scares me the most. I'm glad you were there. I wouldn't have known what to do."

"I'm glad you were there too. That was a first for all of us."

"No kidding. Your life can—" she starts.

"Kate, I know. For goodness sake, don't you think that I know exactly how fast my life can change?" I freeze, my hands clenched into fists at my side. The pounding in my head returns, and a painful pinch in my throat locks my jaw.

"Oh my God, Tanzy. I say that to you all the time. I'm so sorry. Of course you of all people would know that."

"Exactly."

Kate bites her lip as she glances at my face from the corners of her eyes. Her genuine distress makes my fingers uncoil. I'm still not happy about it, but I don't like seeing anyone upset at my expense. "It's okay. You didn't mean any harm."

"I really didn't." She slides her hands in her back pockets.

"We're good. Just forget about it, okay?"

"Okay." Kate gives me a timid smile and we round the corner to the wash racks.

"I picked a stall out for him," Molly says as she hops from one foot to the other, lightening the weight in my chest. Winchester's slow trip must have been torture for her. "I cleaned it out."

"Thank you so much, Molly. It's very important to keep cuts clean, so that was good thinking. Do you want to learn how to take care of a hurt horse?"

Molly breaks into a smile and steps dutifully to my side. I crouch down to examine the leg he props. She mimics me. Her face is so close to mine that I can feel her breath on my cheek. I talk to her about wrapping techniques as we cold hose and bandage his injured leg. Her eyes grow wide as I hand her a pair of latex gloves and ask her to help me inspect his open wounds. She is quickly able to recite the difference between punctures and lacerations. Kate watches, leaning against the wash stall. She offers praise as Molly helps wash out the cuts and pack a deeper wound with antibiotic ointment.

"All right, I think he's good as new," I say as we finish.

"That's so cool," Molly squeals. "Mom, look what I did!" She raises her hand triumphantly so Mrs. Beck can admire the neon yellow goop still clinging to the latex.

"Do you want to go get some hay for Winchester while I put him in his stall?" I ask as I stiffly climb to my feet. The surge of adrenaline has long since left me, and my muscles are tired and achy in its absence.

"Yeah! Mom, can I?"

"Of course, honey." Molly takes off for the hay shed. "Thank you so much, Tanzy," Mrs. Beck says. Her eyes linger on Molly's back as she clomps down the aisle.

"I thought it was important that she didn't go home scared. And I apologize in advance if she tries to doctor any of your pets."

Most importantly, I wanted to make sure November 1st doesn't mean for her what it does to me: the end. The unbidden thought gnaws on the surface of my heart. It takes everything I've got not to wince.

"I really appreciate it. Riding has been so good for her. I'm glad that she doesn't seem the least bit rattled," Mrs. Beck says with a shiver. "I'm doing my best to follow her example."

"She's a great kid. I'd hate for something like this to ruin horses for her."

"I don't think we have to worry about that. She seems to be just fine. I'm sure we'll see you next week," she says pointedly, which comes as a relief. Wildwood can't afford to lose a paying student right now.

"Ms. Dana says that she wants you to meet her in the office when you're done," Molly calls in a sing-song voice as she skips past us, clutching flakes of hay to her chest in a bear-hug.

"Thank you, Molly. We'll follow you to his stall," I laugh as I pluck a couple of stems from her hair.

Winchester moves stiffly down the aisle. The short trip takes twice as long as usual. He perks up as he spies the fresh pile of hay in the corner. Molly and her mother watch him eat a few bites before waving goodbye. Kate and I hang by his door a little longer to make sure he settles in okay before turning for Dana's office.

"Hey girls," Dana glances up from her computer screen. "I just got this community-watch email about several pets missing from the neighborhood that backs up to our pasture."

"So what does that mean?" Kate asks.

"It means we obviously have a coyote problem on our hands. I've cancelled all lessons for today, and we're bringing the horses in from the paddocks. Animal Control should be here soon to set traps. Until then we'll take care of ourselves," she says and points at the shotgun mounted on the wall behind her desk. "Kate, will you go post these signs on the information boards? I don't want anyone riding outside."

Kate nods and takes the sheets of paper from Dana before slipping from her office.

"You're doing a great job, you know," Dana says once her door clicks shut. The sound of her voice makes me jump. "I know it's hard. Being here. Especially today."

My cheeks flush with a cocktail of pride and grief. "It helps and it hurts. This is all I know how to do."

"Well, I'm glad you're here. You've got good instincts. And you're good in a crisis."

"Thanks. That means a lot." *If only you knew what I thought I saw out there. You'd have me committed.* The thought of the face in the shadow makes my stomach turn.

"And Tanzy, you're only eighteen. Don't be so hard on yourself." I shrug again. "You feel okay? You don't look so good."

"I'm pretty wiped."

"That was quite a morning."

"You aren't kidding."

"Feel free to take a nap in here," Dana says and gestures to the low-slung green futon in the corner. "I think it's your turn for night check, so a little shut-eye might not be such a bad idea."

"I'm fine. But maybe I'll do that." My answer sounds as weak as I feel, and she's obviously not buying it. She opens her mouth to say something but her phone rings in her hand. Relieved, I give her a wave and duck out of her office before she asks me a question I can't answer.

Although every cell in my brain begs me not to, I march past the broken gate, down the hill, and toward the tree line. *I am not crazy.* The fact that I can't convince myself is almost more than I can take, and a sudden swell of agitation tingles beneath my skin. A cold wind whips across the dry grass. The wild air has its own voice, wailing a sharp note that lingers in the darkest corners of my mind.

I draw in a deep breath and take a few steps closer to the trees. I could reach out and touch one if I wanted to. But my hands firmly stay in the warm cover of my pockets. Sunlight filters through the canopy of branches overhead and speckles the ground beneath, giving an ethereal dimension to the flat brown surface.

"See, Tanzy, nothing here," I whisper to myself.

I can't help but think of that prank call. *"Please be careful. It's an important day."* His words echo in my head, sending a wave of goose bumps down my arms. Part of me wishes he'd call back so I could give him a piece of my mind. But a bigger part of me just wants to hear his voice again. He didn't sound like anyone I know, but there was something so familiar about it, something about the way I felt with his voice in my ear.

It reminds me of something Dad used to say: "Don't get that mad unless it matters, Tanzy." The thought of my father makes me crash back to the present, staring into the same woods that took his life. I am so close to running back to the farm that my boots are the only part of me still facing the trees.

Tanzy Hightower, there is nothing out here to be scared of. You know plenty well the woods had nothing to do with it.

I clamp my arms protectively around myself and sit down in the tall grass. The cover instantly makes me feel safer and works at the knot in my middle. I pluck a few brittle stems from the cold ground and absently weave them together.

My mother showed me how to make bracelets out of this grass when I was a kid. We must have made a hundred. My father was happy to wear them each time I took one up to his office. I found them in a desk drawer after he died. He had saved every one of them. I swipe at a lone tear burning a trail down my face and drop the bracelet I braided on auto-pilot to the ground, wrestling against a sudden urge to bury it.

The skin on the back of my neck prickles. My eyes lift from the dirt to the knotted tangle of roots at the base of the trees. But my gaze won't venture higher, won't search the shadows. I do my best to mask a shudder and quickly head back to the barn, leaving the bracelet in the tall grass.

Hopewell whinnies as he hears footsteps approaching his stall. I pause by his door and let him nose at my fingers. "You and I are still on for a night ride, okay? There will be some normalcy to this day," I insist to us both.

He snorts and returns his focus to a pile of hay. I lean against the wall and stare across the indoor arena. The barn is completely still. It reminds me of a morgue, expectant and chilly. It reminds me that they never found his body, that we buried an empty coffin with a photograph and his dog tags inside. They said it would help us heal. They lied.

A weary defeat settles on my shoulders. I'm usually better at fighting it off. But I'm tired and it's so heavy this time.

I stifle a bitter sob, thankful that Hopewell is the only witness. *A quick nap isn't such a bad idea. Maybe it'll help me pull myself together.* After another look around confirms that I'm alone, I head to Dana's office, slip inside, and close the door.

3
Lucas

Pardon me." a deep voice breaks through the crushing black.

My eyes burst open, and I draw in a sharp breath as the wail of agony echoing in my head fades away an octave at a time. A towering figure leans halfway into Dana's office.

I jolt upright and my hands fly to my tangled mess of hair. "I'm sorry. Are you with animal control?" I ask, making every attempt to regain a shred of professionalism as I pull my hair back in a ponytail.

"I'm Lucas," he answers.

I stare back without responding. He has to duck to fit inside the door. His eyes are wide set and almost completely black. I search for a delineation between his iris and his pupil but find none. The muscles of his well-toned arms are visible through his fitted black shirt. His square jaw is set and strong. Two parallel white lines run several inches across his left cheekbone, marring his tan face. I have to resist a startling urge to touch them.

My eyes move from the scars to his dark gaze. We lock stares for only a moment, but it's enough to make the air freeze in my lungs. He drops his eyes to the hollow between my collar bones. Even though my heavy jacket nearly covers up to my chin, I reflexively move my hands to the hole his stare is making.

"Can I help you, Lucas?" I finally manage, a chilly fear working its way down my spine.

"Actually, I was just checking on you."

"Why?" My reply comes quickly. I bite down on my lip to keep any other runaway thoughts from spilling out.

The slight smile that plays across his face makes my stomach tingle. *Butterflies. I've never understood that expression until just now.*

"I understand you've had a rather interesting day." His eyes narrow as he says it.

He knows. Instant panic makes my heart hammer beneath my ribs.

"Well, the manager is in the pasture with the other Animal Control officers and she's probably who you'll need to see," I say as casually as I can. "You're welcome to wait in the lobby by the wash racks. It's right down the hall. Can't miss it." His silence hangs in the air between us as he stares down at me. "And I'm fine, thanks. Never better."

His eyes linger on my face for another couple of seconds and then he turns to stare at something in the barn aisle. I use the opportunity to scan the full length of his towering stature. His black shirt is tucked into a pair of jeans and his boots are caked with mud. *I like you better already.* And whatever it is that I'm feeling for him, I can't help but admit that I like that, too. Lucas's eyes burn holes in the top of my head. I hesitate a second longer before meeting his gaze, afraid I'll get locked inside of it again.

"Be seeing you," Lucas says the moment I look up, and then he retracts his looming body from the doorway.

The door clicks shut before I have time to respond.

"Be seeing you," I echo quietly to the empty office.

Will I? I hope so. The thought comes as a shock. But I can't deny it. *Get a grip. I mean he wasn't hard to look at, but you've known him all of two minutes. And "known" is an overstatement.* Still, I can't help but wonder what he might say if I asked him to come to lunch with me and Dana.

What time is it? Shouldn't she be back by now? I round Dana's desk and jiggle the computer mouse. The old machine staggers to life. The small print in the corner of the screen reads seven thirty. *That can't be right.* I move the mouse again and wait for the screen to unfreeze. Seven thirty one.

My eyes scan the rest of her office. No daylight peeks under the closed door. Dana's keys aren't on the hook. The barn is too quiet. *Did I really sleep that long?* I pull open the door. Taped to it is a piece of paper with Dana's scrawled handwriting:

"T— *Animal Control found something. Will fill you in tomorrow. I'm glad you're getting some rest. Be safe. I'll see you in the morning.* —D"

I fold the piece of paper and tuck it into the back pocket of my worn jeans. *If Animal Control has already come and gone, who was that?* The question makes the hair on the back of my neck stand up. I replay our conversation in my whirling brain. *He said he was checking on me.* I can't shake the thought of his dark eyes. And those scars. My pulse quickens at the flash of his face across my mind. *What if he's still here?* Even though my mouth is bone dry, I force a swallow.

I slip out of the office and creep along the aisle wall to the end of the indoor arena. Most of the barn is visible from there. Careful only to expose the top of my head, I watch across the expanse of the barn for any movement. But the farm is perfectly still.

"Nope. Nothing here," I whisper to myself.

But why do I feel like I want him to be here? The earlier tingles return along the curve of my neck and to the spot above my sternum—the place Lucas couldn't stop staring at. I dismiss the thoughts as quickly as possible and head to the parking lot, empty except for Dad's truck.

The new night is clear and bright, the full moon putting off enough light to give me a shadow. *A perfect night for a ride.* I remember the promise I'd made Hopewell earlier in the day—a promise I'd made myself about doing something normal. Being normal. I turn in a slow circle and hunt for a gut reaction. *You should stay. It's not like Mom's got dinner waiting or anything.* The thought of sailing atop Hopewell's powerful gallop lifts my rattled spirit.

"What's the worst that could happen?" I challenge the night air.

I think this day has already had its share of crazy. It owes me. I pocket my keys and walk briskly back inside, determined to hold tight to this rogue wave of enthusiasm. Without another thought, I stop by the tack room, scoop up my saddle, and head straight for Hopewell's stall.

4
The worst that could happen

"Did you think I'd forgotten about you?" I fish for the peppermint in my pocket that Hopewell has come to expect. He noses my chest, impatient. "We'll play it safe tonight, okay?" I say softly as I give him the treat and slide into his stall.

His salty scent works like a salve on my frayed nerves. I inhale deeply, marveling at the welcome silence in my mind. I move the curry comb in firm circles along his muscled body, bringing loose hair and dirt to the surface. My mind shifts into auto-pilot and the rest of the world slips away as I brush the grime from his coat, slide the tack in place, and lead Hopewell from his stall. The sounds of his steel shoes against the concrete aisle echo across the quiet barn. My fingers methodically secure my helmet, and I swing into the saddle.

The glow from the barn quickly dissolves into the inky night. Not a shred of it accompanies us past the mangled gate. But the dark offers little relief from the shadows that plague me in the light of day. The full moon casts a blue glow over the rolling field, making the dark places that sway in the steady breeze look alive. I release the breath I'd been holding as we near the riding ring. Hopewell stands still as I lean from the saddle to let us through the gate.

Once we're closed inside the safety of the lit arena, I take a quick scan of the tree line. The woods and their shadows are still.

"Paranoid," I say, unwilling to admit to myself that it sounds too much like a dare as it drifts across the empty pasture.

I cluck to Hopewell and he strikes off in a floating trot. He stretches his neck and lets out a snort. We track a figure-eight pattern across the broad arena and then I move him up into a canter. His three-beat gait feels like flying. My eyes close in bliss as we sail down the long side of the ring. And then, a break in rhythm. The next two beats come too fast and his typically light step pounds at the ground. My muscles clench, locking my seat into the tack, and my eyes fly open.

"Easy, Hope. Easy."

His pulse skyrockets, thumping through the saddle. I search the dark in a long sweep, anxious to catch sight of something I can define scurrying in the brush. But the field is empty.

"I don't see anything." Panic raises my voice to an unfamiliar octave and every muscle tenses with adrenaline.

Suddenly, he charges for the railing, twisting his head so far to the inside of the ring that I can see the rolling whites of his eyes. Whatever is scaring him is in here with us.

I brace myself in the tack and chance a look behind us. Horror charges through my body as I lock eyes with a dark, ghastly creature slinking along behind us. It lowers its saber head and opens a pair of wide, capable jaws. My breath stills in my throat as it lunges from its crouch. Hopewell spins and bucks, kicking the beast square in the chest and throwing me onto his neck.

Don't fall! I cling to his mane as I try to right myself, but I can't get my feet back in the stirrups.

Hopewell leaps into a gallop and races toward the end of the ring. The distance between us and the fence evaporates in seconds. I push him forward, silently begging him to ignore the routine barrier. He powers off the ground and sails over the rail. I sit up as he lands, and steer him toward the barn. Without warning, he leaps sideways tossing me airborne. I cry out as I land hard in the saddle.

Another animal races toward us from the side. The first creature is closing in from behind.

Dad! Help me! The instinctive prayer makes me feel all the more desperate as helplessness squeezes my throat. *Trust him,* my father's voice washes over my shattered mind. Putting all of my faith in Hopewell's instincts, I release the pressure on the reins.

"Go, go!" I yell, blindly kicking him forward.

Hopewell wheels away from the lights of the farm and gallops toward the trees. The two creatures cackle at each other as they fall in line behind us.

We rip through the dark woods. The branches claw at us, but Hopewell charges on. I know the pasture fencing must be up ahead, reinforced with steel mesh and over five feet high. With no clear place to take off or land, jumping may be more dangerous than whatever is chasing us through these woods. Angry tears leak from my eyes and are then torn from my cheeks by the frigid wind. I fight to ignore the trapped feeling, clinging to Hopewell's mane as he pushes himself even faster.

Moonlight sporadically shoots through the wooded canopy, betraying our dark cover. Hopewell sees the fence just in time to make a hard turn to avoid crashing into it and then gallops flat out alongside it.

But we're not alone. A dark streak gives chase, staying cloaked in the shadows of the trees. Hopewell's right ear swivels back and forth, listening to it close in. I focus on the steady rhythm of air blowing out of his nose like a freight train. His head flings back, nearly cracking me in the face. A scream roars through my parted lips and tears the night in half as another black creature leaps at us head on, claws outstretched and huge jaws open in a wicked grin. Hopewell stumbles and then gathers.

"No!" My voice is shrill with panic as Hopewell flings himself sideways over the five-foot fencing. I wrap my arms around his neck and squeeze my eyes shut as my left leg crushes between his sliding body and the fence rail. Sounds of splintering wood fill my ears.

His legs buckle on the other side and his body flips above me as we roll across the hard earth. The saddle smashes into my face. Blood and leather are hot and salty in my mouth. But I feel no pain, and though I'm sure I'm screaming I don't hear it. A rush of cold air stings like a slap in the face as I am flung free from the heat of his back. Hopewell's labored breathing sounds somewhere ahead of me. I try to call out to him but no sound comes. I spit out blood as it drips steadily into my mouth.

Have to get up. Have to keep moving. But I can barely lift my head, my body still writhing in agony as the air slowly returns to my lungs. My eyes train on the gaping hole in the mangled fence. The panther-like creatures gingerly tread across the broken boards and move silently toward me. My brain commands my body to crawl away but only my right arm responds. The other limbs answer with searing heat.

One of the creatures is within inches of me. The smell of decay is heavy and metallic on its breath. Darkness creeps across the corners of my eyes. The grunts of Hopewell struggling to stand work to ignite any fight left in me. But the shadows win.

5
Lucky

I COUGH AND ROLL TO MY SIDE. MY MOUTH IS FILLED with dirt. I reach inside to wipe the grit from my tongue. I climb to my feet, which are bare, and shield my eyes with my hands so I can see into the distance. My white linen dress is a stark contrast against the endless, rust-colored desert. I turn in a slow circle, surveying my surroundings. And then, a flash of gray. Several faces spin in the sky above me. I close my eyes, take in a breath, and open them again. The faces have left. Cool relief washes over my skin.

Movement in the distance catches my attention. My voice makes a cry that is simultaneously familiar and foreign to my ears. I walk toward the motion, which becomes more distinct by the second. Lucas comes to me, relaxed and unhurried, a bittersweet smile lining his tan face.

"I want to stay here," I say.

"Do you know where you are?" he asks. I shake my head. "Do you know who you are?" Before I can answer, a murmur of voices sounds from overhead like threatening thunder.

"We're losing her again," I hear. My eyes snap toward the sky and a warning hisses through my bared teeth. Another wave of voices yells from behind me. They sound closer now. I whirl and crouch low to the ground.

"Get the crash cart," a male voice calls. A searing white circle of light appears inches from my face. My eyelids snap shut. Lucas takes my hand in his.

"Charge to two hundred," another voice batters against my brain.

"Leave me alone," I scream back.

"It's okay, Spera. It's time," he reassures me, his mouth so close to my ear that his lips brush my skin.

"Clear!" a voice booms. A bolt of lightning screams down from the blue sky and strikes the ground only inches from my feet. Lucas turns his sad, dark eyes to mine and squeezes my fingers in his big hand.

"Be seeing you," he whispers. Instantly I am flying, falling upwards into a sinking black.

The total void begins to liquefy, the inky darkness pressing on my skin, filling my mouth. I try to lift my hand to wipe it away, but it won't budge. *You're dreaming. Open your eyes.* But they won't open, glued together by whatever sticky substance I'm covered in. Behind my eyelids, my eyes begin to burn as desperate tears pool across their surfaces.

Wake up!

Slowly, the weight dissipates along with the darkness, fading into a soft gray. Sensations come back one by one. But all of them hurt. Someone is touching my hand. *Lucas?* My eyelids flutter as I work to make them stay open. Dana's sing-song voice floats into my ears. *Please be real.* Her pensive face finally comes into focus. I draw in a deep breath to keep the tears at bay. The air moving down my throat and into my lungs feels like it's splintering my ribcage. *What's happening to me?*

"Dana?" I rasp.

Am I still in her office? Was that all a bad dream?

"You're awake!" Her head falls into my lap. The pressure floods my entire body with pain and makes me cry out.

"Oh I'm so sorry," Dana sits back from me, her face crumpled with worry. She reaches a worn hand across my face and swipes a messy lock of hair from my eyes. An emerald semi-circle about the size of a marble glows in the palm of her hand. The color looks alive, like she'd caught a lightning bug. I gasp as it passes within inches of my face. Up close I can tell that it's in the shape of a horseshoe.

"Am I hurting you?" she asks, alarmed by my reaction. She sits back and rests her hands palm-down on her knees. If that weird glowing thing is still there, I can't see it.

"Where am I?" The grayish room comes completely into focus. The dismal wallpaper is checkered with handmade posters. Words like "get well" and "feel better" leap out at me from the bright paper. And my name. Countless emotions swell in my chest and rise in my throat. She doesn't have to tell me where I am anymore, but I let her.

"You're in the hospital. UVA Medical."

"What's wrong with me?" My eyes move from the cheery posters to the suit of plaster that covers most of my body.

"Pretty much everything" is all she can manage to say before her voice cracks.

"What happened?" *What's the last thing I can remember? Meeting that man from Animal Control— Lucas. But he wasn't with Animal Control. Why was he there?*

"You don't remember?"

"Don't worry, Dana," a man interjects calmly from the open doorway. I see the electric blue glowing from the crevice of his loosely clasped hands. "Most trauma patients never remember what they went through. We think it's the mind's way of protecting itself."

The shrink they made me see right after Dad died said something similar when I couldn't explain what caused the accident. I'm glad Mom never made me go back. Oh, God. Mom. This will completely destroy her.

"Dana, you didn't tell—" I start, suddenly panicked.

"Of course not," Dana cuts me off, reading my mind. "I didn't want to alarm her unless it was absolutely necessary since she's out of the country on mission work," she says pointedly. Her eyes dart to the man in blue scrubs and back to me. "Oh my God, Tee. You're so lucky." She chokes on her words and dissolves into tears.

"Tee? You haven't called me that since I was a kid," I whisper and try my best to give her a reassuring smile. But it feels lopsided.

"Dana is a good friend. She's barely left your side," the man says and steps to the foot of my bed. He looks younger up close. Too young to be a doctor. Unless he's some kind of prodigy.

Who are you?

His eyes are the same sapphire blue as the glow I won't acknowledge in his hands. But I could look at his eyes all day. They're incredible. I catch myself staring straight into them. *There go the butterflies again. Second time ever.* Of course I can't think about these butterflies without thinking about the first. *For all you know Lucas was just part of a very bad dream.*

"She's the best." I reach out for her with my right hand, the only part of me that isn't weighted down by a cast. "I can't believe someone found me. Who found me out there?"

"One of the firemen. Thank goodness he noticed your truck. I never should've left you in my office. I just couldn't bear to wake you."

"Fireman? Why was a fireman there?"

"She doesn't remember the fire?" Dana pleads with the guy in scrubs.

"It's to be expected, Dana," he reassures her.

"What fire? Tell me what happened," I demand, instantly more alert. The jumbled memory of being chased through the woods floods my battered brain. I press my free hand hard into my eyes as a sudden headache slices between my eyes. "Is Hopewell okay?" I ask through clenched teeth.

"I can't do this," she says and stands up to put more distance between her and my questions.

"Dana?" I plead.

"What if it's too soon to tell her?" she asks, turning away from me.

"I'm right here! Don't talk like I'm not here!"

"She's stable, Dana. She's awake. She's asking questions. She's proven that she's a tough girl," he answers.

I close my eyes and my focus on the last moments that I can remember. *Hopewell jumping the fence. Trying to crawl away from those things. There was no smoke. No one was there but me. How could a fire start? What am I forgetting?*

"How did the fire start?" I ask, desperate to thread the pieces together.

"They're still investigating. There's no one point of origin, so the inspector said that it's going to be harder to tell. But they're not ruling out arson," Dana says.

"There was no one there. Well except—" An invisible finger jabs at my sore ribs and cuts me off. *Lucas. Who probably wasn't even real.*

Dana's face stares plainly into mine as she waits.

"Me. And the horses, of course," I finish. *If he was real I don't know enough about him to be helpful. And if he's not they might lock me in the psych ward and throw away the key.*

Dana collapses limply into the chair. "They're gone, Tanzy," she sobs.

"Who's gone?"

"The horses. All of them."

"They died?" I shriek.

"No, they can't find them. No remains, no bodies, no nothing. They're considering some kind of mass-theft. And then maybe whoever stole them set the farm on fire to erase any evidence. That's the theory they're working on now, anyway," she says, flailing angrily in the stiff chair.

"But Hopewell, he was right there. He was hurt, but he was alive," I answer, distracted as a tinge of orange burns away the green that I'm imagining in Dana's hand. "Did I hit my head?"

"That's an understatement. You had very serious swelling on your brain," the doctor says.

"I'm seeing things. Weird colors. In strange places."

"With the trauma you sustained to your brain, I have no doubt that you'll be seeing halos or have other abnormalities with your vision for at least the next few weeks. And you should prepare yourself to accept that some of it may be permanent. You're a very lucky girl."

"Yeah, I was sure we were goners," I said, shivering under a pile of faded blue blankets.

"What about Hopewell? Did someone hurt him? What do you remember?" Dana pleads.

"We crashed—" Another jolt sizzles through me like I grabbed an electric fence. "A jump. It was a bad distance. A bad take off. Hopewell clipped the jump and fell. I guess that's the last thing I remember." Not a complete lie, but not the whole truth either. The air around me relaxes.

"That makes sense," the doctor muses.

"It does?"

"If you suffered a concussion in the fall, and then went to sleep in Dana's office, you may have lapsed into a coma. Which is likely why you slept through the fire. Sleeping after any kind of head trauma is never a good idea," he lectures.

"I'll try to remember that next time," I answer dryly.

"That can't be right. How did she get herself back to the office if she broke her legs when she fell?"

"Dana, we don't know what to attribute to the fall and what happened when the roof collapsed." He keeps his voice kind and objective.

"The roof collapsed?" I gasp, the air leaving my lungs in a painful rush. Their faces turn back to me. New tears leak from Dana's puffy eyes.

"Tanzy, just relax." The doctor gives my shoulder a reassuring squeeze. "You've been unconscious for over a week. We're just glad you're talking. Don't stress yourself over what you can't remember. You know who you are and that's a great start."

As he lets his hand drop the back of his fingers barely brush the tops of mine. The contact of skin on skin lasts less than a second, but it sends a surge of electricity through my sore body. My eyes swell in their sockets and my pulse surges beneath my skin.

"Who are you?" I ask, more sternly than I mean to.

He smiles anyway, locking his eyes on mine. "I'm Ryan."

"Are you a doctor?"

"No. I've got a long way to go before I'm a doctor. I'm shadowing Dr. Andrews as a student intern. I want to specialize in neurosurgery, and he's the best."

"How long will you be here?"

"Through the holidays. Dr. Andrews says the ER is always crazy during the holidays, so it would be a good time for him to have an extra pair of hands because the hospital staff gets spread so thin. Normally interns aren't allowed to do anything by themselves except grab coffee for the doctors. But he's been so busy that he has me check on his patients when he's in the operating room for long stretches of time. Consider me a glorified messenger. I can't wait to tell him that you're conscious. He's not going to believe it. He was sure we'd be spending Christmas with you."

"How long am I going to be here?" My clenched hands go cold and clammy.

"It all depends on your progress. Dr. Andrews said that he has never seen anything like you. The game plan for now is to take it one day at a time. But I do know that the best thing you can do is rest."

"I feel really groggy." The admission makes it all the more true. I lean back against my flimsy pillow, my head too heavy to hold up any longer.

"I know you just came to but you should try to get some rest. I'll let Dr. Andrews know you're awake. He'll want to see you as soon as he's out of surgery. And he's probably going to run a lot of tests." He turns for the door.

"Will you come back with him?" *I can't believe I just asked that out loud.*

"I'm afraid you're stuck with me, Tanzy," he grins. "Dr. Andrews assigned me to you for the duration of my stay here. You can call the nurses' station any time, day or night, and have me paged. Or Dr. Andrews. He is the head of neurosurgery here. Consider us on speed dial."

"I have the head of neurosurgery on speed dial? That's probably not a good sign."

"Depends on how you look at it. Better than a mortician." His pager beeps on his hip. He glances down at the message and ducks out without saying goodbye.

"That guy has a sick sense of humor," I muse aloud.

"He's been really nice," Dana says.

"Dana, why don't you go home and get some sleep. It sounds like I'm going to be here for a while so think of something creative to tell my mother," I say, trying to lighten the mood.

"She thinks you're in Florida with Kate checking out colleges."

"Colleges? But..."

"Don't worry. She bought it. I wasn't sure how she would ... We're making sure she doesn't find out about any of this," she explains. "I'm just glad you're eighteen. They've asked questions about your mom. I told them she's on a six-month mission trip in Uganda and is impossible to reach. So do me a solid and stick with that story."

"Uganda? You're fast on your feet." I make an attempt to laugh but it comes out more like a cough.

She shrugs and rubs her red eyes.

"Go home, Dana. I'll be fine. And I think you might look worse than me."

She raises an eyebrow in mock offense and then gives me a grateful smile. "I think I'll take you up on that. I need to see what's going on at Wildwood anyway."

"Will you thank everyone for me? This is really too much," I say, waving at the homemade signs with my good hand.

"You got it." She gives me one last half smile before she leaves.

I sigh and look myself over. My neck is braced. My left arm is in a cast from my knuckles to my shoulder, and both of my legs are in casts. *Do I have one of those marks too?* I nervously turn over my right hand. *Nothing.* I try to check my left hand, but I can't rotate my arm enough to get a good look.

A quiet knock makes me look up. A woman I've never met waves at me from the doorway. Her pristine business attire rules out that she's from Wildwood. *Maybe she's with the billing department. I'm sure none of this is cheap.* A reddish gold hoof print shimmers in her palm.

"Go away already," I cry out and rub my eyes with my good hand.

"I'm sorry, would you rather be alone?" she asks. Her lyrical voice is as much of a shock as the green of her eyes, which are the same color as spring leaves in a thunderstorm. A lock of honey blond hair falls in front of her face. She reaches up to brush it behind a small ear.

"No, it's not you. It's a long story."

"I'm glad to see you're finally awake." Her southern accent makes her words long and soft.

"Are you with billing?" I ask. I can't imagine even how much this is going to cost.

"Oh, no," she laughs. "I'm Vanessa Andrews. My husband is Dr. Andrews, one of your doctors. When he's on the night shift I sometimes get a little spooked in our house, so I come here and read to the long-term patients. Studies show it helps with recovery."

"Did you read to me?"

"I did. Mostly trash. You know, tabloids, gossip magazines."

"I don't really keep up with that stuff." My well-practiced tendency to keep people at arm's length responds before I can stop it. Her pretty face falls and she clutches a tabloid magazine to her chest. "Sorry, I didn't mean that. It's just been a bad day. Well, kind of a good day, I guess. I mean, I woke up, right? But bad, too. It's hard to explain," I flounder.

"No, I completely understand. Yes, you're awake and alive. But now you have to deal with everything," she says solemnly as she moves to the side of my bed. "Life is not for the faint of heart," she adds with a wink.

I stifle a gasp at my father's familiar words, something he used to say to me any time I complained. I barely know Dr. Andrews's wife, but immediately I have to stop myself from trying to give her a one-armed hug. "That's really nice of you to spend time with people you don't know."

"Well, it's selfish, too." She sits lightly on my bed. "Everyone's been very interested in your case. It's all my husband talks about when he gets home. So I thought I'd come see what all the fuss was about."

"Why is it so interesting?"

"Well, I don't understand all the doctor lingo they use when they talk about you. But from what I've heard, there's no reason you should have survived. Your heart kept failing. They shocked you multiple times and gave you doses of epinephrine, but nothing worked. You died officially. For several minutes. But Dr. Metcher wasn't willing to give up. He gave my husband some kind of medicine from his own country. Nothing else had worked and David, my husband, he gets so emotionally involved in his patients, especially the young ones. So he was willing to try anything. And he idolizes Dr. Metcher. He's a legend. Anyway, David said the instant the medicine entered your vein your heart restarted."

"What did he give me? And why don't we have it here?"

"No one knows. Dr. Metcher said the formula is a closely guarded secret. He wouldn't even tell my husband what they call it. Just that it's a kind of blood substitute, and it would help you make your own red blood cells faster."

"They have no idea what he gave me?" I ask slowly.

"You were one hundred percent dead. They'd called your official time of death and everything. Since he gave it to you after you died the legal stuff gets a little gray. I wasn't supposed to tell you any of that, actually. I don't know what made me tell you. So please don't say anything." She winces.

"I don't think anyone would believe me if I did. Or care, since I'm alive. And I wasn't. Wow, that's going to take some getting used to."

The weight of it makes me squirm. I scan the room to distract myself. A blue square of fabric is draped over a thin box on the wall.

"What's that?" I ask. She clears her throat and her eyes find the floor. "It's a mirror, isn't it?"

"It is. They covered it." She makes her voice matter-of-fact.

"Do I look that bad?"

"Well, you're still pretty bruised and swollen, but you're a whole lot better than you were a week ago. That's something my husband talks about too. How fast you're recovering. Especially since you lost so much blood. He said he's never seen a surgical site heal so quickly. I think it's safe to say that every staff member in the hospital has checked on you out of sheer curiosity."

"I lost a lot of blood?" I search the back of my head with my free fingers. A fuzzy patch of new hair covers a bumpy row of staples.

"Try all of it. There's no reason you should be alive. They couldn't even figure out what type you are. They tried to give you a bunch of O-negative because it's supposed to be universal, but it didn't do a thing to help you."

"So how…?" I can't bring myself to ask it out loud.

"How are you still here?" she finishes for me. "Basically, you're a medical miracle," she says, her voice becoming sober. "No one should be able to live through that kind of trauma. You probably wouldn't have if Dr. Metcher wasn't here. He'd come to give a lecture on extreme trauma care and just happened to be in the ER when you came in. He's a world-renowned trauma surgeon. You're as lucky as they come."

"This is a strange kind of lucky." I know I sound ungrateful. *I could be dead. Should be. Was.*

"Maybe I shouldn't have said anything," she says and chews on her lower lip. "I'm sure it's a lot to take in. I know you don't know me yet, but I'm here for you," she says and offers her hand.

I close my free fingers around hers and give them a meager squeeze. "Thanks. Actually, I'm glad you told me." The silence that follows makes it too easy to get lost in my own thoughts. "Can we talk about something besides me?"

"Of course. Ask me something," she laughs.

"Well, how old are you?" I decide to stick with a safe topic.

"Twenty-four."

"And you're married to a brain surgeon?" I blurt. *Way to go.*

"It's true," she shrugs. "We got married about six months ago. I guess I'd be considered a gold digger if I didn't come with my own very healthy trust fund."

"Oh, no, I didn't mean—"

"I'm kidding. It's nice that you just come out and ask instead of whispering about me behind my back. We got married pretty fast, which started tons of rumors. A lot of the nurses here make me feel like a freak. Sometimes it's really hard to be here."

"I know exactly what you mean." My father's accident had started more rumors than I cared to count.

"That's a shame. You shouldn't feel that way," she frowns. "Now your ability to come back from the dead, that's freaky. But you, my friend, are otherwise perfectly normal." She glances at her watch.

I don't want her to leave, but I don't know what else to talk about. *How long has it been since I've talked about anything other than horses and the weather? I don't think we have much in common.* But then I realize that we do. Not a something, but a someone. *Ryan.* Even the thought of his name makes my cheeks warm.

"Well, my friend, can I ask you a question?" I ask.

"Of course."

"But you can't say anything."

"I won't." She gives me a funny look.

"How old is Ryan? He's the medical student assigned to me. He is shadowing your husband. Do you know him?" I force the words out as fast as I can, afraid I'll lose my nerve.

She breaks into a wide grin and clasps her hands together. Her excitement makes me wish I'd kept my mouth shut. A sudden jolt makes me shiver as Lucas's scarred face haunts the edges of my mind. *Why does he keep showing up in my head? He wasn't real. I don't think anything you think you remember from that night is real. Just forget all of it.*

I close my eyes and shake my head in hopes that any memory of him and the lasting effect he seems to have on me will fall out permanently.

"Don't be embarrassed!" Vanessa laughs. "If you're going to be stuck here for a while you might as well enjoy the view." The suggestive twinkle in her eye makes me blush.

"So how old is he?" I ask, clearing my throat.

"He's twenty or twenty-one, I think. I'll ask my husband to be sure. I do know that he thinks that Ryan is brilliant. How old are you?" she teases.

"Eighteen," *Barely.* "Not old enough."

"That's not true. Age is a state of mind as far as I'm concerned. And it seems to me that you're eighteen going on thirty. Not to mention that under those bruises I'm pretty sure you're a knock out." Her voice delivers the compliment plainly, as if it's a fact.

"I'm not so sure about that." I paint myself to the back of the lumpy mattress and will her eyes away. I hadn't ever thought about myself like that. She dismisses my discomfort with a wave of her hand.

"Don't be modest. It doesn't do a thing for anyone," she says.

Easy for her to say. She belongs in a Cover Girl ad.

"David has kind of taken Ryan under his wing, so they've spent a lot of time together in the past week. I can find out if he's single," she says and raises an eyebrow. "Or you could just come out and ask him."

"Yeah. I'll do that." *Should I make my move before or after he checks my vitals?* The weight of the casts and the layer of grimy film that covers my skin make me feel disgusting. I swipe at a few loose strands of hair that are stuck to the side of my face but I can't get them to stay behind my ear.

"Do you want some help?"

"That'd be great, thanks." I relent with a scowl. "I don't do helpless well." Agitation crawls across my skin like a line of ants.

"Don't worry about it. I think you're as far from helpless as you can get," she says as she leans over me. Her hair falls away from her neck, revealing huge purple bruises all along her collarbone.

"Wow! What happened to you?" My wide eyes find her ashen face. There are yellowed places on her forearms where older marks have faded.

She quickly sits back and crosses her arms, glancing hesitantly over them. "I don't see anything." Relief is plain in her voice.

I squeeze my eyes shut and then open them slowly. The bruises are no longer there.

"Sorry, I've been seeing some pretty weird things lately. Ryan said it's to be expected with everything I went through. I guess my eyes are still playing tricks on me," I explain.

"Of course. That makes sense." She presses her lips together.

"That's what they tell me," I joke. But my attempt to lighten the air in the room has made it awkward instead.

"Well, I better get going. The hubby's going to want dinner soon," she says after a few seconds.

"I hope you'll come back soon. We can read that magazine."

"I will. Take care." She barely turns around in her haste to get to the door.

"Take care," I echo, but I'm already alone.

6
No one to call my own

A WEEK PASSES. MY DAYS BECOME ROUTINE: DRAW SOME blood, run some tests, make small talk with visitors, make attempts to flirt with Ryan, hurry up and wait, check vitals, think of better things I should've said to Ryan instead of what I'd come up with, wonder if Vanessa is going to stop by again. *I'd kill to read that trashy magazine right about now.*

Nights are long, but they're better. Darker. They expect less from me. And I can pretend to be asleep without people prodding me to make sure I haven't relapsed into a coma. I've gotten so good at faking sleep that the moment the door creaks open my eyes automatically clamp shut. But the burning smell of vodka taints the measured breath I take in and my eyes fly open.

"Mom." My voice catches in my throat.

She doesn't reach for the light switch, but she doesn't have to. The alcohol seeping from her pores is so strong that it makes my eyes water. *She won't be able to handle this. It's too much.*

"You honestly thought I wouldn't find out?" she glowers from the door frame. Silvery white light glows from beneath the hand that she presses against the wall to hold herself steady. Her eyes narrow.

"I'm going to be fine. I didn't want to worry you."

"Worry me? I've called every hospital in Virginia looking for you," she snaps.

"I know. I—"

"Not another word, Tanzy. You listen to me. I don't even have to guess what landed you in here. All I asked of you was to not ride anymore. Do you really respect me so little—respect the memory of your father so little—that you would ride again behind my back? After all I've been through? Was it not enough that you took my husband from me?" Her accusation stings like a slap.

"Mom, please. That accident was not my fault," I choke.

"Don't call me that! Stop calling me that." Her whispers echo in the dark room.

"Call you what?"

"Mom. I am not your mother," she seethes.

She's never been this bad before. She must have had a lot tonight. I hope she didn't drive. I just need to get her to calm down. Then I'll call a taxi. She'll sleep this off and completely forget about it.

"I know you're mad, and I am sorry but I—"

"Listen to me, Tanzy. Hear every word that I am about to say to you. I am not your mother," she says slowly and evenly. Almost calm. "Your father had you before we met. There's not a drop of my blood in your body. And I never officially adopted you. Which means that you don't belong to me at all. You're eighteen now, and I no longer have the energy to keep pretending that I care about you. Do you understand? I have wiped my hands clean of you. As far as I am concerned, you do not exist."

She glares at my still body for a second longer, and then whispers something I can't make out under her breath. The tones don't even sound English. Suddenly, the white beneath her hand changes to pure gold. She closes her fist and walks away without a single glimpse back.

The air thins as if all of the oxygen followed her out. A rumble grows under my sternum. I can't swallow. Thick blood bubbles up my throat and fills my mouth. Red vomit splatters my front and dribbles to the floor. My ribcage and teeth chatter as more blood shoots out of my gaping mouth like a fountain. *I'm dying. This is what dying feels like.* A shriek that can't possibly be mine, can't possibly be human, tears through my soaked lips. Everything sounds like it's screaming as beeps and alarms sound around me, swallow me. The cacophony of anger and fear and panic fade before the first bodies rush through my door. Then they fade too.

Turquoise water stretches as far as I can see from my perch on a smooth black rock. The ocean is perfectly still. Like glass. I reach a bare toe to the water and drag it across the surface. The ripples I make grow into waves as they roll away from me and back across the endless blue. I lose my balance and fall into the bottomless sea. I gasp as I resurface and then swim back for the craggy shoreline.

How did it get so far away that fast? I reach it quickly. But the rocks are too high and too slippery. I can't pull myself out. A face peers down at me.

Lucas. He reaches for me. I don't know whether or not to take his hand. The waves I made earlier double back and toss my body against the hard rocks. Even though I am still afraid, I give a hard kick and propel myself just far enough out of the water for him to reach me. Our hands fit together like a key to a lock. I don't care what he's going to do so long as he stays with me.

My eyes fly open. Several nurses scurry around my hospital bed. I can't distinguish their rapid orders, and their voices blend together into a single, frenzied sound. They freeze and peer down at my face as a moan escapes my lips. The blur of colors and motion begins to clear. Ryan's face appears above my own.

"Tanzy? Are you with us?" he asks, his hand on my face. I can't focus enough to answer yet.

Dr. Andrews appears beside Ryan. His gray eyes study mine.

"Her pupils are dilating normally and evenly. That's a good sign," he says to Ryan. "You gave us quite a scare," he says louder. I mentally cling to his solid voice like a buoy.

"What happened?" I mumble. The nurses that scrub at the blood caking my skin don't respond. Another nurse covers me with a new blue blanket. I think I'm glad I didn't see the one she took off.

"We're not really sure," Dr. Andrews says. A lemon yellow mark gleams in his palm as he rubs his graying brow with the back of his hand. "It appears that you went into sudden respiratory failure and then cardiac arrest. Your body's been through a lot. We'll probably run a couple of tests to check for any new internal bleeding or other complications."

"Am I dying?" I whisper. "Tell me the truth." The wrinkles around his eyes deepen as he frowns sympathetically.

"No. Not right now, anyway. Your vitals have stabilized for the most part. We just need to make sure you're healing properly. It's only been two weeks and you're doing much better than anyone expected. But you're not completely out of the woods yet," he explains. "With all of the surgeries you had, I would not be surprised if there was some kind of complication."

"Tanzy!" I hear Dana cry from the open door. "Are you okay? Why is there blood all over the place? What happened?" She rushes to my side.

"I'm okay," I croak.

"Tanzy gave us a good scare, but she's recovering," Dr. Andrews explains.

"Your mom. She—This was on my windshield." Dana says and holds up a folded piece of paper. "I got here as fast as I could. What do you mean a good scare? What happened?"

"We're going to take her for a few tests and scans just to make sure everything is okay," Dr. Andrews continues firmly. "I'll come get you from the waiting room once we're done, but we need to clear her room of any visitors for now."

"Sure. Of course," Dana says and shoves the note in her back pocket. "Are you okay?" she mouths at me.

I nod. New tears come as she slips from the crowded room. I wish we had our fence to lean on. All these walls and people and machines. They inch in on me. Even the air tastes stale.

"Ryan, let's take her down for a full CT and an MRI," Dr. Andrews orders as he flips pages back and forth on my chart. "Page me as soon as the results are up," he says and strides from my room.

"Looks like me and you will be hanging out today," Ryan says and smiles down at me. His voice feels like warm sunlight on my face. I smile back at him and my heart does cartwheels in my chest. He takes hold of my bed and pushes it out of the door and down the hall.

"There is a patient ahead of you, so we'll just hang out here 'til it's your turn," he says, parking my bed alongside the wall.

Having Ryan as a captive audience is exhilarating and intimidating. *I wish Vanessa were here. I bet she'd know if he was interested in me.* Thinking about her makes me feel braver.

"I'm a little disappointed, I have to admit," I venture.

"What? That your miraculous road to recovery had a speed bump?"

"No." I stumble on the small word, but I make myself keep going. "This isn't what I had in mind for a first date."

The corners of his mouth pull into an embarrassed smile. *Great. He's trying not to laugh.* Heat makes a conspicuous path from the neck line of my faded hospital gown to my ears. *There's no taking that back.* I try anyway. "I'm totally kidding."

"For the record, this is not what I had in mind for a first date, either," he says as he looks up. His blue eyes sparkle with curiosity. If there is such a color that is redder than I already am, my cheeks are well on their way to finding it.

"So what all are you looking for?" I ask, desperate for something else to think about so I stand a chance of returning to my normal color.

"Honestly, pretty much anything and everything," he answers, taking my lead. "They'll make sure there's no internal bleeding. They want to make sure all the breaks are setting properly. The whole nine yards."

"None of this makes any sense. I still don't know what happened to me. Dana can barely talk about it and Dr. Andrews isn't the world's best conversationalist." Ryan lets out an amused laugh. "Sorry, it's nice to have someone to talk to."

He smiles and takes my free hand in his. *Do doctors usually do this? Don't read into it. Well, maybe it wouldn't hurt to read into it just a tiny bit.* Some kind of current flows back and forth between our touching skin. I wonder if he feels it too.

"You're in a very unique situation," he says. His grip is just as cautious. "Honestly, we're all pretty confused. And Dr. Andrews is an amazing surgeon, but no, he's not a man of many words."

"What about the visiting doctor that gave me the illegal stuff? What do you know about him?" I whisper.

"Who told you?" His eyes widen in panic. He scans up and down the hallway before he brings his face closer to mine. "You weren't supposed to find out about that. No one outside of that OR was ever supposed to find out about that."

The sudden fierceness in his face makes goose bumps bloom down my arms.

"Don't worry. I'm not going to tell anyone. Or sue, if that's what you're worried about. Although it would be a quick fix to pay for this extended vacation of mine," I add with a forced laugh. His face relaxes a little. "I'm alive. I don't think I have much to complain about. And I won't tell anyone, if it makes you feel better. Not that anyone would believe me."

"It does make me feel better." He watches my face. His thoughts trek back and forth across his eyes. "You're a very interesting woman," he leans down and whispers into my ear.

I can feel my cheeks turning red again, but I don't care. All I care about is the fact that he just called me a woman.

"And it wasn't illegal. It was unknown. And everything about you so far has fallen into that category," he says as he straightens and slips his hand from mine.

My fingers instinctively follow his before I force them into a fist and tuck them beneath my thin sheet. "What exactly happened when I got here? No one has really filled in the blanks for me. They just tell me I'm lucky," I probe.

"The night you came in was my very first shift here," he says. "You were life-flighted from the local hospital near your farm, and you were considered D.O.A. Your body was—the injuries were catastrophic. They tried for over an hour to resuscitate you, but nothing was working. Dr. Andrews finally gave up and called your time of death. That's when Dr. Metcher stepped in. He completely transfused all of the donor blood with a blood substitute from his home country. He left almost immediately after your heart restarted; he was running late for his flight. I guess he took a lot of your answers with him. And we all swore to each other that what happened in that operating room would stay there. The only reason Dr. Andrews agreed to try the drug is because you truly were officially dead. They were already drawing up harvesting plans for your salvageable organs."

"I guess I am lucky," I whisper.

"You really are. Even the senior surgeons around here are saying you're like nothing they've ever seen before. You're going to be in a lot of case studies," he says as he peeks into the procedure room.

"Can I ask you a question, but you have to promise not to move me to the psych ward?" I venture.

"I don't think you can surprise me anymore than you already have."

"Well, I know I shouldn't expect everything to be back to normal yet, but I'm seeing some strange things. I think something is wrong with my eyes."

"I told you before that halos are perfectly normal following the extent of the trauma your body has handled," he answers and glances at his watch.

"But these aren't halos. They're little horseshoes. I only see them on people's palms. They glow. And they change color," I add before I can talk myself out of the confession all together.

"You're right. That's not normal at all," he says. I wait for more information, but he stands stone still beside my bed.

"Okay, so?" I push.

The blue in his hand turns a cranberry red. *What does that mean?* He closes his hands into tight fists, purposefully concealing his palms. "So that's probably a good question for Dr. Andrews."

"But you know Dr. Andrews isn't going to tell me anything. You said so yourself."

"I don't know how to answer that one."

"Ms. Hightower, we're ready for you," a nurse calls from the open doorway.

I leave my questions in the empty hallway as Ryan silently wheels my bed into the procedure room.

7
Two of a kind

THE TESTS TAKE FOREVER. I HAVE TO STAY QUIET AND perfectly still, which is fine with me since Ryan doesn't seem interested in breaking the wall he's thrown up between us. He won't look at me, and every time I catch him deliberately staring anywhere else it makes me feel even worse. My mind picks apart every interaction we've had in the past two weeks. It's only been a couple of hours since the last time he stared straight into my eyes, but I already miss it. Not just the depth of the blue but the way I feel in their gaze. Like I don't have anything to hide anymore.

The sudden clarity just makes the likely truth that much worse: He thinks I'm certifiably crazy. And possibly contagious. By the time I'm done and ready to go back to my room I don't even try to talk to him. I ignore the quick glances he makes at my face when he thinks I'm not paying attention.

The hurt and tension vanish as I catch sight of Vanessa waiting in my room. "Hey!" I say as Ryan steers me through the doorway.

"Hi, Tanzy," she replies. "How are you? I heard you had a hard night."

"Yeah, wasn't my favorite night ever." *And she doesn't know the half of it.* "They just did a bunch of X-rays and a full CT so I guess we'll find out soon. How's everything with you?"

"Oh, you know," she answers vaguely.

"Girl talk?" Ryan asks with a raised eyebrow.

The instant rebound in his voice makes me stare at him. *Where was that cheerful guy a couple of hours ago?* He even gives Vanessa a playful half-smile.

"Yep," Vanessa says with a laugh and gives him a little wave as he feigns a hasty exit. "Did you two have fun?" she ribs as soon as we're alone.

I can't help watching the empty doorway, digesting the fact that Ryan's bad mood clearly had something to do with me. I sigh as I lean back in my bed. "I wish there was more to tell you. I guess three casts and a neck brace just don't do it for him. So what about you? Your turn." The subject of Ryan makes me queasy. Even though I want nothing more than to talk about anything else, thoughts of him won't leave me.

"Well, I came to talk to you for a couple of reasons," she says. The golden mark pulses in her open palm. She rubs her hands together as she shifts on the bed.

She's nervous. What in the world does she have to be nervous about?

"I think when you meet someone that could be a friend, it's important to be up front and honest. You know, put all your cards on the table and see what happens."

"Okay," I say, even though I don't have a clue what she's talking about.

"You scared me the other day."

"I didn't mean to."

"No, I know you didn't. Let me explain," she says, closing her eyes.

I sit back and watch her face twist as she tries to decide how to continue.

"You scared me because of what you saw. I didn't have any bruises on me last week. But I've had marks on me before. A lot, actually. I mean, it's been better lately. He's been really sweet since—well, the last month or so. Being a doctor can be so stressful, you know.

It's hard, what he does. And I am so much younger than he is and there's a lot I don't know so I frustrate him. I don't mean to. It just happens." The fact that she is near tears makes my stomach knot. "I used to have to cover up all the time. So when you said that, about seeing marks, I guess it just shocked me. Took me to a place I didn't want to ever go back to. I don't know what you saw or how you saw it, but there it is," she finishes.

"Are you saying that Dr. Andrews hurts you?" I whisper. He is always so kind with me. I couldn't imagine him laying a hand on anyone, least of all Vanessa. The doubtful thoughts make me feel instantly guilty.

Of course you only see him for five minutes at a time tops. Anyone can hide anything for five minutes. You should know that better than anybody.

"Not recently. It's been over a month since the last time," she says quietly.

"So what changed? Why did he stop? Did you tell someone?"

"I'm not sure how to explain it to you," she stammers. "No one ever believes me. They just think I'm a freak." I can practically feel her pulling away as the vortex of her thoughts wipes every hint of expression from her face.

"You want freak? Right now, I literally see a horseshoe glowing in your palm. It's gold. Ryan's is blue. Everyone has one," I blurt. "So just try me."

"You can see it too?" she gasps.

Too? Did she just say what I think she did? Her eyes dart to her right palm and then back to my face. "You see them? They're real?" I whisper.

"I used to see them all the time, but I don't anymore. I saw rings, not horseshoes. But I'm sure they're the same thing. The only one I still see is my own." She looks down at her palm again and waves her fingers. "My whole life I've seen things that, well, that don't make sense. Once the colors disappeared other things started happening that I couldn't explain. But I never told anyone about any of it. Not 'til right now," she stammers.

My mouth falls open. I don't know what to call the emotion that races through my veins as she validates the countless things I was sure I'd imagined.

"I never knew there was anyone else out there like me," Vanessa continues, echoing my thoughts. She sits down gingerly on the bed next to me. "What color is yours?"

"I don't have one that I can see." I turn my free hand over and show her my palm. "But I know what you mean. About seeing things that don't make sense. I know exactly what you mean."

"I knew there was something special about you," she says.

"I've never thought of it as special."

"It is. There's a lot I don't understand about it, but I know it makes us special," she says fiercely. "We're two of a kind, you and me. That means we have to stick together."

"What all do you see now? You know, that isn't normal?"

"Once the rings disappeared I started having dreams that would come true soon after. And now I see things even when I'm awake. It can get a little confusing," she says with a grimace.

"What kind of things do you see?"

"I wasn't going to tell you, but I saw what happened the night you came here," she says, lowering her voice. "What really happened. I saw the horse you were riding flip over the fence. I saw those awful creatures. What were those? I've never seen anything so horrible," she says, cringing.

The air around me explodes like shattering glass. In a rush I tell her every detail I can remember from the chase that night.

"They were so aggressive," I remember. "They must have had rabies or something. I've never seen anything like them. Honestly, I had convinced myself that they weren't real. That none of it was.

I'm still not sure if I imagined any of it. I don't remember anything about the fire. Did you see anything about how the fire started or how I got back to the barn?"

"No," she says apologetically. "The last thing I saw was those animals climbing over the fence."

"I can't prove that what I remember is real, but it felt real. I don't remember the fire, but Wildwood was burned to the ground, so that's hard to argue with. There's a giant piece missing somewhere and it's driving me crazy, And now everyone has these glowing marks in their hands. I know they're not really there but I have no idea why I'm seeing them or what they mean."

"I started seeing them when I was six," she says. Her eyes fall to her lap. "After a bad car accident. I woke up in a hospital—just like you. And that's when it all started."

"Do you think they're auras?" I ask. "That was the only thing I could think of."

"I think the colors are just a starting point. It's the first step that your mind takes in learning how to translate a sixth sense. If you're anything like me, the color marks will fade away and you'll get the information in a different way. Like the dreams I have now."

"Will you teach me about it?" I ask, a new hunger rumbling within my core. If I can understand this, maybe I can use it. Maybe I can find out what really happened that night. What that shadow really is. Why it attacked my father. And maybe, just maybe, I can make it pay.

"Of course! Are you kidding? I'm so happy that I have someone to share this with."

"Even though we sound completely crazy?"

"You want to hear crazy?" Ryan's voice calls from the doorway.

We both turn to face him. *How long has he been there? What did he hear?* Vanessa holds her breath next to me. Neither of us offers an answer.

He waves a thick folder in the air above his head. "These are the results from all the scans we just ran on you. Tanzy, there is not a thing wrong in your body. We couldn't find a single fracture on your CT scan."

"Do I need to take another one?"

"Honestly, I don't know. How do you feel?"

"Like most of my body is in a cast. How do you think I feel?"

"I can't imagine how you feel," Ryan answers, his voice thick.

The change in it pulls on my heart strings, and I will him to look at me so I can see his eyes. *Can I see through you like you see through me?*

He clears his throat and meets my stare, but his eyes are stony on the surface and reveal nothing beneath the blue. "Well, the next step is to take off your casts and do a round of X-rays just to be sure there was no obstruction or interference."

I nod along, but I can't help thinking about all the things I'd do differently if we could start over. *Not tell him about the horseshoes, for starters.*

"I'll be back soon to cut the casts off," he says on his way out.

"Is he okay? I've never seen him that tense before," Vanessa asks once we're alone.

"I tried to tell him about the colors earlier. He made me feel like I should be moved to a padded cell, and honestly I've been a brat ever since." I sigh and she gives me a sympathetic frown.

"Don't tell anyone else about the colors. Trust me. I learned the hard way that it only causes trouble."

"I won't. I'm sorry I didn't tell you about it before, and I'm over-reacting, I know. Can we please talk about something else?"

"So what if the breaks are really healed?" she obliges.

"What if they were never there to begin with? I don't know what to believe. Visiting mystery doctors? Magic illegal potions? Glowing horseshoes?" I start to tell her about Lucas, but a clench in my gut stops me.

"Trust me, the breaks were real. My husband said that it took a team of orthopedic surgeons hours to set your compound fractures. You know, where the broken bones stick out of your skin?" she says, making a face.

"That's hard to argue with. I've just got too much time to think, and that doesn't help. It's making me restless."

"Can't imagine why," Vanessa says, rolling her eyes. "I bet you're used to moving around all day and you've been in that bed for two weeks straight."

"I started helping my dad at the horse farm when I was eight. I've been there almost every day since."

"Well, at least you've got school work to make the time go by, right?"

"No. I ... it's a long story," I falter.

"I've got time. If you want to talk about it." Something in her eyes works at the lock I keep on that part of my life.

"My dad died a few years ago. My mom had a hard time with it. She needed a lot of help, so I stayed home a lot. I got really behind. I tried doing home-school but there was too much else that needed doing. After a while I just kind of stopped."

"Do you miss it?"

"Not really. Sometimes though, I miss the idea of it. What it would have been like if everything had stayed the way it was. You know, just be a student. Have homework. For Wildwood to feel like it used to."

My trail of thoughts drifts into dangerous territory, so I dig my heels in and pull back. Vanessa gives me a curious look, which yanks the mental leash right out of my hands.

"Wildwood Farm used to be a sanctuary for me. He died out there, my dad. He was in a really bad riding accident. Afterwards, all I could think about was the day I'd be able to leave. You know, start over. Maybe get my GED and go off to college somewhere out west. But I can't leave Mom alone," I explain, feeling both lighter and heavier now that those words are out.

"No wonder you're old for your age," Vanessa says.

"I'm trying not to think about the fact that I don't have insurance. There's no telling how much debt I'll be in once I'm out. And we don't have a lot of money."

"And your mother?" Her green eyes train on mine again, and instantly I feel trapped.

It's just because you don't like to talk about it. Especially now. What do I say? Where do I start? I draw in a long breath and hold it. Vanessa waits, unblinking. "She blames me for Dad. Like I said, she had a hard time. After."

Vanessa waits as if she knows there's a lot I'm not saying.

"Potential friend should be honest, right? Put it all out there?"

"Of course," she says.

I swallow the knot rising in my throat. "She told me that she's not actually my mother. I don't know whether I believe her or not. She was really drunk. She probably doesn't even remember doing it. But she made it clear that I'm no longer a part of her life."

Vanessa's face clouds over and I have to look away. But I can't help wondering what the note said that my mother gave Dana.

Dana! How long has she been waiting?

"Vanessa, will you do me a favor?"

"Of course." She stands up.

"Will you get my friend Dana? She's in the lobby. Your husband had everyone leave earlier and I forgot to have someone tell her I was done. She's been down there for hours."

"What does she look like?"

"She's got reddish-brown hair. And she'll probably be the only one wearing boots."

"Got it. I have to scoot anyway, so that's perfect."

"Thanks. I'll see you soon?"

"Wild horses," she says with a wink. *Couldn't drag her away.* She deliberately waves with an open palm before disappearing into the hallway.

I smile to myself as I lean back against the stiff bed and replay our conversation in my head. *She never finished telling me about what made her husband stop. Maybe it's too hard to talk about. And that's something I can definitely relate to.*

A soft knock on the partly opened doorway breaks my train of thoughts. A guy in blue scrubs sticks his head through the cracked door. "Ms. Hightower?" he drawls kindly.

"That's me."

"I'm Steven. I'm an orthopedic resident. Ryan asked me to get these casts off and take you down to Radiology for a set of X-rays."

"Ouch," I mutter to myself.

"Oh, it won't hurt any."

"Right, I know." The crack I feel spreading under my ribcage isn't going to show up on any x-ray.

"This won't take long," Steven says and begins sawing through the hard plaster. I watch the whirling blade slice through the cast and wonder how he'll know when he's all the way through before carving into my skin. My fingers reflexively tighten into a fist. The cast pops open and he peels it from my arm.

"Huh. Well, I've heard nothing about you has been normal," he says.

I inspect my newly freed arm. A red, thick line streaks across my forearm. "What's that?" I ask and point to it.

"That's where both the bones in your forearm came through your skin. That's where your stitches should be," he says slowly. "That's where bruising and swelling should still be."

I don't know whether to be elated or scared. I watch Steven scan my skin. His eyes widen as he points at a little pile of metal staples.

"And those are the staples they used to close your arm after surgery. Your body must have rejected them. I'll need to get my attending to examine this, but I'll go ahead and take the casts off your legs first."

He works quickly, cracking open both casts in just a couple of minutes. "I've never seen anything like this," he mumbles.

I follow his gaze to my bare legs. My left leg is riddled with angry, red streaks. A long, ridged welt runs the length of my thigh with several red limbs branching from it. Even though I heard about the countless surgeries I had the first few days I was here, the map of scars across my pale, shrunken limbs still don't seem real.

"Were staples there, too?" I ask.

"Yes. This is, I mean I've never seen ... I'm going to go get the attending surgeon that set your fractures. I'll be back as fast as I can. I know your casts are off, but don't move a muscle," he says in a rush. He turns on his heels and races from my room.

As soon as I'm alone, I reach back and touch the place Dr. Andrews cut into my skull. But I can't find it. The staples are gone. I fight the urge to squirm, feeling like a freak again. I press my thumb into my empty palm. For the first time I feel disappointed that I don't have my own little horseshoe.

8
Visitors

Some people heal faster than others," the orthopedic surgeon explains to Dana and me. A second round of X-rays
had shown exactly the same thing as the first: absolutely nothing.
"Although I have to say that this is quite remarkable."

He launches into a tangent about "the amazing human body," and
I half listen as my mind revisits every encounter with Ryan. His
blue eyes pierce my mind, and if I focus on either time we touched
I can still feel the effect he had with the simple brush of his fingers
on my skin; the warm comfort that pulsed like a heartbeat when we
held hands. Even though I try to stop it, every memory circles back
to the fact that he isn't here now. And as much as I don't want to
admit it, I added as many bricks to that wall between us as he did.

"Remember, we don't know how strong the bones are. So don't
try anything physical yet until we get you with a therapist," the surgeon says. I agree automatically. He gives some more instructions
that don't register and turns to leave.

"I don't know what to say," Dana says, rubbing her face.

"I know. It's almost scarier to be healed. Where am I going to go?
Maybe I'll call Mom and see if she remembers what she said. What
did her note say?" I look away. If there's pity in Dana's eyes I won't
be able to hold myself together.

"That she was leaving town. And that we shouldn't bother look-ing for her." Dana clears her throat and takes my hand. "I am in this with you, Tanzy. You aren't alone."

"But what will you do? Are they rebuilding the farm? How much damage is there?" I keep my tone even and frank, leaving no room for the clench in my gut to work its way into my voice.

"They'll have to rebuild the barn. The whole structure was destroyed when the roof collapsed. I mean, it went up like kindling. And I didn't want to tell you this, but I know I should."

I wait while she steels herself against whatever she's about to say.

"They're sure it was arson now. They've found traces of acceler-ants. Even on the floor in front of the office. Tanzy, if something had happened to you—" She chokes on her words.

"But it didn't. I mean, it did. But I'm fine," I reassure her and clasp my hand on top of hers.

"I meant what I said. You have a home with me no matter what. We're family." She bites down on her lip as she hesitates. "I got a really good job offer at a training farm in Kentucky. If it's okay with you, I'm going to take it." Dana makes her words soft like they might hurt me. But they don't.

"I think you should," I encourage. The idea of Dana moving on with her life makes me feel lighter, like maybe I can finally move on, too. Like there's no reason to keep myself tied to Wildwood Farm.

"It's just that the investigation is going to take even more time, and they have yet to find any leads on any of the horses. I just … I can't stay. It's too hard."

"You know I understand, right?" I insist.

"Of course you do, you better than anyone." Her weathered face softens with empathy.

"Dana, you've been amazing. But go. You don't need to spend every free moment here. I'm okay. I'll figure it out. And I'll call you if I need anything—like a ride to Kentucky," I joke. "Actually, I do need one thing."

"Sure."

"Clothes. Now that my casts are off, I don't ever want to see a hospital gown again."

"I already got you covered," she says and points to the small chest of drawers under the window sill. "I brought you a couple of my things when you ... before you woke up. Just a pair of jeans, some sweat pants, a few shirts. I figured we're about the same size. I thought if I acted like you were going to wake up then it would help."

"Thanks," I whisper. Seeing her get emotional is almost too much to bear. "You must've done something right."

"And your boots," Dana continues, making a lightning fast wipe at her face. "They made it, actually. They're in the bottom drawer. The nurses were going to throw them away with the clothes they cut off you, but I saved them." She stands up and pulls a sleeveless white shirt and a pair of gray sweatpants out of the drawer. "Are these okay for now?"

"Anything is better than this," I answer with a grimace. She sets them on the end of my bed and sits down beside me. "You are unbelievable. I don't know what I would've done without you," I say. Her face falls, heavy with guilt. "Dana, no. You have to go. It's time for you to take care of yourself."

"Promise?"

"I promise. I think Vanessa is going to be a really great friend. I have a feeling she'll want to help once they let me out."

"I almost forgot," Dana says and pulls her purse into her lap. "Vanessa gave me something for you. She said she forgot to give it to you earlier."

Dana retrieves a black velvet pouch from her purse and hands it to me. I pull apart the drawstring and pluck a delicate silver ring from the bag. The band coils around an oval jewel. Its iridescent surface shifts with every movement. As I slip the band around my finger, the stone turns a luminous shade of purple.

"What is that? A mood ring?" Dana laughs.

"Probably," I smile, although somehow I'm sure it's not.

Dana's face is suddenly serious. "She seems like a good person. I'm glad you have her."

"Are you leaving soon?" My throat constricts at the thought of not seeing Dana every day.

"Tomorrow. If I got the go-ahead from you, that is. This job offer came out of left field. They needed an answer pretty quickly."

"Well, you've got it. But you better stay in touch." I work to keep my voice from cracking.

"Are you kidding?" She pulls me into a fierce hug. "I'm going to miss you, Tee." She tugs at a strand of my hair. It looks darker in her fingers. "Your hair has gotten really long," she muses, cocking her head to the side. "Of course I only see it under baseball caps."

"Yeah, yeah." We stall in the silence, neither of us particularly comfortable with parting words.

"If you need anything…"

"Dana, I will. Go on, I'm sure you've got lots to do before tomorrow." The burning behind my eyes won't wait for much longer, and if she sees me cry she'll never be able to leave. And she needs to. We both do.

"Bye, Tanzy," she whispers.

"Good luck." I squeeze her hand, and then watch her walk from the room. As soon as I'm alone I press my fingers into the corners of my eyes and wait for the sting to subside. I draw in a ragged breath and silently send her the words I couldn't say aloud.

Once I'm sure I'm not going to cry, I slip off the hideous floral gown and pull on the clothes that Dana picked out. They are soft and worn. They even smell like her, which helps and hurts. The confidence that made me feel so sure moments before seems to have left with her. I twist the new ring on my finger, desperate for a distraction. The color shifts again. A red glow burns at the center, bleeding outward. I stare harder into the whirling colors. It's hypnotizing. I can't look away. The room slowly spins.

"You okay?" Vanessa's voice makes the rotation stop. She frowns and moves to the side of my bed.

"Yeah, just dizzy all of the sudden," I say and shake it off. "I'm glad you're here. Wait, why are you here? I thought you were leaving."

"I thought I was too," Vanessa says with a shrug. "We'd pulled onto the main road when my husband got paged to the ER for a bad car accident. We rode in together, so it looks like I'll be here a little while longer. Perfectly fine by me. It's just the two of us at home and I get really lonely sometimes." Her eyes find the floor.

"What's wrong?"

"Nothing. Nothing I want to talk about, anyway. Hey, check you out with real clothes on and cast free," she says, changing the subject. "My husband told me that your breaks really are healed."

"I know. It's pretty weird. I meet with a physical therapist for testing first thing tomorrow."

"Freak," she winks. Her devilish smile makes me feel better instantly. "Oh, did Dana give you something from me?"

"She did! Thank you for the ring!" I raise my hand to show her that I'm wearing it. "I love it."

"I have one too," she says and pulls an identical black velvet pouch out of her purse. "I saw them at a quaint little store yesterday. I wanted to give you something as an apology—" she starts but I cut her off with a wave of my hand.

"You have nothing to apologize for."

"Then maybe they can be friendship rings? Or is that lame?" she asks, making a face.

"Not at all. It's perfect."

"Okay good." She slips the ring on her finger and smiles down at it. "Don't laugh, but they are supposed to be magical."

I give her a dubious look. "What are they supposed to do?"

"Lots of things."

"Like what?"

"Well, for starters, they're supposed to be protective," Vanessa says tentatively.

"How?" I ask and glance down at the little ring.

"By increasing intuition. Supposedly it gives the wearer warnings if something bad is going to happen." I raise a wary eyebrow but Vanessa ignores it. "What sold me is that the shopkeeper said if two people are very in tune with each other these rings will let them communicate with their minds," she says. She tries to make it sound like she doesn't believe it, but I can tell that she might.

"Telepathy? Seriously?"

"Hey, they were on sale," she says in mock defense.

"So what should that tell you?"

"Would you at least try?" Vanessa says, failing to cover up her enthusiasm.

"Ok, fine," I say and close my eyes.

"You're mocking me."

"I'm really not," I laugh and open my eyes. "I am trying to concentrate."

"Okay, say something. Well, think something," she says.

Hi, Vanessa. Can you hear me? I wait. The air around my ears feels like its thinning.

Hi, Tanzy. I hear you! Vanessa's voice sings in my head. My eyes fly open and I stare at her face. *Maybe I imagined it.*

"Nope," she says smugly.

"Well, that was too obvious," I argue. *There's no way these rings can really let us hear each other's thoughts.* But the possibility piques something deep within me, something that wants this to be real.

"There's no way these rings can really let us hear each other's thoughts," Vanessa repeats verbatim. She even adds inflection in the right places. "Did I get it right?" My incredulous face answers her. "Think something else!" she says, clapping her hands.

I wonder what Ryan is doing. I don't want to think about him, especially right now, but I can't help it. I wait for Vanessa to tease me but her face falls with disappointment.

"I don't hear anything. It's like a door just closed."

"Maybe we just have to practice?"

"You're probably right," she concedes. I turn the ring wistfully on my finger, unable to keep more thoughts of Ryan away. "Hey, we'll get it! I have faith in us," she says brightly.

"No, that's not it. I just can't get Ryan out of my head. I mean I never thought we'd see each other once I leave or anything, but I didn't think it would end like that," I admit, regretting our last exchange.

"You okay?"

"Yeah, it's just hard to shake him when I know he's in this hospital somewhere. I think some fresh air would help clear my head. Maybe take a walk."

"Tanzy, I get that you're bored out of your mind but I don't think that's a good idea."

"Look at that sunset. How can you not want to be out there?" I plead and gesture toward the narrow window. A smile tugs at her lips as she glances at the hospital courtyard, which is washed in the evening's rusty orange.

"You'll tell me if anything hurts, right?"

"I promise. Trust me, I don't want to do anything that's going to keep me in here any longer than I have to be." I start to push off the bed, but Vanessa stops me with a hand that is stronger than I expect.

"Not so fast, medical miracle. Let's at least put you in a wheel chair 'til we get you outside," she bargains.

"Okay, it's a deal." *Whatever it takes to get me out of here even if just for a minute.*

Vanessa returns quickly from the nurses' station, wheelchair in tow. I let her help me into it and she spreads a bed sheet across my lap, covering my scarred legs.

"Now I feel like a little old lady."

"You've already got the ornery part down." Vanessa laughs. I give her a half-hearted glare. "Come on, Granny. Let's go for a walk." She giggles and wheels me out of the room.

Our journey through the maze of identically dismal halls feels like it takes an hour to navigate. Finally, Vanessa pushes me through the automatic exit doors and into the open air. I inhale until my lungs feel like they might pop. Reluctantly, I release the deliciously clean air and gulp in some more.

"This is my favorite time of day," Vanessa says, taking a deep breath. "Right after the sun goes down. It's so quiet and peaceful. It feels magical out here, doesn't it? Like anything could happen."

"I like sunrise best. But this is a close second," I say, admiring the mystery in the purple shadows of twilight as we make our way down the paved path to the landscaped courtyard.

She wheels the chair to the edge of the lawn. I start to push myself up but she stops me with a hand on my shoulder.

"Are you sure you want to try this?" Vanessa asks. "What if something happens to you?"

I close my eyes and concentrate on my body. My muscles respond instantly, buzzing with the possibility of movement. "I think it'll be okay." I scoot to the edge of the chair and set my bare feet on the brittle grass.

"Tanzy, you're not even wearing shoes. You'll catch a cold," Vanessa warns.

"I'll pay the price." I wave off her concern. Without waiting a second longer, I stand up.

"Oh my gosh! How do you feel?" Vanessa asks, clasping her hands in front of her chin. I take a few cautious steps.

"Great, actually. Like I could go for a run. But don't worry, I won't," I add.

The dry grass tickles the bottoms of my feet, which have softened considerably in the past two weeks. Every sensation feels amplified, like I can feel the entire path between the nerve endings and my brain. *I feel so … alive.* I grab the sheet from the wheel chair and practically skip to the center of the courtyard.

"Are you coming?" I call over my shoulder. Vanessa hurries to catch up.

We spread the sheet out across the grass and lie down on our backs, staring up at the smoldering remnants of day. Even here I can't help but think of Ryan. What we might talk about out here. What it might feel like to kiss him. The thought blooms on my lips.

A ringing sound pierces through my daydream.

"It's David," Vanessa says, sitting up. I make a face as she answers the phone. "Hey honey," she says. She winces at whatever he says through the speaker. I turn away, feeling like an intruder. "I know, I'm sorry." She pauses. "Yes, of course. No, you're right." She waits again. "I'll be there as fast as I can." She puts the phone down in her lap.

"Is he okay?" I ask. "That sounded important."

"He's hungry and I'm late bringing him dinner," she answers, her mouth twisting with worry.

"He's a brain surgeon and he can't find his own dinner?" I blurt.

Vanessa lets out a gasp of surprise and stares back at me. I press my lips together to keep any other opinions from slipping out. *Did I cross a line?* Relief trickles down my back as she bursts into a fit of laughter.

"What's so funny?" The sound of Ryan's voice attracts my eyes like a magnet.

I regard his approach briefly and then turn back to Vanessa. My insides hum with excitement and I don't want it to show. "How helpless you doctors are," I quip.

"Good thing I'm not a doctor, then." He smiles at me, which makes my heart leap.

"Perfect timing. Now I don't have to leave you alone," Vanessa says and climbs to her feet.

Part of me instantly perks at the possibility of being alone with Ryan, but the other part is dreading it. "You're still going?" I ask, although I knew she would.

"Yeah," she says. Suddenly, my ears get hot. *As pathetic as he is, I don't want to find out what would happen if I don't go.*

I stare up at her in disbelief. *I heard you just then,* I call back. We lock eyes and she gives me a thrilled grin.

"So Ryan, she's your responsibility now," Vaness says quickly, filling the silence we left.

"I'm not his patient anymore, apparently," I retort.

"Go ahead, Vanessa. I'll take my chances," he says.

"See y'all," she says and gives us a little wave. *Have fun. Don't do anything I wouldn't do.* Her parting thought nestles into my middle, warming me from within.

Ryan lowers himself beside me without saying anything. I study his face in silence. A hundred possible first sentences filter through my brain but none of them make it to my mouth. He holds my gaze for a few moments before dropping his eyes to his lap.

"Aren't you cold?" he finally asks.

I look down at my bare arms. It's been so long since I wore anything other than a hospital gown that I forgot to grab a jacket. "I'm okay." I rub them anyway, feeling exposed.

"It's near freezing out here."

I don't answer.

"I know why you're upset with me," he says. "I gave you mixed signals and that wasn't fair, and it also wasn't your fault. But there are a lot of complications between you and me."

That's what his attitude was all about? He doesn't think that I'm crazy? My insides leap and then tense. "What, because I'm a patient?"

"No, it's not just that."

"Because I'm younger than you?"

"I think 'younger' is a mild way of addressing the age gap."

"I'm eighteen. You're not that much older than me. If you're just here to make fun of me then you can leave. I am fine out here by myself. I don't need a babysitter," I say sharply, and instantly regret it.

What would Vanessa do? She'd probably put all her cards on the table and let them fall where they may. I can practically hear her voice in my head telling me to do just that. *What do you have to lose?* The thought is strangely comforting. I pounce on the surge of confidence before it can escape.

"For starters, I'm well aware that I'm younger than you. But I feel like when you look at me, you see me. Really see me. I don't know what that means, but I know it means something."

"Tanzy, there's still so much you have to learn; so much you have to decide for yourself," Ryan says vaguely.

He might as well have petted me on the head. Embarrassment paints a hot line up my throat as it makes its way to the corners of my eyes.

"I don't even know what that means, but I think that was answer enough for me." I clench my jaw shut and climb to my feet.

Ryan's strong hand is quick around my wrist. I start to jerk it away from him, anticipating his pull, but his hold is tender and patient. "Please," he says. He shakes his head in frustration. "I'm just not good at talking about how I feel. I'm kind of a guy that way."

I can't help but smile down at him. His blue eyes draw me in and I ease myself back down on the grass. His fingers trace the veins on my wrist to my palm and he takes my hand in his.

"But, Tanzy, I do see you. Don't think for a second that I don't," he says, his eyes grave.

No one has ever looked at me like that before.

Under his hot stare, all of the uncertainty and nervousness burns away. I tug at his hand, pulling him closer to me. He gives me a half smile as he brings his face to mine. There is no hesitation. His lips are warm and full against mine. We melt together effortlessly, sending little shockwaves all the way to my toes. I push myself even closer, drawn to the taste of him. He quells my rushing body with a slow kiss and I cave into his solid chest. He brings a strong hand gently to my throat, and my pulse hammers under his thumb.

An icy gust of wind tears through the courtyard. He protectively wraps his arms around me as the air whips around us. It sounds like it's screaming. I've never heard anything like it. And then it's gone as fast as it came. Without warning he pushes away from me, rocking back on his heels.

"I have to go, Tanzy. I'm sorry."

"What do you mean?" I ask, bewildered. I bring my fingers to my tingling lips.

"I'll explain later, but I can't be here right now."

My eyes dart to his pager, but it's not glowing with some urgent message.

"Was that bad for you?" I stammer. The words hurt to say but it's the only explanation I can come up with.

"What are you talking about?"

"That, just then. Did you not feel the same thing I did?" *Because that was one of the best moments of my life.*

His face softens as my words fight their way through whatever is storming behind his wild eyes. "It's not what you think," he says gently. "Close your eyes."

I stare suspiciously at him for a second before obliging. His worn hands take the sides of my face and he tilts up my chin. The kiss is quick, but it's enough to shore the break he'd made.

"I don't have time to explain right now. But I will when I can," he says. His touch fades away. I reach out blindly for him, but I don't feel him anywhere.

"Ryan?" I ask, feeling ridiculous. He doesn't answer. I open my eyes. He's not in front of me. He's not anywhere.

"Pathetic," a low voice snarls behind me.

I spin toward the threatening sound. A man I've never seen before stands rigidly beside a bare tree. His raven hair is a stark contrast against his translucent face. He is horrifically beautiful. I am startled to recognize how much he resembles Lucas. But his beauty scares something deep and unnamed in my very center as he assesses me with colorless eyes.

"You shouldn't tease the poor boy," he mocks. "You shouldn't waste your time with him, either. Or did you learn nothing last time?"

He glides a step closer. And then another. My eyes instinctively jump to his hands, but no color glitters off his smooth skin.

"I'm sorry. Do I know you?" *Is this a psych patient? Could he be dangerous?*

A throaty laugh sounds from his pale lips. "If you still don't know who I am, I imagine you don't yet know yourself."

"What's that supposed to mean?"

"Who you are. What you're capable of. Why you're back." His words stir in my mind, tugging at something long-forgotten. "When you're ready, when you know yourself, you'll find me. And I'll be waiting for you, Spera. But you of all beings should know that I'm not patient."

He takes two smooth steps backward and then fades into the shadows.

What just happened? Who was that? My brain replays the strange man's words, his face, his white eyes, the weird name he called me. *He must be a psych patient. Amnesia or Alzheimer's or something like that. His eyes are so freaky.* I feel a pang of sympathy for him.

I hug my legs to my chest and rest my face on my knees as my heart rate returns to normal. The scars on my arm are silver under the moon. I trace each line with a finger. They're already flat and smooth. I close my eyes, suddenly exhausted, and mentally replay the kiss with Ryan over and over. And what happened afterward, wondering what made him run away like that.

The thought works itself under my skin like a splinter. I let out a loud sigh and lie back. The ground is surprisingly comfortable. Too comfortable. My eyes feel heavy. I fight back, knowing I should go back to my room and sleep in bed like a normal person. I'm still arguing with myself as the sounds from the hospital fade away.

⌖

"Are you coming?" Lucas asks. "There's something you need to see."

He guides me the short distance to a dirty black rock that is taller than I am. It's caked in red sand. I wipe at the jagged surface. The images I knew would be there become clearer as the rusty grit falls away. Six stick figures ringed in red spirals. Even though they are identical I focus on the last one. I trace her with my finger. A sharp pain sizzles through my hand and I instinctively draw it away. Black-red blood seeps from my torn finger. A drop of blood falls to the beach.

The ground beneath me begins to tremble. The sea churns violently as the ocean floor quakes, and the waves that crash ashore grow more powerful. All at once the wild surface charges forward and thousands of white horses race onto the beach like a tidal wave. They gallop in tight formation and make an impenetrable circle around Lucas and me. I hold my breath as the horses halt in perfect synchronization and turn to face us. They stand still and ready like a silent army.

"They've been waiting for you. We all have," Lucas says.

"Why?" My eyes move to his scarred face.

"It's almost time."

"For what?"

"You'll have to make a choice."

"What kind of choice?"

"It's not for me to tell you," he says, bringing his hand to my face. "Just be ready. Nothing comes without a cost."

"Will you be there?"

"In my heart I've never left you. Keep this on you and I will always be able to find you." Lucas slips a delicate, silver chain around my neck and wordlessly fastens the clasp.

I bring my fingers to the pendant. It's a simplistic horseshoe, more basic than any I've ever seen. Like it's from another era.

"I wasn't sure it was really you. Never believed he could really do it," Lucas says, staring at the necklace.

"Do what?"

"Bring you back." The moment the words leave his lips, the horses dissolve into an ocean. "Be seeing you," he whispers as we watch the white water flow back to the sea.

9
Marked

W HERE AM I? IT'S ALMOST AS DARK WITH MY EYES OPEN as when they're shut. I blink rapidly as I try to focus. *Am I outside? The courtyard. I must have fallen asleep.* I sit up and rub the sleep from my eyes. Moving my hand makes it burn. The ring Vanessa gave me has already rubbed my finger raw. I slip it back off and drop it in my pocket.

"Hey! What are you doing out here all by yourself?" Vanessa asks as she steps onto the courtyard lawn.

"Ryan just left me. I think he got paged to the emergency room," I lie. I want to keep that memory just for me for a little while longer. *And what happened afterward.* The thought makes me cringe.

"That's pretty. Did Ryan give you that?" she asks and reaches for something around my neck.

"What?" I look down. The little horseshoe glimmers against my skin. A deep sense of calm washes over me even as my heart starts to hammer in a sudden panic.

"No, Ryan didn't give it to me," I answer, dodging the truth. *What is the truth?* "I found it."

"It's really pretty. I'll check with the hospital to see if anyone's reported it missing. Do you want me to put it in my purse so you don't have to keep up with it?" she asks as she folds the sheet.

I cover the pendant with my hand and press it into my skin. "I'll just wear it. I really like it. I hope no one claims it, honestly," I say, unable to keep the possessiveness out of my voice.

"Well then, so do I. It suits you." She pats the back of the wheelchair but I wave it off.

"I'd rather walk. It feels really good to stretch my legs."

"But you'll let me know if you get tired?"

"I'll let you know."

"I heard some news today that I think you'll like," she says as we walk into the main lobby.

"What's that?"

"If your test results and vitals look good over the next forty-eight hours, they're going to discharge you." She grins sideways at me.

"I like that news a lot." *But where am I going to go when I leave here? Maybe I'll call Dana.* I keep my worries to myself and give her an appreciative smile.

"And I have even better news," she adds. "When I took David his dinner he mentioned that Ryan is quite taken with you."

I've replayed our kiss a thousand times in my head. That part felt amazing. But what happened next … I still can't make heads or tails of it.

"We kissed. While you were gone. I thought it went well. But he left right afterwards. It was really weird."

"You did? Why didn't you tell me? What do you mean he left? What happened?"

"We admitted that we had feelings for each other, at least I think we did. But he kept talking about 'complications.' I don't know. He was saying some weird things."

"Like what?"

"That I had decisions to make. I'm telling you, he was really cryptic."

"Boys." She rolls her eyes. "Don't take it personally. None of them ever know how to talk about what they're feeling."

"I don't know why he ran off like that. He said he had to go and that he'd explain it later," I say, deflating like a balloon.

Vanessa lets me walk into my room ahead of her and then parks the wheelchair in the corner.

"So tell me about the kiss," she says and sits down next to me on the stiff bed.

"It was intense and amazing and…"

"And what?"

"And not like anything I've ever felt before. I mean I've kissed a guy before. But not like that."

"What made it so different?" she asks.

I relive my new favorite memory one more time, letting every detail play in slow motion as I consider her question.

"It felt like … the start of something. And I could feel it in my toes." The confession makes my face hot, and I bring my cool fingers to my cheeks.

"A kiss isn't just touching your mouth to someone else's. A real kiss is a full-body experience," she says and raises an eyebrow. *Full-body experience. That's a perfect description.* "Tanzy, I think you just had your first real kiss."

"Maybe. I mean, I guess so. It was the first something, I can tell you that much." *I just hope there's going to be a second.* "Oh!" I say, straightening beside her. "There's a lot more I have to tell you. Something crazy happened while I was out there."

"It's about time. I've been dying to hear about your visitor," she says with a wink. My mouth falls open. "I had a dream yesterday that felt, well, you know, not so normal. I wasn't sure when it was going to happen."

"What all did you see?" I ask.

"Just bits and pieces. They're like a movie that's gone through a blender."

"Did you see his face? His eyes were insane. I think he might have been insane, actually. I feel a little bad for him."

"Really? Because I only saw your face, and you seemed really angry." Her voice lowers on her last words.

"I was," I answer, thinking back to the strange encounter. My fingers wander unprompted to the silver horseshoe, the most impossibly possible thing yet.

What would Vanessa say about Lucas? I press my lips into a firm line, debating whether or not to tell her about him. *Maybe just start with the necklace.* But before I can tell her the truth about where the necklace came from, it warms against my bare skin and Lucas's voice echoes in my listening mind. *Don't.*

Although I'm not wearing the ring, my eyes dart sideways and watch Vanessa's face for a reaction. *Had she heard him just then?* Her gaze doesn't lift from its focal point on the speckled tile.

"So what did he say?" she presses.

"Weird stuff," I answer. "He called me a strange name. Spera. I guess he thought I was someone else. Honestly, I kind of felt like I knew him too, but I know I've never seen him before."

His chiseled face surfaces in the front of my mind and makes my pulse speed up. His eyes seem to burn into me from within my own memory. The racing blood makes whooshing sounds in my ears and my muscles respond to the adrenaline pumping full force into my body.

"Is it hot in here to you? I think it's hot in here," I say, waving my hand in front of my face.

"No, I don't think so." She regards me with a puzzled face. "Are you okay?"

"Yeah. I'm just really hot all of the sudden."

"You're turning red," she says, alarmed.

I roll up my pant legs and fan at my sweaty skin. "Do you think that window opens?" I ask, pointing at the narrow pane of glass.

"No, I'm sure they keep it locked for—Tanzy, your legs," she gasps. I follow her gaze. "What? They look okay. They're ... fine," I repeat, stunned.

They are fine. Perfect. Not a single scar blemishes my skin. Not even older scars from years of working on a farm. Just smooth, pale skin. Cold shock douses the internal heat wave like a bucket of ice water, leaving me chilled and clammy. We search the rest of me for any trace of my accident. I turn my back to her and rip my shirt over my head.

"Do you see anything else?" I turn in a slow circle. Her wide eyes and open mouth say plenty.

"Somehow I don't think that happened during your accident," she says and reaches toward my sternum. I instinctively cover the necklace with my hand but she touches the skin just underneath. "Unless you got that before."

"Got what?"

"That." She traces three small interlocking circles that are scarred into my skin like a brand. The raised mark is still a fresh red.

"No. That wasn't there before," I answer in a strangled whisper. "What do you think it means? What's happening to me?" The adrenaline coursing through my veins demands me to move, but my nerves flat-line and root me to the spot.

"I don't know. I think it's glowing." Vanessa stares at the mark.

"Maybe it will go away." I cover it with my hands.

"Maybe," she agrees. But she sounds skeptical. "Can I see something?"

"Sure." I drop my hands, expecting her to move closer, but she quickly crosses the room and flips the light switch.

"Oh, Tanzy. You are not going to believe this," she gasps as soon as the light goes out.

"What?"

"I can't describe it. You're going to have to see it for yourself." Vanessa motions me over to the mirror. With a slow and careful hand she lifts the bottom of the sheet that covers the glass.

The scar looks like it's glowing. Alive, even. The hot pink brand brightens and dims in time with my pulse. I trace it with my finger tip.

"It's hot," I say more to myself. Too hot. I can barely maintain steady contact with it. The overwhelming heat returns and begins to spread throughout my body. I dizzily take a step for the window.

"I've got to get this thing open," I say, and search the frame for any kind of latch.

The instant the moonlight touches the scar it cools off. I let out a sigh of relief and rest my forehead against the cold window pane. The sensation of someone watching drills a hole into my bare skin. I glimpse down at the courtyard below and lock eyes with Lucas. He stands like a statue in the center of the lawn. I stifle a gasp and press my hand against the glass. *What are you doing here? I thought you were all in my head.*

"Tanzy! What if someone sees you?" Vanessa hisses from behind me.

I whirl to face her and back against the window so she can't see past me. *I don't know whether or not he's really there, and if she doesn't see him and I do, I'm going to completely lose it.*

"I forgot that I didn't have a shirt on," I mumble, covering myself with my hands. It takes every bit of self-control I have not to glance back out of the window. *I'll check again when she leaves.*

I will myself to move to the mirror. As I draw even with it, I can't help but lean away, quivering with dread over what I might see in my reflection. Finally, I let out a hard breath and meet my own eyes.

Vanessa laughs. "Stop scrunching up your face."

"Oh, right." I relax my face and concentrate on each feature one at a time. I don't look that different. But I don't look the same, either. My hair is definitely longer and nearly black. I lean toward my reflection. *Are the shadows playing tricks on my eyes or is my face ... sharper than it was before? And my eyes.*

"Will you turn the light back on?" I ask without turning away. The harsh fluorescent lighting washes over my pale skin. But it doesn't soften the lines of my face like I thought it would. I press my fingertips into my cheekbones. *They feel the same. Don't they?* I bring my face so close to the mirror that my breath fogs up the glass.

"What's wrong?"

"Nothing," I say, straightening. "Everything is just a little different."

"I think that's to be expected."

"You're probably right." I frown at myself in the mirror, startled to note that my hair is still nearly black even with the light on. I run my fingers through the dark waves. *I finally look a little like Mom.*

The thought tastes bitter, especially since I have no idea where I'm going to go once I'm discharged. I consider the idea of calling her to see if she remembers what she said, but the possibility that she might have meant it is more than I can bear. *I can always call Dana.*

"Are you okay? You're doing that thing with your face again," Vanessa asks.

"I'm really freaked out." Admitting it makes me feel a little better, and my muscles start to let go of each other.

"It's almost normal now," she says and motions toward the circular scars. They're the traditional angry pink of new scars, and the strange glow has disappeared in the light.

"No, it's not that. I mean, it is that. But I don't know what's going to happen after I'm discharged. Part of me is so excited about getting out of here that's all I can think about. But I don't know how I'm going to explain this to anyone. I can't hide it forever."

"Actually, I was hoping you'd come stay with us for a while," Vanessa says with an easy shrug. "I've been meaning to talk to you about it. We just always get a little sidetracked whenever we're together."

"Are you serious?" I hold my breath and brace myself for her to reconsider.

"First of all, our house is enormous. Ten people could live in there and never see each other. My husband and I talked about it and we both want to help you. He'll probably ask you a million questions about your recovery though," she laughs. "And I would love to have you stay with me until you figure out what you're going to do. I feel like we were brought together for a reason. We're two of a kind. Please say yes."

"Yes, yes. Of course. Are you kidding?"

My whole body feels lighter, immediately shrugging off the weight of so many unknowns. For the first time in weeks, they don't matter, and I'm going to live with the only other person who knows what it's like to see the world so much differently than everyone else.

"Good! Then it's settled. I'm going to go home and get a room ready for you. I am so excited!"

"Are you sure—" I start but she waves me off.

"I have a lot to do so I probably won't be back much between now and when you're discharged. Have them page my husband if you need anything," Vanessa says and quickly gathers her things.

I don't want her to rush out, but I am dying to see if Lucas is still there. "Vanessa," I insist, feeling guilty. She stops at the doorway. "Thank you."

She gives me a wink and slips out of my room. As soon as I am alone I step to the window pane and stare hard into the dark night. The courtyard is empty.

10
Pinch me

FOUR HOURS. THAT'S ALL I HAVE LEFT BETWEEN NOW and when Vanessa picks me up. More doctors than I care to count have stopped by to wish me well. None of them were very good at hiding their curiosity. But one doctor, well, almost-doctor, hasn't come by. And his absence is driving me crazy.

I haven't seen Ryan since he left me in the courtyard two nights ago, but he's pretty much the only thing I've thought about since. What had seemed so intriguing at the time now feels nothing short of insulting. I bristle every time I think about it. *So I will not think about him again for the next four hours.* My fingers absently fiddle with the little horseshoe necklace while I stare out the window. *I could always think about Lucas.* Real or not, he is very easy to think about.

"Can I come in?" Ryan calls from my open door.

My pulse quickens at the sound of his voice, but I refuse to let my excitement show. *If he wants to play hard to get, he's met his match.* "It's your hospital," I shrug.

He crosses the room and sits beside me. My heart thumps against my ribs. I'm sure he can hear it. I hug my arms to my chest and beg it to slow down.

"I heard you're leaving today," he says without turning his face.

"You heard right."

"I will miss you. I wish we had more time together."

"I've been right here the last two days."

"I know." His answer etches itself into my mind and makes my stomach sink. The few seconds we spend in silence feel like they might go on indefinitely.

"What happened? In the courtyard?" I blurt.

"I want to explain it to you, but now's not the time or place."

"That's just an excuse. I'm discharged. I'm not a patient here anymore."

He doesn't respond. Each of us picks a different part of the room to stare at. I clasp my fingers together to keep from drumming them.

"I heard you're staying with Vanessa and David for a while."

"Yep."

"Can I call you sometime?"

"I don't have a phone yet. I don't really have anything anymore, actually. Just Vanessa. And that," I say ruefully and motion toward a plastic bag that holds everything I own. It isn't much: the ring Vanessa gave me and the rest of the clothes that Dana brought. I still haven't taken off the necklace.

"But I guess you can call me at their house."

He stands and moves to the door. Part of me wants to tell him to stay and spend these last hours with me. The other part of me is searching for something to throw at him. I lean forward and reach for him instead. The instant my fingers touch his arm he turns to face me. His sapphire eyes smolder a darker, deeper blue, almost navy.

"Stay."

"Is that what you want?"

"Is that what you want?" I counter. "Don't stay just because you feel bad."

I drop my hand and cross my arms. Our eyes meet and I stare unwaveringly into his. In a fast, fluid movement Ryan sweeps me from the bed and pulls my body into his. I gasp and wrap my arms around his shoulders, startled by the relief that floods through me. He steps to the cabinets and gently sits me on the counter top, gazing at my face as he brushes my loose hair behind my ear.

"There's so much I want to tell you," he murmurs.

"What are you talking about? What's there to tell?" *Does he already have a girlfriend or something? That would explain why he's been acting so torn about this whole thing.*

He opens his mouth to speak, but instead a deep growl rumbles in his throat. I gasp and lean back. His strong arms tighten around my back as he brings his lips to mine. They are full and hot and I can't get close enough. *This is definitely a full body experience.* His wide palm glides smoothly over the side of my face and his thumb gently moves between our lips. I open my eyes and study his face.

"Are you sure you're ready?" he whispers, his eyes still closed.

"Ready for what?" I ask, trying to keep my voice from shaking.

"Ready to know."

"Yes." It is the only possible answer.

Ryan opens his eyes, and the black of his pupils bleeds into the irises as two white lines appear across his right cheek. *Scars. It can't be.*

"Lucas?" I jerk backward, struggling to create more space between us. "How did you ... who are you? What is this?"

I want to scream but can only manage a choked whisper. He drops his gaze to the floor without answering. The sadness in his eyes makes me stop fighting.

"How did you do that? I didn't think you were real. What are you? You were there that night. Why were you there?" I demand.

His strong hand moves slowly to my chest, and presses gently against my mark, which is covered by Dana's worn sweater. "It wasn't supposed to happen that way," he starts. I go completely still under his touch. "I was trying to make sure it never happened at all."

"What are you talking about? Make sure what never happened?"

"I failed you. They came for you and I failed you." His face clouds over with rage and grief as his fingers move to the little horseshoe. It's tiny in his big hand.

"Who came? You aren't making any sense."

"It's not safe for you to know yet. I will tell you as soon as I can. As soon as you can defend yourself. I will come for you."

"Defend myself? Against what?"

"I will tell you when you are ready. When you are finished. But you aren't done yet. And I can't compromise the process now that it has begun."

"What process? I think maybe you have me confused with someone else, because I don't know what you're talking about."

"If I had been successful, you never would've known me at all. I would have had to give you up, but you never would've had to know any of it."

"Give me an answer, Ryan, Lucas, whoever you are. One solid answer."

"What is your deepest concern? What is in your heart?" he asks and his black eyes soften.

My earlier panic is replaced with something deeper, something older. "Whether or not I can trust you," I whisper.

I don't even have to think about it. Above all else, that's what I need to know most.

"I can't decide for you whether or not you should trust me. But I can tell you that I exist for you. That I belong to you. That I have loved only you for a thousand…" He bites back the rest of whatever he was going to say. His face contorts and then relaxes as his eyes wander my face.

I watch, spellbound as he leans forward and whispers in my hot ear. "Be safe for me, Spera. I have waited too long for your return to lose you now."

"You love me?" I ask cautiously. I know he said more after that word but it's all I can think about. I didn't hear a bit of the rest of it.

"Yes." His answer is beautifully simple and sure. His full lips brush along my jaw as he runs the back of his knuckles along my throat. I close my eyes, hypnotized by his soft touch.

He said something else. Something familiar. Something important. Spera. I've heard that before.

"Wait. That name, why did you call me that name? Spera? Someone else called me that too. Someone that looks a lot like you, actually."

"You will learn in time. You must have patience. I've already given you too much information—thrown off the balance."

"Really? Because I don't feel like I know any more than I did before."

"About me. About who I can become. Don't tell anyone what you know."

"Lucas, I don't understand!" Tears spring to my eyes for reasons unknown to me.

"You will." The blackness lightens in his eyes as the blue seeps back in like an incoming tide. "I am never far from you. This is the way it must be for now."

I nod, too overwhelmed to argue anymore. *And because I trust him. I don't know why, but I do.* "Be seeing you," I offer, echoing the parting words he used the first time we met.

The words have an obvious, bittersweet impact on his face, which has returned to Ryan's smooth features. But the haunted look from Lucas's eyes remains as he stares at me long and hard before silently gliding from the room.

Did that really just happen? I slip off of the counter and step to the little sink. The cold water on my face is a welcome shock to my system. All I want to do is tell Vanessa. She'd know how to make sense of this. But he told me not to, and for some reason what he wants seems to matter. I gaze down at my ring finger, still red with irritation. *I guess it's a good thing I have an excuse not to wear that ring just in case we get good at hearing each other. I don't think I'll be thinking about anything other than Lucas. Ryan.*

I shake my head, nearly dizzy with the vivid memory of the past few minutes. A soft knock on my door brings me out of my head.

"Ms. Hightower, I just wanted to let you know that your paperwork is all set. You're good to go. Just make sure you sign out at billing before you leave. It's beside triage," a short, older woman says to me without stepping all the way into my room.

"Right. I'll do that."

"I hope you enjoyed your stay with us," she drawls.

"Best hospital visit ever," I try to keep the sarcasm out of my voice.

"That's good to hear. Take care, now," she says and moves back into the hallway.

Billing. And I thought a man who could change into a completely different person was scary. I glance at the plain clock on the wall. Three hours to go. *Well, no point in putting it off. I'll just wait for Vanessa outside when I'm done.* I pick up the plastic bag and leave my room without so much as a wave to my temporary home.

As I make my way to the billing desk I can't help searching for Ryan. *Lucas. That's going to take some getting used to.* I can tell he's not here. I can literally feel it. But I can also feel something else when I think about him. A new kind of connection. Even though he's not here, he could get here if I needed him. The thought is comforting and unsettling at the same time. *Why would I need him like that?* I round the last turn by triage and reluctantly walk to the billing office. *Unless of course he can save me from this hospital bill.*

"Can I help you?" a prim, middle-aged woman asks from a desk.

"I'm here to set up a payment plan for my bill." The words make my mouth dry.

"Last name?"

"Hightower."

"Hightower, Hightower," she repeats as her eyes scroll the screen. "Tanzy Leigh?"

"That's me."

"You're all set," she says, looking up. "Just sign right here." She points at a signature line.

"All set? What does that mean?"

"You don't need a payment plan. Your balance has already been paid."

"Did the hospital do all that for free?" I ask as I scrawl my name across the line.

"No." She laughs like I made a joke. "Someone already came and paid your balance in full. You owe someone a very big thank you," she says and gazes pointedly at me over the wire rims of her glasses.

"Does it say who did it?"

"No. It was paid with cash this morning right before my shift started. My gracious, I wish I'd been here to see that."

"Cash?" I nearly choke on the word. *This must be some kind of mistake.*

"Mmhmm," she confirms, staring at her screen. "Are you feeling all right, honey? You're a little pale."

"No, I'm good. Great," I insist, backing away. "Thanks." *I have got to get out of here before they realize they credited the wrong patient.*

"All right. Take care, now," she says and turns back to her computer. "Cash. Lord have mercy," she mumbles to herself under her breath.

I turn on my heel and try to walk as casually as I can manage across the lobby and out of the main doors. Vanessa and I agreed to meet in the courtyard, and I don't mind the idea of spending a couple of hours in the sunshine. But she's already waiting for me.

"You're early," I greet her.

"It's probably a southern thing. Daddy always said 'if you're on time, you're late.' He was a bit old-school that way." Her face softens as she recalls her father. She talks about him like I think about mine. Like he's gone.

"When did he die?"

"The car accident I told you about earlier. My parents were in the car with me. I lived. They didn't."

"I'm sorry."

"It's something I don't talk about." She says, her words neat and well-practiced. "Is there anything I can carry for you?"

"Nope, everything I own fits quite nicely in here." I raise the plastic bag.

"I had a feeling you were a light packer. I hope you don't mind but I got you a few things—a few changes of clothes. If they don't fit I'll take them back."

"Please take them back. I wouldn't feel right accepting anything else. You're already letting me stay with you. And, I know this sounds crazy, but did you," I hesitate and train my eyes on her face. "Did you pay my hospital bill?"

"Of course." She answers so casually that at first I think she's kidding.

"No, really."

"Really." She reaches out to take my plastic bag but I don't let her.

"But why? How?"

"Please, do you have any idea how much money my husband is going to make off your case? He's already got a dozen offers to give lectures, and every medical journal wants an article about your recovery. Just don't tell anyone that I paid for it because it would be a conflict of interest for David," she says and gives me a mischievous grin.

"You paid cash," I blurt.

"I know. So that should tell you that it was no problem." I stare at her, incredulous. "Anyways, I just guessed on your size. We can take back whatever you don't like," Vanessa changes the subject as she leads the way to the parking lot.

"You didn't need to do that. Any of it."

"Of course I did. I can't let you run around without clothes on. What would the neighbors think?"

"I'll pay you back," I say automatically. *I will find a way to pay her back. For everything.*

"Don't be ridiculous. I'm just happy that you're coming to stay with me," she says and threads her fingers through mine. "Where's your ring?"

"In here," I answer, showing her the plastic bag again. "I put it back in the little pouch and wrapped it in a shirt. It's totally safe."

"Why did you take it off?" Vanessa asks, frowning with disappointment. "You don't like it?"

"Of course I like it. It's beautiful. I just have really sensitive skin," I say and show her the red line on my finger. "I think I just need to get used to it. I've never worn a ring before."

"You've never worn a ring before?"

"Does that surprise you?" I ask, raising an eyebrow.

"Sorry I got weird about it. I just wanted to practice, you know, with the rings," she explains tentatively and taps her head.

The mind reading. Something about the whole idea doesn't sit right with me but I try not to let it show.

"You, Vanessa, are never, ever going to believe what happened today," I tease her with a sly grin in an attempt to change the subject.

"Does it have to do with Ryan?" she asks, her face piquing with interest.

I don't say anything, but I'm sure the redness creeping across my cheeks at the sound of his name is a dead giveaway.

"It does! What happened? Did you kiss him again?"

"Understatement."

"Tell me everything," she says in a rush.

I do. Almost. Reliving my last encounter with Ryan makes me shiver as I talk about it. By the time I'm through telling her, my lips feel hot against my tongue again. I do not tell her about his eyes … about his secret.

"I am glad you two, eh hem, talked it out," Vanessa chides as she moves toward a black sports car parked alone in the back corner of the lot.

"That's yours?"

"It's a Maserati," she says proudly. My mouth falls open. I'd never seen one in person before. "Hey, I like to go fast."

A daring glint makes her green eyes a shade darker. I shake my head in disbelief. The better I think I know her, the more I have to learn.

"Anyways, aren't goodbye kisses the best?" she says, changing the subject back to Ryan.

"Not goodbye," I correct, my voice more defensive than I mean it to be. "He gave me his number. And he might call me at your house. I hope that's okay."

"Of course it is," she says and unlocks her car. "I'll be glad when they get home safely."

Home safely? The surprise on my face must be obvious.

"He didn't tell you?" she asks as we climb into the sleek coup.

"Tell me what?"

"About the trip. It was a last minute thing. He probably forgot all about it once you guys started … talking."

"Where is he going?" I absently clutch the little horseshoe in my hand.

"The hospital is sending a medical team to Puerto Rico for a ten day free surgical clinic. Someone dropped out and my husband recommended Ryan to take his place," she explains. Vanessa zips the car out of the parking spot and accelerates to sixty miles an hour before we make the quick turn on to the main road.

"It's such a good opportunity for him. Medical schools love stuff like that," she continues, and I forget all about her wild driving.

Puerto Rico? Why didn't he say anything? My hand tightens its grip on the charm and instantly Ryan feels closer. "That's really good for him, then. I wonder why he didn't tell me."

"Like I said, it was really last minute. He'd only just found out about it when I ran into him in the lobby about twenty minutes ago. He may not have even known yet when you saw him."

"Do you know when they're leaving?"

"Tonight. They're taking the red-eye. My husband is going too, so we will have the house all to ourselves," she says with a grin.

"Are there beautiful women where he's going?" I try to joke, making every effort to cover up the sudden paranoia from creeping into my voice.

"Uh oh." Vanessa smiles at me over her shoulder. "I know that look."

"What?"

"You are head over heels," she says with mock disapproval. I don't answer. "You are, aren't you?" She smiles. "Now Tanzy, when Ryan comes over I'll expect you to leave your bedroom door open."

"Vanessa. You have got to be kidding me," I gasp.

She laughs so hard that she closes her eyes. *We're pushing ninety miles an hour on this two lane road and she's closing her eyes.*

"Sorry. I'm sorry." She tries to compose herself. But with one sideways glance at me she bows her head with another round of giggles. "I really do feel bad now," she says as she catches her breath and rights herself in her seat just in time to make a hairpin left turn.

"You should." I grin, relieved that she must somehow still be paying attention to the road. And the teasing is actually kind of nice. Kind of like family. "Where do you live?"

"Don't worry. I think you'll like it. We live in Keswick, about twenty minutes north of the hospital. Smack in the middle of horse country."

"I don't know if I'll ride." The words slip from my brain before I can stop them.

"Are you afraid?"

"No. The accident wasn't the horse's fault. It's just my mother. I mean, I did promise her, and—"

"She's not your mother," Vanessa snaps. My eyes go wide as my lips clamp shut. "I'm sorry. I shouldn't have said that. But what she did makes me so angry." She plucks a pair of sunglasses from overhead and drops them in place. "Tanzy. You should do absolutely everything that you want to do, whether that means riding all day every day or never seeing a horse again. Don't let anyone tell you any differently, either."

"You're a really great friend," I say, watching her stony profile. "Thank you, for everything. This all feels too good to be true, honestly."

"You're adding to my life too, you know."

"You'll have to explain that to me one day."

"I will. But I don't think I'll have to."

I can't imagine how that could be true.

"We're right up here," she says a second later and points at the only green grass I've seen on the whole drive.

The unblemished land is neatly dotted with hardwoods and rolls on as far as I can see. No house is visible from the road. She slows the car down and whips expertly into a cobblestone driveway, which is guarded on each side by a stone pillar. Mature trees line the cobblestone drive in perfectly spaced, checkered rows. Their trunks are so wide that I can't see what's past them. The driveway curves to the right and then back to the left, cutting a gentle switchback climb across the steep terrain. As it straightens out again, the neat forest curves symmetrically away from the cobblestone.

The house sits atop the hillcrest, surveying the flawless land like a fortress to its kingdom. *House is an understatement. Mansion is an understatement. What do you call this thing? A castle?*

A diagonal divide slices through the driveway as the cobblestone changes to some kind of shiny marble. The fiery-colored rock resembles the surface of the sun. The driveway loops in front of the spectacular stone house and doubles back on itself, leading back to the tree-lined entrance. An ornate fountain made of copper and the same rust-colored stone babbles in the center of the circle drive.

"Is that fire real?" I ask as I do a double-take.

A metallic statue of a woman spins smoothly in the center of a stone ring. Water flows from one hand, and some kind of liquid flame drips from the other. Steam rises from the pool beneath her as the drops of fire are extinguished at her submerged feet.

"You should see it at night," is all Vanessa says about it.

Someone pinch me.

Vanessa stops the car behind a black truck, which still has a temporary dealership tag on the back. I nod appreciatively at the make and model. A new Ford F-150. She doesn't strike me as the truck type. *It's probably Dr. Andrews's. I wonder if he'll let me drive it.*

I open my door as Vanessa pulls the key out of the ignition. Land rises and falls around us like a wind-swept ocean. Her spectacular house claims the highest hilltop for miles. *And she was worried about neighbors?*

"You have a lot of land." I say. It's a gross understatement.

"Almost a thousand acres. It's been in my family for a very long time."

"What do you do with it?" I've never met someone with so much land. *With so much, period.*

"Enjoy it. And let it be," she says.

I can't think of an answer that would sound better than that.

"Your home is ... unbelievable."

"Our home, Tanzy. For as long as you want."

"Thank you. There aren't words, really." My eyes drop to the glittering red marble beneath my feet. My worn boots look ridiculous against such an exquisite backdrop.

"There's no need to thank me."

"I'll find a way to repay you. I'm actually pretty handy, if you need anything fixed."

"You don't owe me anything. I want you to be here. You're my friend and I want to take care of you. We're two of a kind, you and I."

Something in those words makes me uneasy, but I can't put a finger on why. *You're just not used to relying on anyone.* The thought instantly makes me feel more settled.

"Are you hungry? I'm starved," Vanessa says from a few feet ahead of me, snapping me out of my fog.

"Lunch sounds good, actually," I answer absently as I shake off the lingering doubt. I'm not the least bit hungry, but doing something normal sounds like a good idea.

"We'll eat and then I'll take you on a tour," she says, and I fall into step behind her.

"I like the truck."

"I'm glad you like it. I got it for you," Vanessa says without turning around.

Her simple words make me freeze. "For me? Why?"

"Dana told me. About your dad's truck. That it wasn't salvageable after the fire. I thought this would make you feel more at home. If you had something that reminded you."

Dad. How long has it been since I've thought about him? The thought hurts like a punch in the stomach. I draw in a ragged breath and blink back the tears that come immediately. "This is too much."

"Please, don't be upset. This is something I wanted to do," she says as she moves back to me.

"It's not that. I mean, it is partly that. I don't know." She waits and watches my face as I sort out what I'm trying to say. "I'm just not used to anything like this."

"No one has taken care of you in a while," Vanessa says. "Life isn't supposed to be as hard as you've had it. I've been very fortunate in my life, and I love being able to give something back."

Her face and words are solemn. She makes me want to believe them. I take a step toward the brand new truck. My truck. "Thank you. Thank you so much." I run my hands over the smooth hood.

"It's unlocked, so feel free to check it out. If you don't like it—" My sharp glare cuts her off. She smiles as I take a mock defensive stance between her and the truck. "Okay, good. Take your time. I'm going to get lunch ready."

Vanessa strides to the mansion and slips through a pair of tall glass doors. I watch them click shut and then turn back to the truck. *Unbelievable. I can't wait to tell Dana about this.* I gently pull open the driver's side door. The rich scent of the calfskin leather interior makes me giddy as I breathe it in. The elaborate dashboard is equipped with all the bells and whistles. *She didn't spare a penny.* My eyes land on stitched cursive that runs across the chair-backs of both front seats. The letters make my breath stop in my throat. "Hightower" is embroidered perfectly on each chair. I rest against the seat as I trace the letters of my name.

Memories of my father fill every inch of the truck. I can picture exactly the way he would sit in the driver's seat. I know what radio station he would pick and how he would adjust the mirrors. I know that he would use the far cup holder because he would complain about bumping the close one with his knee.

Suddenly, I can hardly breathe and I need out of the truck. I hop out like it's on fire and slam the door closed. *Get a grip. Pull yourself together, Tanzy.* A strong wind whips across the foothills. Miles away, dark clouds grow on the horizon. The coming storm feels like a warning sign. *This is way too good to be true.* I shove my hands into the worn back pockets of Dana's jeans and try to ignore the gnawing uncertainty.

"People dream of a life like this," I scold myself under my breath as I stride to the grand entrance. The sound of my voice reassures me a little. I pause long enough to fish the ring out of the plastic bag and slip it back on, concentrating on how grateful I was for Vanessa's companionship at the hospital. Her understanding.

We're two of a kind. I repeat it to myself all the way to the engraved front doors.

"Perfect timing." Vanessa's voice echoes from somewhere deeper in the house as I close the door behind me.

The wood floors shine a dark mahogany and pay expert complement to the rich green walls that seem to climb skyward forever. A pale green, marble staircase carves a slow spiral along the cylindrical foyer wall. The stone railing chills my fingertips as I slide them along the detailed engraving that runs along the top of the solid banister.

"It's jade," Vanessa explains from behind me. I hadn't heard her approach. Her bare feet are a bright contrast to the dark floor.

"Oh, sorry." I quickly kneel to untie my boots.

"It's not a rule or anything. Just a personal preference."

"You?"

"Only in my own home." She winks and turns back to wherever she came from.

Luxurious velvet curtains drape the length of the towering walls and puddle on the cool floor. *These ceilings must be twenty feet high.* Original artwork is perfectly centered between each pair of covered windows. We cut through a spacious oval shaped room. The curve of the wall is made out of glass. An intricate oriental rug takes up most of the floor space and feels impossibly lush under my bare feet.

"This is my favorite room," Vanessa says.

"I can see why," I whisper back. I can't help but stare at the grandeur of every detail as we wind our way deeper into her home. *My home.*

"We'll gawk after we eat," Vanessa jokes without turning around.

"I've never seen anything like this," I say.

"It takes some getting used to. But you will in time." She steps aside and motions me ahead of her into a kitchen fit for the castle. "I hope sandwiches are okay. I'm not much of a cook."

"Sounds great," I respond in an awed whisper. The afternoon sun filters through the windows that stripe the quartz wall and casts streaks of light across the marble island. Two places are already set. We each claim a barstool and a plate.

"Welcome home," she says and raises her glass.

"Thank you," I smile. The clink of our glasses makes a little echo in the lofty space. "Do you ever get lonely here?"

"Sometimes. Actually, a lot. Does it make more sense now? Me wanting you here?"

"I think so. My old house felt big and lonely sometimes, and it could fit in your kitchen."

Vanessa throws her head back with a burst of laughter. "So, you see, you're helping me too."

I've never seen her so carefree. "Dr. Andrews works a lot?"

"He does. And this time of the year is always busier than usual. But it's better. When he's not here."

"Why do you let him stay? I mean the house is yours, right? Why not just kick him out?"

"Not everything is black and white. It's more complicated than that."

"Do you love him?"

"That's not a simple question either."

"It sounds simple to me."

"This coming from the girl who just had her first real kiss? I'd love to hear what you think you know about love." Her words come out like a bark. Vanessa narrows her green eyes as she glares at me and then at her sandwich. She puts it down without taking a bite.

"Sorry, I crossed a line."

"My life is an open book for you, Tanzy, except for one thing. My marriage is off limits. I know I told you some personal things earlier, but it would be better if from here on out we leave my marriage alone."

"Of course," I answer automatically. I would've agreed to anything she said if it meant this side of her would go away and the Vanessa I know would come back.

Then again, do I actually know her at all? Not really. Maybe it was a mistake to come here.

"Good. I appreciate it," she says.

A sudden clanging sound pierces the uncomfortable silence and makes me jump so hard that I almost fall off of my bar stool.

"It's probably David," Vanessa mumbles and moves for an old fashioned black phone on the far end of the counter.

"I'm going to go outside for a minute," I mouth to her as she picks up the receiver. She nods, a new heaviness settling on her face. My lips press into a firm line as I consider making sure she's okay, but she turns her back to me as she starts her conversation. *Her marriage is off limits.* She wouldn't need to tell me twice.

The temperature has dropped considerably in the short time we spent inside. Of course I can't tell if the shiver that passes through me has to do with the air outside or what just happened between Vanessa and me. I walk to the black truck and lean against the front bumper. If I knew where the keys were I'd be tempted to go for a drive. *A long drive. Maybe all the way to Kentucky.* My ears burn with shame at the thought. *Travis Hightower did not raise an ungrateful daughter.*

I turn away from the truck and walk around the side of the house. The hills are steeper in the back. Warning clouds have closed the distance between the house and the horizon. At this high altitude the clouds seem just out of reach. I stand on my tip toes, extending my raised arm a bit further. But they still elude my touch.

"I'm having an affair."

I drop my arm and whirl to face Vanessa. Long golden strands of hair whip across her face as the wind picks up.

"Do you think less of me?"

"No."

"I'm sorry. About earlier. I've been really stressed about the whole thing. I mean, if David ever found out … I took it out on you."

"It's okay. I shouldn't have said anything."

"You were only trying to support me. It's just a very complicated situation. One I shouldn't have gotten myself into." She clasps her bare arms in front of her chest.

"I think we're in for a good storm," I offer, moving my gaze to the angry sky.

"So you're not going to ask me?"

"About what? The affair?" I ask.

She nods without turning to face me.

"No. You'll tell me what you want to. That's your business," I say. And I mean it.

"Thank you. For understanding. I know my life seems extravagant, but it's not easy."

"Easy? Nothing about this looks easy. It's a lot to maintain."

"Yes. Yes, it is," she says, clearly appreciative. "Come inside. I've got some hot water on." She motions toward the back entrance, which is carved into the glittering black stone wall.

I'm sure it's just as gorgeous as everything else about this place. But all I can see is her right palm, which is bare. No horseshoe. No nothing. Just a plain hand. *It's gone.* I don't expect the panic that gives my heart a squeeze. I thought I'd be thrilled the minute those things went away. But they're why I'm here. That's what brought Vanessa and me together. *Maybe they'll come back.* I can't believe I want them to. But I do.

I don't say anything about it as we fix our tea and then walk from room to room, each more extraordinary than the next. Instead, I make too many comments about how much I appreciate the décor. Vanessa leads me into a great study. Books line the set-in shelves that climb the treacherous height of the cylindrical room.

"See, kindred spirits," she says as she shows me a life-sized black marble statue of a horse.

His head is raised; his still eyes defiant. The stone radiates warmth and life. I almost expect him to snort in annoyance. I move toward him and reach out to see if he feels as real as he looks.

"Don't touch him!" Her words come out in such a rush that I draw back my hand like I've been burned. "Sorry. He's very valuable. And the stone he's made of is very porous. Any oil from our fingertips would decrease his worth tremendously."

Vanessa continues down the hall, but I chance a last glimpse of the black horse. His smooth ears seem to be pricked harder than before, more focused. His gleaming eyes are trained on mine. *You're just imagining things because she made such a big deal about it.* I hurry to catch up to Vanessa. She chatters on about importing the jade for the banister during a recent remodel as we climb the long, curved staircase.

"I picked out a room for you and put your clothes in it, but there are plenty of other rooms to choose from, so let me know if you'd like to switch."

She swings open the heavy door and steps aside, bidding me to enter ahead of her. The walls are made of an ocean blue stone. The deep color is endless and satisfying. A king-size bed commands the center of the room, its four-poster frame draped in sheer, white curtains.

"Wow." My shock escapes my mouth in a whisper. My ears hum as my mind hears Vanessa keep a lewd joke about Ryan and the size of the bed to herself.

"I heard that." I flash her a grin.

Her face twists in confusion until I raise my hand and show her the ring.

"Do I get points for not saying it out loud?" she asks, clearly excited.

Sure. Why not? I think back to her. She claps her hands in delight.

"It's working!"

"I can't believe that these are for real." I glance down at the ring. It's already starting to hurt again.

"Can we practice tonight?"

"Sure," I say, still bewildered.

"I need to take care of a few phone calls, so why don't you get settled. If you need anything come find me," she says.

The burning sensation intensifies and I blink back a wince. "Sounds good." I turn to face her, but she's already gone.

Immediately, I try to yank off the ring. But it's stuck. My finger throbs as I wiggle the band back and forth until it finally crests the thickest part of my knuckle and slides off. Relieved, I shake the sting out of my hand and look for a safe place to store it until tonight.

A little ivory table sits beside the bed. I carefully run a finger across the oval table top. The material is soft and hard at the same time. Almost like weathered bone. *Maybe it is,* I think with a laugh. Nothing seems impossible in Vanessa's world. I set the ring down on the table and turn my attention to the canopy bed. The comforter feels like I imagine clouds do; like I could sink into them forever and never find the bottom. I double-check to make sure I'm alone, push the curtains aside, and leap, spread-eagle, into the middle of the giant bed.

"Definitely cloud like," I say to myself as I roll onto my back.

My body feels adrift, and I can't help but wonder at the thought of Lucas in my bed. Of the weight of him. I close my eyes, holding tight to the thought, and let the world fall away.

11
Surprise

PALE MORNING LIGHT FILTERS THROUGH THE SHEER white curtain, casting an ethereal glow in my new room. *Morning?* I bolt upright.

"Hey, sleepyhead," Vanessa calls from the cracked doorway.

"Hey. I'm so sorry. I can't believe I slept all the way through. I am a really great house guest, huh?" I scold myself as I run my fingers through my tangled hair.

"Tanzy, you're fine. I know how uncomfortable hospital beds are. I'm sure you haven't gotten a solid night's sleep in weeks," she says as she crosses the room and sits down beside me.

My hand catches on a knot and I look down to work it out. A thick snarl is caught on the band of my ring. *I don't remember putting that on.*

"I treated it for you," Vanessa says and motions toward my finger.

"Why? When?" Instinctively, I lean away from her. My eyes dart from the ring to her face and back.

"I ran some errands yesterday evening and stopped by a jewelry store. I told them about how sensitive your skin was and they offered to seal the metal with something hypoallergenic. Since our rings are the same size I just had them do mine and then I took yours." She shows me her hand.

I glance down at mine. It doesn't hurt anymore, but something about the whole thing makes me nervous. "And you put it on me while I was sleeping?" I ask. She flushes pink as her gaze drops to her lap.

"I'm sorry. I know how weird that sounds. I was getting bored all by myself. I was hoping you'd wake up." She frowns. "Are you mad?"

"No, I'm not mad. That's pretty weird, but I'm not mad." I can't help but laugh.

"Good." She opens her mouth to say something else but then closes it again. The expression on her face reminds me of a cat that's just swallowed the family goldfish.

"What?"

"I have a surprise for you." She's so excited that she looks like she might levitate right off the bed.

"What is it?"

"I'm not telling."

"You know I can't let you do anything else for me. I'll be doing odd jobs for you until I'm eighty just to pay you back for the hospital bill."

"It's not for you. It's something I did for myself that I think you'll appreciate." She purses her lips. My eyes narrow with wary interest.

"You are one of the most impulsive people I have ever met."

"So. Life is short," Vanessa retorts. "Get dressed. I put some clothes for you in the closet. I stuck your boots in there too."

"Okay, I'll be down in a sec," I say and swing my legs over the side of the bed.

"I'll meet you downstairs," she says and hurries through the door.

I let my eyes wander the rest of the room. My room. *For as long as you want*, Vanessa's words echo in my head. But as I pull on a pair of jeans and a sweater from the closet, I can't help but wonder at what price. Nothing comes without a cost.

"I grabbed a jacket for you. It's pretty cold out this morning," she says as she watches me descend the staircase, her fingers drumming impatiently on the glass doors. *She gave me the truck with as much enthusiasm as a hand-me-down t-shirt. What could possibly have her so excited?*

"I don't usually like surprises," I caution as I reach the bottom.

"We'll see about that." She hands me a green quilted jacket, pushes the doors open, and practically drags me outside. I shrug on the sleeves and follow her around the far side of the house. She covers my eyes with her hand as we turn the corner.

"You're starting to freak me out, Vanessa. What the heck did you do?" I playfully tug at her hand, but she lets it fall. "Did you build a ..." *barn.* The word stalls on my tongue. A stone-front barn peeks out from a grove of oak trees tucked into the side of a gentle slope.

"What do you think?"

"This wasn't here yesterday," I stammer, waiting to wake up.

"Yes, it was. You can't see it from the back of the house because of the hill over there." Vanessa points at a steep rise in the landscape. "I've always wanted to have a couple of horses and maybe even learn how to ride. And it increases the property value."

I can't even fathom what this property must be worth. But right now I don't care. I don't care about anything other than that perfect barn, and that it's within walking distance of my bed. *My whole life, this is all I've ever wanted.*

"Ouch," I laugh as I pinch the skin on my hand. *This is really happening. Maybe things do happen for a reason. If I hadn't been riding out there that night, if I hadn't been in that accident, I wouldn't be here.* I resist the urge to sprint the distance to the curved iron gateway that marks the entrance to the farm, deciding instead to savor every step.

The barn's exterior reminds me of a fortress. Polished black stones are placed together so intricately that whatever adhesive they used isn't visible between them. Black fencing lines a neat row of large paddocks. Water troughs dot the front corner of each enclosure. I hold my breath as I turn back around, prepared for the perfect barn to have vanished off the hillside. I let out a laugh as Vanessa watches me from where she leans against a wide doorway.

"This is the most incredible day," I shout up to her.

"You don't know the half of it," she calls back and waves me up to her.

She leads me down the single walkway that cuts the stable in half. Three generously sized stalls line each side of the aisle. A tack room and a wash stall cap the end of each row.

"So, you like it?" she asks.

"Are you kidding? Understatement." The smells of cedar and hay tug at a locked door under my ribs. My eyelids blink as fast as they can, and I'm glad Vanessa is behind me.

"I haven't shown you the best part." She moves toward a little black box mounted halfway up the wall by the entrance. "No one is taking horses from you ever again." She presses a red button and instantaneously thick metal doors descend to cover every door and window. Automatic lighting kicks on as the sunlight is completely snuffed out.

"Wow." The word escapes in a whisper.

"Isn't it great?"

"It's definitely effective," I manage.

"You know what we need now, right?" she asks as the security doors retract.

What else could she possibly need?

"Try to guess."

I look around, perplexed. Pitchforks and brooms are neatly hung on the walls adjacent to the doorway. A stack of fresh hay bales and two bags of feed sit outside the tack room. Each stall has two buckets for water and a bucket for grain. The scent of leather is strong in the air, which means there's probably at least one saddle in the tack room. Two helmets dangle from a hook beside the wash stall. Everything she would need to buy a horse. *Horses.*

"Vanessa, I don't know if that's such a good idea right now. There's a lot to consider before you get into owning a horse," I say.

"I've always wanted to learn how to ride. And it's not every day that you have the number one junior rider in the country living with you."

"That was two years ago. Who told you?"

"I don't care, and it was Dana."

"She can't keep a secret." I laugh and shake my head. "Dana would not believe this place. I need to call her. Can we have her out sometime so she can see it?"

"Of course. She knows all about it. She even helped me name it," Vanessa says.

"What did you decide on?" I can't imagine a name special enough.

"Let me show you. The name plate just came in this morning." She tows me to the tack room. Two saddles rest on their pegged holders, and a stack of white saddle pads rests on a custom wood tack box. The corners of a large metal plate peek out from a velvet covering.

"Voila!" Vanessa strips the sheet from the copper name plate. Three interlocking circles—my mark—gleam from the smooth surface. "Moonlit Farm" is inscribed underneath in beautiful cursive. I try to swallow the crush of feelings but I choke on them instead.

"Are you okay? You hate it," she says, crestfallen.

"No," I stammer. "I don't. Not at all."

"Then what is it?"

"The name. How did you come up with the name? Did Dana tell you?"

"She did," Vanessa answers. "She told me that your dad picked Moonlit out as a baby and trained her for you. I wanted to honor them both. I hope that's okay."

"It's perfect," I whisper. A long forgotten dream of running my own farm comes roaring back. I close my eyes and imagine what it would be like to teach and train here. I'd wanted to breed Moonlit and start my own line of show horses. This could be the perfect place to get started.

"So you'll help me?" Vanessa asks. Her voice snaps me out of my daydream.

"Help you what?"

"Find a horse. And teach me how to ride."

"If and only if we find a horse that I think is suitable for you to learn on."

"And one for you."

"No."

"Tanzy, we can't have just one horse in this beautiful barn. I worked so hard … okay, that's not true. A few very nice men worked so hard on this place. One horse would be lonely. Just say yes, for goodness sake. Why are you so against good things happening to you?" She scowls at me and I have to stifle a laugh.

"Vanessa, I just think it might be a little rash to—" She holds up a hand and cuts me off.

"Wait, what am I asking you for? I'm going to buy six horses. Now. So you can have a say in what I buy or not."

"I think bringing in six horses at one time is not a good decision," I reiterate, even though I can't help but wonder at the possibilities.

"Did I ask you?"

"Vanessa."

"Are you coming or not?" She crosses her arms across her chest and cocks her head to the side. I sigh and study her stubborn face.

"Fine. I'll come. But let the record show that I think this is a disaster waiting to happen."

"You can thank me later. I'll meet you at the car," she says and jogs ahead to grab her keys from the house.

I guess when she said 'now' she wasn't exaggerating. I slow my steps as I head back to the circle driveway, steeling myself against the dread that I expect to hit me like a runaway train at any moment. But it doesn't come. I lean against her car and close my eyes. *Maybe I really could pick up where I left off. Start a show farm with Vanessa. It takes money to get started, and she seems to have plenty.* My imagination cautiously fires up again, teeming with possibilities. I smile and reach for the horseshoe, but my fingers come up empty. My eyes drop to my chest as my hands feel frantically at my neck.

"All set?" Vanessa calls as she closes the glass front doors behind her.

"Have you seen my necklace?"

"What necklace?"

"The one I found in the garden. I haven't taken it off since. Have you seen it?"

"Oh, yeah." She waves her hand in my direction as she opens the driver's side door. "You were wearing it when you fell asleep yesterday. I put it in the drawer of your bedside table. It's such a delicate chain. I didn't want you to break it in your sleep. I know how much you like it."

Well, I guess that was thoughtful. I reluctantly pull the door open and start to move inside the car, but for some reason I can't stand the idea of leaving it behind. *Lucas told me to keep it on. It seems important for some reason. He can turn into a different person, for crying out loud; if he says it's important, it probably is.*

"Do you care if I go get it? I will be really fast." I ask as casually as I can manage.

"We're already running late for our first appointment."

"You made an appointment?"

"I got really excited yesterday while I was waiting for you to wake up. So I looked up some horses for sale online. I made some calls about a few that I liked the most."

I bite my lip and glance back up at the windows lining my room.

"It's safe, I promise," she says.

I can't explain why I need to get it without telling her about Lucas. *And he was very adamant about not doing that.* I grudgingly relent and slide into her car.

"Okay, where are we headed?" I beg the excitement that had found me earlier to make an encore appearance, but it seems to have disappeared.

"I'm not telling. All I'm going to tell you for now is that you're in for a very busy day." She hands me a thick folder. Pedigrees and photographs are organized between tabs for six different farms.

"I can't believe you did all of this. You think I'd stop being so surprised by you."

"I really like surprises," she says as she adjusts her sunglasses. She gives me a devious grin and then floors the gas. I should've asked if we could take the truck.

12
Horse crazy

THE FIRST FARM IS ONLY FIFTEEN MINUTES AWAY. THE red and white barn is lined with evergreen hedging. An outdoor arena bustles with trainers and their students. The sights and sounds are like regaining a lost memory.

As we wander through the sale barn, I explain to Vanessa that there are three main things to consider when evaluating a prospective horse: how it's built, how well it uses its body, and how it feels about work. Vanessa hangs on every word. She scrawls notes on a pad of paper. After a few minutes she begins to point things out herself.

"You're a quick study," I say. She beams and smiles down at her notes.

"Good morning ladies," a burley voice calls down the aisle. I immediately recognize the leathered face and dark eyes peering out from beneath a red ball cap as Jim Dunn, a trainer my father knew from the show circuit. I catch myself holding my breath, reluctant to let my old world and my new life collide. But if he recognizes me, he doesn't let it show. Still, the newfound certainty swelling in my chest begins to deflate. *Is there such a thing as a fresh start?* Vanessa shoots me a worried glance, her green eyes piercing straight through mine until they soften with understanding.

Nobody has to know, her voice calls out in my brain. Her words instantly make my back relax and my fingers uncurl. She gives me a little wink, and without missing another beat, returns Jim's welcome and extends a nimble hand.

"You must be Ms. Andrews," Jim says.

"It's nice to meet you. Thank you for fitting in an appointment on such short notice. This is my sister, Sarah. She's the rider in the family," she says and motions to me. I shake Jim's hand, maintaining eye contact for the briefest of moments.

"Do I know you?" he asks, cocking his head to the side.

"I'm sure you've seen each other at a show or something. Sarah used to show all the time," Vanessa explains with a wave of her hand. Jim responds with a nod of acceptance. *Sarah Andrews.* The name works like a salve on my nerves. It's easy. Classic. *Sarah Andrews doesn't sound like a girl without parents. She doesn't sound like a girl with anything to hide.*

I shoot Vanessa a grateful smile as we follow Jim down the wide aisle. He rattles off statistics and show histories as he shows us prospects that fit our criteria. My eyes wander ahead of him. A solid bay neck sticks out of a stall, a well-sculpted head swings in my direction. The horse lifts his nose in greeting as I approach. A low whinny rumbles in his throat. Down the aisle, a bored horse noses over a metal trash can. The horses on either side shy at the sound and spin into the back corners of their stalls. But the big bay acknowledges it with just a flick of an ear. The rest of him is steady and calm.

"Is this one available?" I ask, interrupting Jim as he talks to Vanessa about another horse.

"Yep. They're asking too much for him though, I'll be honest with you. I mean, he's a heck of a horse and has a lot of potential but he doesn't have a single mile on him outside of the farm," Jim says with a shake of his head. Vanessa glances at me for clarification.

"He hasn't been anywhere to compete. Some horses are perfect at home but don't reproduce the performance in a new environment."

"Well, I don't want to show," Vanessa says.

"How much are we talking?" I ask.

"Forty. But since I think the price is high and you two seem like you'd take good care of him, I'd be happy to wave my commission. You can have him for thirty-two." I grimace at the price, way more than I expected.

"We'll take him," Vanessa says firmly.

"Vanessa, we haven't even seen him go yet. And a vet needs to check him out."

"Okay. We'll watch someone ride him, a vet can check him out, and then we'll take him."

"You're welcome to hop on him. He's a saint. Or we've got a few exercise riders that can work him for you," Jim offers.

"Will you give us a second?" I dodge the question. He obliges and steps a few feet away from us. I lower my voice and turn to face Vanessa. "You know he means thirty-two thousand, right?"

"I know," she says without blinking.

"And you do remember saying that you want to buy at least two, right?"

"Yes," she says, genuine confusion on her face.

"All right. Let's watch him go."

An hour later Jim graciously accepts Vanessa's deposit check and we shake hands with him. "I'll call you in the next couple of days to iron out the details. Let me know when his vet-check comes back," I say as we head to the parking lot.

"Of course. If you're looking for anything else I hope you'll keep me in mind," he says, failing to keep the enthusiasm out of his voice. *I can't blame him. That was probably the easiest sale he's ever made.* Vanessa had even insisted on the full purchase price, including his commission.

"That was fun!" she practically sings beside me as we head to her car, which looks comical nestled in a row of diesel trucks.

"Are you sure you want to keep going? We can call it a day. That's one of the fastest sales I've ever seen, and we've already spent a lot of money."

"You could've had any of them, you know."

"None of the other horses sparked my interest." We climb into the car and she starts the engine.

"I wasn't talking about the horses." Her words paint me to the back of my seat. She giggles at my obvious discomfort and then drives too quickly down the gravel driveway.

Vanessa reaches into the back and plucks the folder off of the floor behind her seat. "The next place is ten minutes from here. I know right where it is. I printed out the email they sent me. Take a look and see what you think."

I flip through the printouts under the second tab and then thumb to the back of the folder.

"Wait, one of these farms is in Kentucky." I straighten in my seat as my mind fills with images of rolling blue hills dotted with some of the nicest horses in the world.

"I know. There's a great bed and breakfast not far from the farm. I figured we'd drive there tonight, eat somewhere fabulous, and get a good night's sleep. Then we can check out the horses in the morning. We'll drive home when we're done. There's no rush."

"Are you serious?" Even though I'm sure she's very serious, every nerve ending waits for her response.

"Why wouldn't I be?"

"You didn't tell me to pack," I say, unable to keep the excitement out of my voice.

"I packed for both of us." Her answer makes me snort. *Of course she did.* I peek at the other farms as I settle back into my seat, but all I can think about is tomorrow. Kentucky is proud of its horses for good reason.

I force myself to focus on the next farm we're going to. "I've actually been to this next place before."

"Do you like it?"

"Honestly, I wasn't impressed," I say frankly. She purses her mouth in disappointment. "There's no reason for you to waste time at the dime-a-dozen farms. I want to make sure you see the best of what's out there. Let me make a couple of calls to some people I know."

"That's what I'm talking about!" she exclaims and hands me her phone. I dial a familiar number.

"Hello. I have a client who is in the market for a couple of horses. No, there's no price limit…" The role slips back on like a pair of perfectly broken in boots.

We stop for lunch and then head west. Virginia's mountains peak around us as the speeding Maserati grips the winding road. In total we have three more stops for the day, the last one on the western edge of Virginia. But I can't stop thinking about tomorrow. *Tomorrow we'll shop Kentucky's horses without a budget.*

"The turn should be up here on the left," I say, glancing up from the directions I'd written on a napkin during lunch. Vanessa turns up the gravel driveway, which winds through the property. A faded, metal barn sits on a plain lot. The pitched roof is rusted in places and the scattered shrubs marking the entrance are in sore need of attention. But the farm has an air of seriousness about it that I like.

"This place seems kind of run down," she says without concealing her disappointment. She pulls into a parking space.

"Don't let that fool you. This is a working farm; it's not dressed up to impress boarders or students because the primary focus is turning out six-figure horses. And the horses don't care if the barn isn't pretty, as long as their stalls are spacious and their meals on time."

"It's nice to hear you so confident. I like this side of you," Vanessa says, which makes my face flush with pride. She turns back to the mirror and inspects herself before we get out of the car.

"Well, I'll be. You're Travis Hightower's girl. All grown up, aren't you?" A familiar man calls to us from the simple entrance.

"I'm sorry, I don't remember you," I admit, glancing down at my boots.

"No need to apologize. It's been a long time. I was friends with your pop. I'm sorry to hear about his passing." He extends a hand. "Name's Avery. Travis and me used to work the circuit together. Last I saw you, you was belt high. Kept his shadow good company. I can't believe it's you. I saw 'Hightower' written down on the appointment notebook and I don't know too many of those, but I never would've counted on you walking up on my farm." His eyes sober as they take me in, which touches my heart and rips it in half inside the same breath. I swallow back the surge of emotions climbing my throat and blink away the sting of grief.

"Avery, I'm Vanessa Andrews. Tanzy's going to teach me how to ride," she says, giving me a minute to gather the pieces of myself scattered on the gravel parking lot. They shake hands, and Avery gestures Vanessa ahead of him through the open doorway. I linger outside for a moment longer, allowing a few slow breaths to shore the old wounds before stepping inside.

A couple of hours later Vanessa signs two deposit checks, one for a snow-white thoroughbred gelding that had captivated her instantaneously and another for a chestnut mare that had a soft mouth, a rocking-horse canter, and a smooth jump. Even though memories of my father and Wildwood snuck up on me each time I thought I'd shut them out, it was still easy to appreciate the care and effort Avery and his staff took with their horses. What the farm lacked in appearances, the horses made up for in sheer brilliance.

"You've got some great horses here." It's probably the longest sentence I've said to Avery in the time we've been here. He gives me a kind smile.

"We like to think so. We're keeping them as safe as we can. It's a durn shame what's been happening around here."

"What are you talking about? What's happening?" A wave of adrenaline jumpstarts every muscle into readiness as I watch his eyes cloud over.

"That's right. I'd forgotten Wildwood was the first." He studies my face.

"The first?"

"No other farms burned down like Wildwood did, but a few others had their horses stolen overnight. You were there, weren't you?" he asks. In an instant, the memory of being chased through the woods slams into my brain. I close my eyes instinctively, willing away the sight of the trees blurring past as Hopewell ran for his life, but I can still hear the frantic rhythm of air rushing from his nostrils, his shrill whinny as he flipped over the fence. I throw a hand out for Avery's desk as my legs surrender beneath me.

"Whoa, Tanzy. Are you okay?" he says and sweeps his burly arm under my bent waist. I cling to his shoulder as the memory fades and the room stops spinning.

"I'm okay. I'm okay," I insist weakly to us both.

"She hasn't been out of the hospital long," Vanessa says, running a gentle hand through my hair. The three circles are suddenly hot under my layers of clothing. My hand covers my chest instinctively. I peek down, making sure they haven't burned through my jacket.

"I'm okay," I repeat as I right myself and wipe my face with the back of my hands.

"Take good care of Tanzy, Ms. Andrews. She's one of a kind."

"That she is," Vanessa says warmly.

"I'm going to head to the car. I need some air," I whisper to no one in particular and hurry outside. I swallow a sob and stare up at the darkening sky. A cold mist makes the air thick, which soothes the tightness in my throat. I close my eyes and lean back against the car.

Vanessa's even footsteps move across the lot. Her unconditional support and acceptance makes me want to hug her, but my arms stay locked in place in front of my chest, guarding my heart against another wayward memory of Wildwood Farm.

"You sure you're okay? What happened in there?" Vanessa asks quietly as she claims a spot next to me.

"Coming back into this is harder than I thought it was going to be," I say. She gives me a sad frown and tucks my hair behind my ear. "I can't stop thinking about what happened that night at Wildwood. Or about Dad."

"Do you want to go home? We can do this another time. I'm sorry I pushed," she says, toeing at the ground in a pair of brand new paddock boots.

"No, this is what I want to do. It's what I was meant to do. I know it is. It's just going to take me some time, I guess."

"Do you think we'll find good horses in Kentucky?" she asks.

"If you can't find a good horse in Kentucky then it's your own fault."

"Well then, why don't we skip the last two farms and head straight for Louisville?"

"I think that's a fantastic idea." Daydreams about what we might find are a welcome change to the dark memories that I can't completely shake. I begin to build the perfect horse in my mind: sweeping tail, long legs, deep ribs, wide chest, sloping shoulders, developed, smooth neck, and a sculpted, brilliant head. I start over each time that panther face reappears.

As we merge onto the highway and head for Kentucky, the images I've created take on a life of their own. The horses in my coming dream rear and strike at the blackness surrounding them, their eyes rolling white with fear.

13
Kentucky

WE'RE HERE!" VANESSA'S EXCITED VOICE PIERCES MY sleeping mind and shatters the brutal nightmare I am having into a thousand fragments. All I can remember is shades of red. And a feeling. A terrible feeling. But it all becomes a distant memory as I catch sight of Louisville sprawling in front of us.

"Sorry I slept for so long," I rasp and straighten in my seat.

"Don't be. It just means you can't use being tired as an excuse to not go out tonight." She sounds very pleased with herself. I glare at the side of her face.

"I'm not so sure that's a good idea."

"Tanzy, when is the last time you really went out?"

"Define really going out."

"You know, get all dolled up. Let a guy buy you a drink. Dance like you don't care what anyone thinks."

"I'm eighteen. Guys can't buy me drinks. I can't even get into a bar. I've never really been big on that scene anyway," I push back and fold my arms across my chest. We slow to a stop in front of a red light.

"You already don't care what anyone thinks. It's probably what I admire about you the most. Just live a little. You might actually enjoy it. What has playing it straight your whole life really done for you?"

She has a point.

"Live a little," I repeat. "I can do that." She lets out an excited squeal and floors the gas an instant before the light turns green. I swallow a gasp as my hands strike out for anything to hold on to. Vanessa laughs at my reaction.

"That's a good song. Turn it up," she says and starts to dance in the driver's seat. "Come on, Tanzy."

I turn up the volume and nod along to the beat.

"Aw, you've got more than that."

"I don't know how to dance," I admit.

"You don't have to know how to dance, you just have to know how to let go," she says, and promptly releases the steering wheel. She twirls her hands above her head as we fly down a straight road.

"Vanessa!"

"I'm not stopping until you start," she teases.

I do my best to copy her.

"Do you feel that? How can you not want to move? Close your eyes and feel it, Tanzy."

Well, at least this way if we crash I won't have to see it coming. I hold in a breath and close my eyes. The deep bass thumps like a heartbeat. My hands drum against my knees as the sounds flood my veins.

"There you go!" she says. I open my eyes and Vanessa grins in approval as she rocks her hips in her seat. I mimic her movement, feeling the little twists in my waist. My shoulders join in, rolling side to side with the music. Before I can stop them, my fingers press against the ceiling of her car and my body sways to the pounding rhythm.

Louisville's lights fly past like a whirling disco ball as we speed through the city. Vanessa throws her head back with laughter, and I can't help but want to feel just how she does in this exact moment. At last, I let go of the final thread of hesitation. I brace myself, sure it will feel like falling. But it doesn't. Not at all. I'm soaring. I'm free.

The drive is over too soon. She turns the volume down as we pull into a small parking lot across from the bed and breakfast. I swipe at the loose strands of hair that have fallen across my face. She gives me a wink and turns off the car.

"This place is really pretty," I say, regaining a little composure. But already I miss the rush as it evaporates from my skin and leaves me hungry for its return.

"I think so too. I always stay here whenever I'm in town," she says, her voice descending from the high. But her eyes are still wild. I wonder if my eyes are every bit as bright. Every bit as unpredictable.

"You come here a lot?"

She answers with a nod and doesn't add anything. Only one thing, or person, rather, can make her clam up like that. I let the topic drop and look up at the bed and breakfast. The quaint, three-story brick building is nestled between two high-rises. Its white wrap-around porch is completely out of place in the urban surroundings, but immediately it's what I love most.

We grab our bags from the trunk and head inside. An older gentleman in traditional bellhop attire takes our bags and swings the white door open for us. The interior is made entirely of wood. Unfinished beams line the tall ceiling. Vintage lace curtains cover the old fashioned window panes. The foyer smells like cedar and pancakes. I follow Vanessa the short distance to the front desk. The concierge knows her by name and calls a personal greeting to her the moment he spots us. *Yes, I'd say she comes here a lot.* She finishes checking in and hands me a room key.

"Oh here, take this back. I'll just lose it," I say and hand it back to her.

"I hope not. I got us two separate rooms."

"I don't need my own room," I say. *I can't afford my own room.* The lingering adrenaline from our drive leaves me like a sunset, and there's no way to hold on to the glow.

"I do." She bites her lips as she pauses. "He's coming to visit me later tonight." My mouth rounds in a silent response. *I'm guessing the "he" she's talking about isn't her husband. No wonder she comes here a lot.* She turns away from me and continues up the next flight of stairs. "We're on the third floor. This place only has six rooms. I like it because it's nice and private. And the customer service is the best," Vanessa adds without missing a beat.

"Vanessa, this whole day has been too good to be true. I need you to think of a way that I can repay you. I don't want to feel like I'm taking advantage of you."

"Don't be silly. There's no need to repay anyone anything. And I know if I ever needed you that you would do everything in your power to help me. That's what friends do. It's what family does. And you're like a sister to me. You know what you could do?" she asks, instantly brightening.

"Name it."

"Go out with me tonight. And be that girl you were when we pulled in to the parking lot. She was a hell of a lot of fun," she says with a wink.

"Okay, I can do that."

"Good," she says in mock seriousness. "Take some time to get settled. Let's meet in the lobby in about an hour," she says as we finally reach the third floor. "Your room is to the left and mine is to the right. It's just us up here so make yourself at home." Her cell phone rings in the pockets of her stiff jeans. She looks at the caller ID. Her eyes light up as she sees the name.

I'd bet the farm I know who that is.

Vanessa gives me a wave and starts toward her room. "Look cute. I know you know how," she calls over her shoulder before answering the phone. I can't hear what she says, but the silky sounds flowing into the receiver make her message clear: this conversation is just like her marriage. Off limits.

I walk to my end of the floor and swing open the heavy, unfinished door. A bed with a side table, a weathered rocking chair, and an oval, full-length mirror each claim a corner. I hoist my overnight bag onto the bed. It's so full that the zipper seems in danger of busting at any moment. *This is a lot of clothing for a one night trip.* A gold, silky something sits neatly on top of the pile. I try to unfold it with no success. It's just that short. I cringe and lay it carefully on the bed spread. The neckline plunges almost to the end of the fabric. *Why not call it for what it is and not wear anything at all?*

I swallow a lump of dread and nervously peek to see what else she'd packed. A pair of jeans. *Well that's not so scary.* My relief doesn't last. The jeans are skinny-cut and have the shortest zipper I've ever seen. A little yellow piece of paper is taped to the thigh. *Wear these tonight. And yes, the top you hate, too. —V*

But I don't hate it. "Maybe it is time to live a little," I whisper to myself in the empty room. I rally every bit of nerve I have and slip out of my customary attire. Goose bumps rise on my bare skin. I wriggle into the skinny jeans. The tight denim clings to every inch of my lower body. I hadn't expected them to fit. They actually feel good, and that makes me more curious about the revealing top than I'd like to admit.

As I pull it over my head, the slinky fabric glides down my waist and leaves more than a hint of skin between its end and the low-cut top of my jeans. I make sure the door is closed and then practice swaying my hips in little circles. *I can't believe I'm doing this.*

I fish through the rest of the bag, forcibly denying any acknowledgment that maybe, just maybe, I'm getting a little excited. My hand bumps against something that feels like shoes. Black patent heels. *Great. This will be the closest I've come to killing myself all day.* I hold on to the footboard of the bed as I work my feet into the two-inch heels and thank my lucky stars that Vanessa didn't pack stilettos. The full-length mirror I've been ignoring tempts me. I take a couple of cautious steps and then stride slowly to meet myself. My reflection takes my breath away. I take another step, marveling that she mimics my every movement.

"That's a girl that gets what she wants." I jump at the sound of Vanessa's voice and whirl to face the door I know I didn't hear open.

"I didn't hear you come in."

"You left the door cracked," she says and shrugs a bare shoulder. *No, I didn't. Did I?* Thoughts about whether or not the door was open disappear as I take in the sight of a very dressed up Vanessa. A steely silver dress cuffs her long neck in a mandarin collar, clings to every inch of her sculpted torso, and glides the very short distance to the hemline. Beautiful green earrings twinkle through their cover of loose blonde hair. The huge emeralds deepen the jade color of her eyes. If you didn't know her, you'd never guess that stones that size would be real. But I know better.

"You look amazing. He must be quite a man," I tease, still a little apprehensive about touching the subject.

"Oh honey, this isn't for him. I dressed up for you. And you look pretty amazing yourself."

"I feel amazing. I feel … different. It's hard to explain. I've never worn anything like this."

"The clothes don't make the woman, the woman makes the clothes. I think you're finally realizing your worth. That's a good thing," she says as she inspects me. "You just need one little thing."

"What's that?" I ask. To answer she pulls a tube of red lipstick from her jeweled clutch.

"Are you going to run away?"

"Nope. I trust you."

"It's about time," she says as she makes two quick swipes across my lips with the deep red lipstick. "See what a difference a little color makes." She takes me by the shoulders and turns me to face the mirror. Coal black hair cascades to my elbows, framing in my hazel eyes, which burn amber in response to the gold top. Red lips pout back at me, daring anyone who's looking to make them change their shape. *This girl's been in there the whole time? I wish I'd met her sooner.*

"Met who? Me, or that woman in the mirror?" Vanessa responds.

"Hey! You're tuned in, or whatever," I say, flashing the ring on my hand. She grins and lifts hers, too.

"It's getting easier," she says happily. "So you didn't answer my question about who you wish you'd met sooner." She pulls my hair back behind my shoulders as she locks eyes with my reflection.

"I hadn't thought about it like that. Both."

"Better late than never. Are you ready to take her for a spin?"

Vanessa doesn't have to ask me to crank the music as we peel out of the parking lot. We roll the windows down despite the cold night. The air that rushes through her speeding car whips our hair in every direction. I've never felt more alive.

She pulls to a smooth stop under the club's valet tent and glides from the driver's seat in one fluid motion. The valet's mouth drops open, words completely failing him. Vanessa pats him on the shoulder as she slinks around the front of the car and takes me by the elbow. The doorman lets out a low whistle as we approach. He waves us over and without a word lets us in ahead of a line of roped off people. I expect someone in the line to protest us cutting in front, but not a single complaint is made.

"Told you," Vanessa says. Every eye turns to watch us as we move through the groups of people to a booth in the back corner. "Do you feel that?" she whispers.

"Feel what?"

"Their desire. And the power it gives you." Even though the word "desire" makes my cheeks hot, I can't help but notice that she's right. The air is thick with it. Vanessa orders us a round of drinks. We silently watch the thriving crowd, trading opinions without ever opening our mouths.

We're getting really good at this, she marvels silently.

I know. I still can't believe these rings actually work. I wonder if it will come and go like it did before.

I hope not. Out of habit, we stop our silent conversation as the waitress approaches with our drinks. Vanessa quickly dismisses her with a little wave.

"Cheers," she purrs and clinks her glass to mine.

"What is it?" I ask, inspecting the drink.

"It's good. That's all you need to know," she teases and takes a sip. I quickly follow suit. *It is good.* Even though there's ice in it, the liquid feels warm as it slides down my throat and leaves a numb trail. I take another sip. My cheeks begin to tingle.

By the time we move to the throbbing dance floor, I feel a new confidence making itself at home inside my skin. The pounding bass pulses through every fiber in my body. I am practically dizzy with wild energy and whatever drinks Vanessa ordered another round of. She walks ahead of me. People part like wind-whipped grass as she strides ahead. She pauses and motions me beside her.

"Do you mind if I put you through a little test?"

"What do you mean?"

"I want to see how you are progressing. You know," she says and points at her colorless palm.

"Okay." Nervous heat crawls up the sides of my neck. *What if I fail?*

"Take a good look around. What do you see?"

"People?" I say, confused. "What am I supposed to see?"

"Let your mind go blank and tell me what you see."

I start to ask for clarification, but something inside of me seems to instinctively know what she's asking me to do. I let it take over, slowing my breath and quieting my focus. My heart slows down, but the pulse is louder, pounding in my ears above the music and noise of the crowd. My mind begins to systematically analyze the building.

Four ways in and out. Nine places to watch from unseen. I hadn't counted, hadn't known what I was supposed to see. It just happened. A chill of surprise flutters across my shoulders. But Vanessa doesn't seem the least bit startled. Instead, a satisfied grin spreads across her face.

"Very good." *She knew I'd be able to do that? What else does she know? What else can she do?* I press my lips into a hard line, wondering if she heard those thoughts. But her expression doesn't change as she stares out across the dance floor.

The tempo changes to a harder, faster rhythm. The crowd responds to it like gasoline to a match. Vanessa's body is set loose, free from its proper boundaries. The air crackles around her, torn apart by the energy that radiates from her gleaming skin. The sensation beats under my ribs like caged wings and I finally give in to it. Our movement flows, practically synchronized as the music consumes our deepest, darkest places.

A pair of eyes burn holes in my bare back. It feels like some kind of challenge. A tall, clean-cut man leans against a long, steel bar. We lock eyes. He turns to the man standing next to him and points in our direction.

You have an admirer, Vanessa's voice enters my mind. "They could be fun," she whispers in my ear.

"Not my type," I answer back without taking my eyes off him. The way he stares at me fills me with an instinct that I don't understand, but I'm having a very hard time staying still.

"Not because of Ryan, I hope."

"No. Well, maybe." My fingers wander over the bare space where the necklace should be.

"You kissed. Once."

"Twice." I cross my arms and wrap my fingers around my side, protecting the warmth that spreads across my skin from the memories.

"Whatever. You're not married. You're not even dating. He's half a world away," she scoffs.

I look down, immediately feeling young and out of place.

"All I'm saying is that he'd be none the wiser," Vanessa says, softening her voice. "It's time that you started looking out for you. Letting yourself do what you want without worrying so much about consequences. You've spent your whole life trying to make everyone else happy. That's a job, not a life. Live, Tanzy."

Without another word, she raises her hand at the two admirers and waves them over. They respond instantly, which makes the muscles in my arms feel jumpy. I shove my hands in my back pockets to keep them from trembling with the sudden flood of adrenaline. The tangy scent of whatever cologne they're wearing grows stronger as they close the distance. I can't read their minds, but what they're thinking is painted all over their faces.

Never gonna happen. Vanessa giggles at my thought.

"Have fun," she says loud enough for all of us to hear. My admirer gives her a smirk and steps in front of me. His friend slides a hand around Vanessa's waist. She moves her arm across his and pulls it tighter.

You already have two to keep up with and you want another one? The thought crosses my mind before I can stop it.

Mind your own good-looking business. That tall drink of water would eat out of your hand if you asked him to, her voice echoes a response in my mind. I swallow a gasp and glance at her over my shoulder. She directs a hard stare my way and then turns her attention back to the man who has already pulled her body so close to his that they touch.

"What's your name?" my admirer asks as he takes my fingers in his. I hide the cringe that shudders down my spine and resist the urge to yank my hand away.

"Do you really care?"

"Sure," he says and steps closer. It takes every ounce of self-control I have not to shove him back.

"What's your name?" I counter.

"John," he says after a pause. On a hunch I glance down at his left hand. A band of lighter skin is visible on his ring finger where a wedding ring usually sits.

"That's the second lie you've told me tonight."

"I like you. You're feisty." He slides his arms around my waist and pulls me so close to him that I can feel the sweaty dampness of his shirt on my bare midriff.

"Hey, stop." I take a firm step back and push a resisting hand at his chest.

"Stop? That's not what you really want. Not dressed like that," he growls as he lowers his face to mine. The sudden need to get away from him is so over-powering that I can hardly breathe. In one quick motion I rip myself out of his grip and spin away from him, blending quickly into the crush of people.

Vanessa, can you hear me? Nothing sounds back in my racing mind. *This guy is no good,* I try to call out to her again. Suddenly, his unmistakable scent floods my nose. *Get out,* my brain commands. Currents of air I hadn't noticed before move past my hot face, guiding me like an invisible map for the nearest open door.

I slip outside and work to slow down my breathing. Even though a thousand sounds bleed from the open door, I can pick out his footsteps as he approaches the exit I took. The only thing I can think about is getting away.

I scan the street for a place to duck into. The alley between the nightclub and the next brick building is just twenty feet away. I hurry the short distance and round the corner. I know he saw me. I can feel it. But cloaking myself in the shadows of the dark alley feels like the right thing to do. The only thing. I draw in a deep breath and wait.

14
Nothing can be the same after this

THERE YOU ARE," HE GLOWERS AS HE STEPS IN FRONT OF me. I don't move a muscle. "How did you know I like it when girls play hard to get?" He gives me an awful grin and reaches for my neck.

Without a single hesitation my body flies into action. My hands shoot forward and twist his arm so hard and fast that his shoulder joint explodes with a sickening crack. A punch rockets from my fist and smashes his teeth into the back of his mouth before he can utter a first scream of pain. A second swell of strength drives my left hand through his jaw, splitting it in half. The force of the blow sends him clear across the alley. He crashes against the brick wall and slumps in a heap on the pavement.

I stand stone still, panting and dizzy as I stare at his limp form. *What just happened? How did I do that? Did I . . . is he dead?*

"Tanzy." Vanessa's voice is low behind me. A jolt of heat zips through my body, followed by an icy wave of dread that wraps around me like a wet blanket and starts to squeeze. I can hear myself gasping, but my lungs don't recognize the oxygen each time it rushes in and out. I'm suffocating on air. I wait for her to gasp or yell, but she is silent. She walks over to "John," in a plain, unhurried stride and then toes at him with her silver shoe. He lets out a low moan.

"We need to call an ambulance," I stammer, wrapping my sweaty arms around my trembling frame.

"The hell we do. He'll be fine," she says and glares down at him.

"I think I really hurt him."

"I saw what he was trying to do. That's no way to treat a lady," she scolds. He tries to yell but it comes out as a gurgle. "See, he's fine," she says as she kneels beside him and fishes his wallet out of his back pocket.

"What are you doing?" The whispered words claw their way up my throat.

"What do you know? His name really is John," she says as she tucks his cash into the neckline of her dress and drops his credit cards and driver's license down the storm drain. I hear her toss his wallet into a stack of cardboard boxes piled against the brick wall, but I can't tear my eyes away from John's face, which is such a bloody mess that I can't remember what he looks like underneath.

"Come on, let's go," Vanessa says and puts a hand on my back.

"We're just going to leave him here?"

"Of course we are."

I stare at her, incredulous.

"This is his fault. If he hadn't tried to do God knows what to you out here, then none of this would've happened," she says. "Someone will find him, don't worry. I'll make sure of it, if it makes you feel better."

I nod, too overwhelmed to say anything. She takes me by the elbow and guides me back toward the main street. I cast one last glance at John over my shoulder. He isn't moving. I let out a jagged breath and lean against Vanessa as we make our way to the front of the nightclub.

"One too many," she winks at the valet as she helps me to the passenger side of her Maserati. I have to brace myself on the open door frame to keep from falling down in the street. She distracts him with a generous tip and then closes my door. "Did you hear that?" I hear her say to the valet.

"Hear what?"

"I thought I heard someone yell in that alley. Never mind, it's probably nothing."

"I'll check it out just in case," he says. A wave of nausea burns the back of my tongue as I watch him start down the sidewalk.

"Are you okay?" Vanessa asks me as she slides into the driver's seat.

"You didn't freak out. Why didn't you freak out?" I ask, ignoring her question.

"What's there to freak out about?" She sounds genuinely confused.

"Did you see what I just did?"

"I know. I'm pretty jealous."

"Are you serious right now?" I shriek.

"You should be proud of yourself. You showed incredible self-control," she says as she puts the car in drive and merges onto the street. Her placid composure makes me feel all the more reckless by comparison.

"That was self-control?" I cover my eyes with my palms, unable to stop reliving the last ten minutes of my life.

"He's alive. That's self-control. You could've killed him at any point."

"I know," I whisper. *How is that possible?* My hands shake harder against my face. I drop them to my lap and squeeze them together.

"He had it coming," Vanessa insists.

I need to go turn myself in or something. He's married. What if he has kids? What if he dies?

"Don't feel bad," she says, reading my mind. "You probably saved a lot of girls from him in the future, from whatever he was going to do to you. And you didn't kill him."

I didn't kill him. Repeating it to myself makes me feel a little calmer. "I don't understand how I did that. He *flew*, Vanessa. His bones broke. I felt them."

"I think it's all part of those circles. I'm sure it's connected. And it's fantastic," she says with a grin.

"Are you kidding?" I cry out, near tears. "I almost killed someone. And he might still die."

"And the world would be a better place without him."

"I feel like I don't even know you right now," I whisper.

"Think of what you could do, who you could help," she says. Her words make my spinning thoughts slow down. I hadn't considered that part of it. "I'm positive you aren't the first girl he tried to force. This has to be a gift, Tanzy."

"What do you mean?" I stare down at my hands, suddenly torn.

"I think something bigger is at work, something we don't understand yet. But I feel sure that you have a higher purpose, and that this super-human strength is just the beginning," she says.

I mull over Vanessa's theory as I stare through the windshield. *He was easily twice my size. There's no way I should've been able to hurt him like that.*

"We're just about there," Vanessa says gently, breaking through my heavy thoughts. "Sorry I kept you out so late. For everything, really."

I nod a response and slip the ring off.

"Your thoughts about tonight are that bad, huh?"

"It's not that, I promise. I just need to turn everything off for a minute." I can't remember being this exhausted in all my life.

"Totally understandable. Are you sure you're okay?" she asks as we start across the parking lot.

"Yeah. I just want to go to bed." But I doubt I'll sleep. Every time I close my eyes I relive what happened in the alley.

I have to hold onto the railing as we climb the front stairs. Concern lines the night-watchman's face as we pass through the open door. Vanessa silently hands him a fifty dollar bill. She's so fast and smooth that I barely see it happen. He tucks it into his pocket without looking at it and straightens at his post. *At least she'll be able to bail me out of jail.* The thought makes me feel sick.

"Well, do you want to meet for coffee in the morning?" Vanessa asks as we begin the long climb to our floor.

"Sure," I answer without really hearing her question.

"They'll have a big continental breakfast buffet in the main lobby. It's always delicious." The mention of food makes my stomach rumble. But I refuse to acknowledge the sudden pangs. Who could eat after what I'd just done?

"Are you hungry? We never had dinner. Can I have them send you something up to your room?"

"No, thanks. I just want to go to sleep. The faster this day ends the better."

"Don't be too hard on yourself."

I give her a shrug and stare down at the carpet.

"We're still on for coffee in the morning, right?" she asks again once we reach the top.

How can she talk about tomorrow like everything is still the same? Nothing is the same. Nothing can ever be the same. I manage a feeble smile in response, too spent to argue.

"Our first appointment is at ten. How about if we meet at eight o'clock? That way we can take our time," she says.

I nod, barely hearing her.

"I'll see you in the morning. And Tanzy, none of that was your fault."

"Right. See you in the morning," I mumble. I can feel her watch me walk the whole way to my door.

My clothes smell like stale sweat and smoke. I peel them off and hang them over the towel bar and then turn on the shower as hot as it will go. The scalding water makes me cry out as I step underneath the hard spray, but the pain feels good. I stand under the pounding water until the heat makes me so dizzy that the memories from the alley spin into a dark oblivion.

Sleep still feels impossible. I ease under the comforter and stare out of the window. The night is clear and the moon is bright. I wish I had the necklace Lucas gave me. I would hold it as tight as I could and maybe he would know I'm thinking about him. Maybe he'd even show up here. *Would you really want him to after what you've done tonight?*

"I don't even know who I am anymore." My voice sounds small in the hollow room.

I know who you are, I imagine Lucas's voice in my brain.

How did I just come up with that? I guess because something about him makes me feel safe, despite of everything. If I didn't know better I'd swear he was right beside me, whispering in my ear.

"I miss you."

I miss you, too.

Even though I know it's all in my head, I hold tight to his words and wait for sleep.

15
Blueblood

W AKING UP IS A MIXED BAG. BECAUSE IF TODAY IS REAL, if I get to shop the world's most pedigreed horses without a budget, then last night was real. And I almost killed a man. The first thought makes me want to leap out of bed. The second makes me want to jump out the window.

I glance at the clock on my bedside table. Seven-thirty. Time to get moving. But the simple action of swinging my legs over the side takes everything I've got. I blink and John's face is in front of mine again, smoke and beer on his breath. Another blink and all I see is red. Salty, warm, red that smells like rust and is every bit as corrosive, eating straight through my flesh and deep into my soul.

Even now I can feel the drops of blood that splattered my cheek the moment my fist made contact. I catch myself wiping at it, sure I'll see stains on the back of my hand. But there's nothing there. A man could be dead because of these hands but they don't look any different. *Shouldn't they look different?* They start to tremble all over again. I shake them at my sides, shake them until they hurt.

Focus, Tanzy. One foot in front of the other. I repeat it to myself from the bed to the dresser. There's a red shirt in my bag. I throw it away as fast as I can. A sob escapes my dry mouth and hangs in the air, waiting for company. But I force the rest down and press the heels of my traitorous hands into my eyes. *He could be someone else's father. You don't get to cry about that.* But the thoughts have an opposite effect, drawing an untamed emotion from my chest and making my insides heave to quaking. I cling to the lip of the dresser, no longer able to support the weight of it all. *Did someone find him in time? Will he see the sunrise?*

I brave a glimpse out of my window, sure I'll see police cars lining the street below. Instead, a clear, bright dawn shines unaware on the outskirts of Louisville. A few people dot the sidewalk. Every exhale they make vaporizes in front of their mouths. Do they know what happened? Is my name in that cloud of warm air leaving their lips?

Self-preservation awakens within my muscles, bullying grief for space. A damp chill runs its icy fingers up my spine. I clench my teeth to keep them from chattering and blindly pull on clothes, but the extra layers offer no shield from this kind of cold. I draw in a long, staggering breath and step into the hallway.

My swollen eyes catch on the morning paper waiting by my door. I almost walk right by it. But the headline in the side column makes me stop short: "ER Nurse Alleges Prior Assault by Comatose John Doe." My heart pounds against my ribs as I fumble the paper open and lean against my door frame. "An unidentified, comatose man brought to Louisville Medical late last night was recognized by a nurse as the man who she alleges assaulted her six months ago. Although his face suffered extensive damage, she says she clearly remembers the tattoos on his arms." I stare down blindly at the rest of the article. I don't have to read another word. I know it's him.

Vanessa was right. I had done a good thing. And I hadn't killed him. *He was caught because of me.*

I hurry down the stairs, pausing at the balconied landing on the second floor that overlooks the cozy lobby. Vanessa sits with her back to me. She has picked a small, circular table by a window. The morning sunlight makes her glow. I watch her from above, reliving the moment she walked into the alley, unfazed and ready. The way she took charge of the mess I'd made. The way she took care of me. She'd said he'd probably hurt other girls. Her instincts were dead on, and I'd treated her like she was the criminal. Regret pinches the back of my throat. I swallow it away, silently vowing to make it up to her, and make my way to the lobby below.

"Hey," she calls as she glances at me over her shoulder. "Did you see the paper?"

"Yes." I press my lips in a firm line to keep from smiling again. Something in her dark gaze triggers another mental replay of the horrible fight. The sound his face made as it caved in. The way his ribs gave out under my foot.

"Told you." Vanessa breaks into a smug grin as I mask a shudder.

"I guess it makes me feel a little better about everything."

"Feel better? You should feel great. I hope that guy never wakes up," she says between sips of coffee. My back stiffens at her words, but I force it to relax.

She's right. He's the only guilty one here. Still, the memory of her stepping in a pool of his blood in silver high-heeled shoes blooms within me and lingers like I might enjoy the way it smells.

"Go get something to eat. We have a big day ahead of us," she says, switching the subject.

"Yes, we do," I agree, more than happy to focus on anything else. And for the first time since last night, recognizing the pangs of hunger doesn't douse me in guilt. I pile my plate until the paper starts to give under the weight and head back to the table.

"This place is great, Vanessa. I can see why you come here," I slide into my chair.

"Actually, that's something I wanted to talk to you about. How would you feel about staying another night or two?"

"Sounds great to me," I answer brightly.

"There's a local tradition around here that I want to introduce you to. You'll like it, I promise. It's outside."

"What is it exactly?" I ask, hiding my doubtful face behind a slice of cantaloupe.

"It's called a drum circle. It's this secret thing that the locals do during the full moon."

"Seriously?" My resolve stumbles.

"Yes," she says, drawing the word out. I give her a sideways glance that begs for further explanation. "There are drummers, of course, and a huge bonfire. Fortune tellers, fire dancers, mountain witches, and singers—"

"Wait, I thought you said this was just locals?"

"It is," she says in all seriousness. "There's fantastic music and story-telling about the ancient spiritual beliefs of our pagan elders. It's a great way to relax and recharge."

"So if it's a secret, how did you find out about it?"

"I went to the University of Kentucky. I dated one of my professors."

I will my face not to react, but I lose.

"What? So I have a thing for older men. Not that it's any of your business."

"Right. Sorry," I say and avert my eyes.

"Tanzy, I'm kidding," she says, swatting my fist with her fingertips. "Anyways, he was a sociology professor and did a bunch of research on hidden local traditions. That's how he discovered the drum circle. He took me with him one night. Since then I go whenever I can."

"Are you serious?"

"I know, I know. But the experience is amazing. Look, I feel horrible about what happened to you last night."

"I do too," I interject, but she stops me with a shake of her head. "I feel totally responsible for the whole thing. I want to make it up to you. I wouldn't take you somewhere tonight unless I was sure you would enjoy it. Would you trust me on this?"

"I'm in," I say and shrug my shoulders. She's been right every step of the way. It's time I stop second-guessing her.

"Good. Now, is it okay with you if we talk about horses?"

"Yes, please." I lean across the table. She pulls the folder out of her tote and hands it to me. I leaf through the printouts of today's prospects and tap the top page.

"I don't know why, but I have a good feeling about this farm," I say. She glances down at the sheet.

"It's our first appointment," she says, checking her notes.

"You did really well setting all this up on your own. And I know I was reluctant, to say the least, but you were right, I'm glad we came."

"You're welcome." Vanessa beams with pride as she gathers her things. "I won't even say I told you so."

The cloudless morning makes a perfect backdrop to the sprawling countryside. Thoroughbreds dot the rolling pasture, which still boasts various shades of green despite the winter temperatures. We make our last turn. The huge white barn from the printout is immediately visible even though we have half a mile to go. I beat a rhythm on my knees. Vanessa glances down at my busy fingers and smiles.

"This is really nice," she breathes as we turn into the driveway.

"Welcome to Kentucky horses."

We step out of her car and are greeted by several barn dogs. They sniff us eagerly, registering where we've been. I open my hands and they lick my fingers.

"Come on, boys. Leave the ladies alone," a kind voice calls to the pack. They bound over to him, a good first impression in my book. "You must be Vanessa." He extends a hand.

"Yes, hi. Thank you for seeing us today."

"Tanzy," I say, and then inwardly cringe, wishing I'd said Sarah instead.

"I'm Russ. Nice to meet you both. Let's head inside and talk about what you're looking for."

We fall in step behind him as he explains the layout of the incredible facility. The farm is home to a hundred horses in three different barns, which are shaped in a horseshoe around the biggest covered riding arena I've ever seen. We stop and watch as exercise riders take their horses through morning workouts. "As you can see, we've got a bunch of sale stock right now. Tell me any specifics you have in mind and I'll narrow it down from there," he says.

"Just something reliable, comfortable, and bombproof. Doesn't have to be too flashy," I start. Vanessa clears her throat.

"Well, it can be a little flashy," she says, which draws a chuckle from Russ.

"What's your price range?" he asks.

"That's a non-issue," she says bluntly.

"Ma'am, the prices here vary a great deal. I just need to know your ceiling before we get started."

"It's a non-issue," she repeats evenly. I raise an eyebrow at Russ, who lets out a low whistle.

"Well, all right." He raises his eyes in wonder, but his pulse doesn't quicken at the thought of a big sale. My appreciation for his professionalism is quickly swept aside by the fact that I can hear the rhythm of his body from three feet away. And it's more than that. I can feel it. I understand it. I resist the urge to clamp my hands over my ears and stare across the large arena, ignoring the new current of information until it blurs into the other sounds around us.

"Let's start with that bay Hanoverian mare working over the line of jumps right there," Russ says and points.

I step back and let Vanessa ask Russ the few questions she knows, giving my own heart a moment to steady. *It's okay. You're okay. It's probably all part of whatever gift this is. Vanessa will know what's going on. She always does.* I shake off the residual adrenaline and join them on the rail. He gives us the statistics on several of the horses working in the riding ring and calls instructions to their riders to show off what they're capable of. Vanessa is mesmerized, studying a gray horse cantering circles on the far end. I keep quiet, unwilling to disrupt the admiration in her eyes. Russ excuses himself and walks into the arena to set up some higher jumps, making her finally turn away. I take the opportunity to see if she's got her heart set on anything yet.

"Do you see any you like?"

"I think the real issue is going to be deciding which ones I don't want. I think I need a bigger barn."

"Let's just start with the stalls you have now. That way you can learn what you like and what you don't, so when you're ready to buy more you'll know exactly what you want."

"Okay, I can accept that. But next time we're coming here first."

"I couldn't agree more. Dana would love it here."

"We should bring her next time."

"She's working on a farm around here somewhere. I should ask Russ if he's heard of her, see if he knows which farm she's at. I feel bad that I haven't called her."

"Don't worry, she called me this morning. I'm sorry I forgot to tell you. I got so distracted when I saw the newspaper."

"How's she doing? Does she like her new farm?"

"I told her we were in Kentucky. She's in Florida for a big horse show or something. She said they've got her traveling a lot already. She couldn't talk long."

"Good for her," I say, keeping a smile in place. But my heart sinks a little.

"Well, ladies, do you see anything you like so far?" Russ calls from the arena. We slip under the white rails and meet him in the center of the ring to talk about Vanessa's favorites.

An hour later we're in Russ's office going over paperwork as Vanessa signs deposit checks four and five.

"I love this facility. Would you mind showing me the rest? I want to get some ideas for back home," she asks as she hands him the checks.

"I'll be happy to," he says. We follow him down the barn aisle toward the pasture, which is divided with white fencing into a checkerboard of paddocks. Most of them are empty. My eyes catch on a gray horse standing alone. Her black-tipped ears are pricked so hard that they're almost touching. She lifts her nose in search of a scent on the steady breeze. Her black eyes zero in on my face, and she screams in recognition.

It can't be.

"That right there is a sad story. I'd love to show her to you but she's not ready to be sold yet. We're still trying to figure out how to keep somebody on her."

"Oh my God. That's Moonlit." My body ignites with motion as my insides go still, waiting in disbelief.

"How'd you know that?" Russ asks without hiding the shock in his voice.

"That's my horse." *My horse.*

I don't wait for either Russ or Vanessa to respond before I take off toward her. The mixture of cold air and hot tears makes my eyes sting. I run at a dead sprint, terrified she'll disappear if I don't reach her fast enough. She screams and canters to the paddock fence. In a fluid motion, I plant my hand on the top rail and swing my body over the fence. Without hesitating I throw my arms around her neck. She stands still in my hold and noses at my hair with her lips.

"You're Tanzy Hightower," Russ says as he approaches quietly. I nod a response, my face still buried in her black mane.

"I knew your name sounded familiar but I couldn't place it. And I durn sure didn't think you were Tanzy Hightower. You don't look quite like the pictures I saw of you in riding journals. But that was a long time ago," he says, trailing off as he glances from me to Moonlit. "Your mother sold me that horse. Told me you couldn't stand the sight of her and wanted her gone."

"She lied to you," I whisper, too many emotions surging through my veins to articulate a longer explanation.

"Well, if you want her back you can have her." His offer startles me. I size him up, immediately suspicious. My father had nearly broken the bank when he bought her as a yearling for fifteen thousand dollars. At the time my mother essentially gave her to Russ she was worth a quarter of a million.

Why would he offer to just give her back? My face must beg the same question.

"You're still the last person to ride her. No one has been able to stay on her for longer than two minutes in nearly two years. And I've tried everything. We were going to breed her this spring if we still couldn't get anybody up on her," he explains. I stare back at him.

"So you'd just give her back?"

"Well, I guess it would only be fair if I sold her back to you at the same price I bought her for. You know she sold her to me for a dollar. I never told anyone what I paid for her. Figured they'd think something underhanded was going on."

"Russ, I don't even know what to say or how to thank you."

"Will you try to ride her while you're here?" His request makes me laugh. "I know she can't do a lot since she's out of shape, and I heard you'd stopped riding a couple of years back. But if it's all the same to you I'd love to see what you can do with her."

Before his last words have left his mouth, my hand finds a familiar hold on her withers and I swing onto her bare back. Moonlit doesn't flinch as I slide behind her shoulders and give her a pat.

"I've waited a long time to be up here."

"Look who's impatient now," Vanessa jokes. I barely hear her as I move Moonlit away from them with the faintest pressure from my calf. *Do you remember, girl?* She snorts in response. We walk a couple of wide figure eights to get in tune with each other and then she moves up into a smooth trot as soon as I think to tell her. *Canter.* The three-beat gait begins the moment the word enters my mind. I open my arms to the cold air as my body moves with hers in perfect rhythm. I close my eyes and the world falls away. The only things I hear are her steady exhales and the muted beat of her unshod hooves on the earth. *Easy.* She breaks smoothly to a walk. I reluctantly open my eyes. Russ and Vanessa stare at us from the fence, mouths agape.

"Well, Tanzy, I don't think that horse is ever going to belong to anyone but you."

"Not if I can help it," I say.

"That was like magic," Vanessa says as we pull away from the farm several hours later. Russ let me groom Moonlit. I even cleaned her stall and scrubbed out her buckets. Finally there was nothing left to do. I am still so reluctant to leave her that I have to force myself not to jump out of Vanessa's car.

"It felt like magic. Moonlit and I just fit together," I answer, squirming in my seat. Russ agreed to ship the three horses to Vanessa's free of charge once the other two passed a vet-inspection. *It's going to be a long week.*

"It's like she's been waiting for you all this time. And only you."
Vanessa's face contorts into a grimace. Moonlit had lunged to bite
her any time she got within striking distance.

"I never thought I'd see her again. And I have you to thank. If
you hadn't made me come, I never would have. I don't know how
to thank you."

"Teach me how to ride like that."

It makes me laugh. I drift back to the reunion with Moonlit and
daydream about what our future might hold. I finally have a piece
of my family back. *I can't wait for Lucas to see me ride, to see what
I'm like outside of a hospital.*

The foothills fade to black as the sun sets behind them. I stare
hard at the horizon, holding on to the daydream that Lucas is
watching me from the trees, happy and proud. But the coming twilight is still. There's no magic left in it for me tonight.

16
Playing with fire

WHILE I TOOK MY TIME WITH MOONLIT, VANESSA HAD called to cancel our other appointments now that her barn was full. *Our barn.* I can't wait to get back to Moonlit Farm, to get started where I left off. Where Dad left off. We'd had so many plans for Wildwood. Before he died I knew exactly how my life would go, exactly what I wanted. Afterward, I wasn't sure about anything. But now everything was back on track. *Except that he's not here to see it. And it's my fault.*

"What are you thinking about over there?" Vanessa asks from the driver's side. Even though her voice is soft, the sound of it makes me jump as I crash out of my head.

"My dad."

"What about him?"

"That he should be here. How thrilled this would make him."

"So why do you seem so sad?"

"Because it's my fault that he's gone," I answer in a whisper. Admitting it out loud for the first time hurts just as much as I always feared it would.

"What do you mean?"

"The accident was my fault."

"If it was an accident how could it be your fault?" she counters.

For the first time, I tell someone the whole story about the day he died. About looking down into the flooded ravine and seeing Teague's unmoving body floating broadside in the muddy water. About waiting for my dad to surface. About the three seconds of silence between the moment they went over the edge to the moment the worst sound I'd ever heard filled my ears. About the instant Teague took off like a shot through the trees lining the ravine. About letting Dad go ahead of me on a trail we didn't usually take to see if he'd see it too; that black, shimmering, crackling nothingness that had been there the last time I rode the seldom-traveled trail alone. About how it lunged at him from its hiding place among a thicket of blackberry bramble.

He didn't see it. Teague did.

"What about Moonlit?" Vanessa asks, nearly breathless.

"She didn't flinch the first time I saw it, which is why I thought it was all in my head. I just wanted to see if he noticed it, too. But when it jumped at Dad, Moonlit spooked and ran back for the barn. I jumped off but I was too late. Teague was basically side-swiped by it and took off. Dad never saw it coming. And it's my fault." I hide my face with my hands.

"That was not your fault," Vanessa insists. "Accidents happen. It was awful, yes. But it was no one's fault. If anything is to blame it's whatever that thing was that jumped at his horse."

"It still feels like my fault. He wouldn't have been there in that moment if I hadn't asked to take that trail."

"Would your dad want you to feel like that?"

Even though I know the obvious answer, I turn the question over in my head. Nowhere do I find a reason he would want me to blame myself. *Intentions are everything, Tanzy. You can't always control how the chips fall.* His voice repeats within me, what he always said when a plan went awry. The warmth of his voice lingers even as the sound of it fades.

"No. He wouldn't." I whisper, studying my hands in my lap. Hightower hands. They're shaped just like his.

"You deserve to have good things happen to you. He would want this for you, wouldn't he?"

"He really, really would," I answer, swelling with bittersweet joy. *He would be so proud of me.*

"I know how you can be sure."

"Sure about what?" At first I think I've misheard her. I swivel in my seat, studying the side of her face. My insides hum like they know what she's about to suggest.

"If you could talk to him again, would you want to?"

"What are you talking about?"

"There's a woman that usually shows up for the drum circles. She does all kinds of voodoo stuff. Reads tarot cards, palms. I bet she could try to contact him for you."

"No way," I answer, shaking my head.

"Okay," she relents immediately. "But if you change your mind, I'll see if I can find her." We let the topic drop, but the offer buries itself in my brain, refusing to be tossed out. It reappears each time I let my guard down.

The lights of Louisville fade as Vanessa drives away from the city and into the dark countryside. She makes several quick turns down roads without street signs, and then pulls into a grassy field. A handful of other cars are tucked into a curve in the tree line. She carefully maneuvers the Maserati into a protected space and turns off the engine. The field falls into inky black the moment she extinguishes the headlights.

"See there? That's where we're going," she says quietly and points at a glow of flame light at the bottom of a long hill. We get out of her car and silently follow the line of trees until the mouth of a trail appears. "Are you okay?" she asks over her shoulder before she starts down the path. The question is more loaded than I'm willing to admit, so I muster a smile in place of the words I can't find. She gives me a knowing look and then moves into the trees.

The rumble of the drums below peppers the air like closing thunder. My breath quickens so I hold it, listening as every beat defines itself from the din. A rustle behind us whips my head around. Two glinting eyes flash in the thick black. They disappear a moment later.

"Vanessa, I think something's out here," I whisper.

"There are lots of things out here. We're in the middle of the woods. We're the outsiders here." Her confidence catches me by surprise, challenging the girl within me who used to feel perfectly at home among the trees and darkness. She stirs beneath my skin, stiff and out of practice. But she's there.

The riverfront is aglow with a ring of torches. A huge bonfire that sends a column of smoke into the clear night sky. People dance around the bonfire, backlit by the flames. Their bodies move in time to the drummers' music like a heartbeat. My pulse reacts the instant we step inside the throbbing fray.

"Come on!" Vanessa says, towing me toward the bonfire. She finds a spot just big enough for two people and lifts her hands above her head. Every strike of a stick on the taut surface of a drum pushes and pulls at her body as she sways to its rhythm, setting her free and keeping her prisoner. And I want it—I want to know how it feels to need everything and nothing at the exact same time.

"Who do we have here?" A woman's voice rasps behind me. I spin toward the words, somehow sure that they're for me. "Now you're something special, aren't you?" she says as she reaches a curled finger toward the mark hidden under my clothes.

I want to take a step back, but there's nowhere to go without bumping into someone. The whites of the woman's hazel eyes leap from her bronze skin. Twists of waist-long dreadlocks spill over her shoulders. Shells and pieces of sea glass are woven into her black hair. She brings her finger within a hair's width of my jacket and then snatches her hand away with a hiss.

"What do you want?" I whisper, still frozen in place. I can't believe Vanessa hasn't intervened. The woman's nose is so close to my neck that I can feel the air rush past me and into her nostrils as she inhales. She leans away from me and cuts her glowing eyes to disbelieving slits.

"Don't let her scare you," Vanessa says, breaking the intense spell that had settled in the sliver of air between us. "Why are you scaring my friend, Maris?"

"She came with you?" she asks, her bright eyes moving from Vanessa to me. "But of course she did."

"You two know each other?" I finally ask, flexing my hands at my sides.

"I know everything," Maris says with another sly grin. I can't place Maris's accent, her voice tropical and worn like a piece of driftwood. It's unlike anything I've ever heard before.

"Don't let her scare you. She's harmless," Vanessa says with a wave of her hand. "She lives here. Illegally, I'm sure. She just takes some getting used to. This is the woman I was telling you about. The one who might be able to help, if you want."

"Right," I answer slowly, studying the woman's face. Something about her glows. It's not something I can see with my eyes, but I can feel it. She has a draw on me like the moon to the tide. "I don't want any help. But thanks." Maris tilts her head and stares straight at the location of my mark again. Her eyes burn through my coat and make my skin hot.

"How do you know about the scars?" I cover the place on my coat with my hand.

"Because I know you. And I know your mother," Maris says. As soon as the word mother leaves her lips, every other sight and sound around me blurs.

"What are you talking about?" My world spins. Vanessa moves between us but Maris waves her back.

"You come with me. I will tell you what I see," she says and stretches out her hand. I reach back and then pause, my hand suspended over hers. "I can cause you no harm, girl. You have strength beyond any other human, do you not? You have nothing to fear from no one. Not like that anyway." She stares straight through my eyes. Her pupils dilate so far that they blot out her gold-green irises. I've only seen one other person do that before. *Lucas.*

Without a second thought, I clamp my hand around hers. Her lips pull back in a satisfied grin as she leads me through the crush of people and toward a little tent at the water's edge. Vanessa follows close behind us.

"Ah-ah, *bella*. This is not for you," Maris scolds Vanessa once we step clear of the crowd. I hold my breath, waiting for Vanessa to argue. But she obediently steps back and gives us a wave. I cast her one last glance over my shoulder as Maris pulls me forward.

We step inside the little tent and she takes a seat on the ground, which is covered with a heavy blue blanket. A weathered wooden chest is nestled in the corner. It's the only thing in the tent besides the two of us. *She lives in here?* I cautiously lower myself to the floor. Crystal prisms dangle from the low ceiling. They catch light from sources I can't see and paint dark rainbows all over the canvas walls. She strikes a match and brings it to the wick of an antique lantern. The rainbows fade a bit in the new light. With a start I realize that the prisms had been reflecting Maris's invisible glow. *What are you?*

"I am the hand in the undertow. I am the rainbow in the mist," she says as she settles to the ground.

"You can read my mind?" I ask, trying to keep my voice from shaking. Quick on the heels of my question comes the startling realization that it won't seem strange if she says yes. It just means

I will have to watch my mouth and my thoughts. I will them both to silence.

"I know everything," she repeats. But this time it sounds like she's trying to reassure me. It does little to help. My eyes dart from Maris to the opening and back. I can beat her to the door, and that does help.

"What do you want with me?" I finally ask.

"I must fulfill the promise I made to your mother."

"How do you know my mother?"

"We go way back," she says, her eyes softening.

"She said she wasn't my real mom. Is that true?"

"It was the best thing. The only way to keep you protected. To keep us all protected." Her cryptic answer makes me ball my fists at my sides. I let out a hard breath and lock stares with Maris, silently begging her to say anything that makes sense.

"So is she my mom or not?" My question obviously takes Maris by surprise. She closes her eyes and a knowing smile spreads across her face.

"A piece of wind and sky, she was," she says, her voice low. "It's the only reason they finally had to let you come back."

"Say something that makes sense!" My cheeks flush, betraying my desperation.

"I have already wasted too much time. Now then. You need to quiet that tongue and that mind of yours and listen to me."

"Maris, please!" I cry out, smacking my palm against the ground between us. She jumps, clutching her fingers to her chest. My wild breaths come out wet and ragged, each one squeezing past the sob I won't let out. *You're only mad because it matters, and that's okay,* my father's favorite bargaining chip haunts the edges of my mind. "She matters, Maris. It matters."

"No, girl. You are mistaken. You matter. You matter to us all."

"What are you talking about?" The sting of threatening tears finally breaks free, dripping unchecked down my face.

"About his mark. About your purpose." She reaches for the rings again. I close my eyes, but I don't move away. I can't. My body is heavy, useless—weighted down by these half answers that act as a paralytic instead of a springboard. "And yours is marked with a purpose that will affect us all."

"What do you mean? What is my purpose?"

"The same as anyone's purpose. To make a choice."

"That doesn't make any sense." Everything in me is suspended over the gap between what I'm sure of and what I'm not, and the ground is crumbling beneath my feet. The meager space inside the burlap walls begins to whirl, picking up speed with every evolution.

"But it makes perfect sense. You are not destined to complete a single action. You are destined to choose between two. And the choice you have to make is truly dreadful. I know now why your mother made the decision she did."

"What decision? What did she do?" I steel my hands by my sides.

"I say too much and waste precious time. I must fulfill the promise I made. Which is to keep her secret, and to show you yours." The word secret instantaneously stops the slow spin in the tent, making me pitch forward. I catch myself on my knees.

Does she know about what happened to Dad? Thoughts of my mother vanish from my head the moment his face appears in the same space. I don't feel like a traitor for choosing his face over hers. She's made it clear she would've rather lost me in the river instead of him. For the first time in years, it seems we're on the same side. The recognition brings a new round of bitter tears.

"Your father has no part in this," Maris says as she leans back and unlocks the wooden chest. It groans with protest as she lifts the heavy lid. "But what happened to him certainly does."

"Part in what? What is this? What does it mean? You know something. I know you do," I demand, motioning to the mark on my sternum.

"Asher. And what he intends to do." She plucks a little red bottle from the chest and snaps it shut.

"Give me one straight answer," I seethe, quaking with desire to burn her little tent to the ground. In a flash of a vision I can even see it smoldering on the riverbank. My mind begins to toy with whether or not Maris is inside when I set it ablaze, but I catch the thought and toss it from my mind, horrified and embarrassed. She levels her eyes at me and I wonder if she saw what I saw. The pile of ash I wish for her home.

"This life is not your first." She delivers the sentence in even words, each one a puzzle piece. They click together one at a time. They paint a picture I can see. A picture that starts to make sense. A wave of doubt overtakes them, scattering the pieces far and wide.

"That's not possible." I shake my head, agitation drying up the wells behind my eyes.

"I have no time for your doubts, girl. Listen to what I have to say now and reject it all you like once you leave." Arguing with her has only served to march me in a circle. My father's voice whispers in my mind again, reminding me of something he told me about the pecking order in a herd of horses: the one in charge moves the least, instead showing dominance by forcing the movement of the others.

Be still, Tanzy.

"Okay, I'm listening." I press my lips together in a hard line and focus on inhaling slowly and deliberately.

"Before this life, you were given form once before, nearly a thousand years ago. During that life, your soul was marked for a terrible choice. So terrible that once your physical form perished, the powers that be took every measure to make sure your soul would re-enter this world as seldom as possible. Never, they hoped."

"What am I choosing between exactly?" My voice doesn't shake, but my hands do. I ball them into fists and press them against my thighs. Maris's hazel eyes drop to the floor. She absently spreads her long skirt across her lap. Finally, she meets my gaze.

"Endings." She blinks the shine in her eyes away as her answer hangs in the air between us. My blood understands her meaning before my mind catches on, speeding up in my veins and drumming in my ears. My hands twitch reflexively, remembering the way it felt to reach into John's flesh and shatter the bones beneath.

Endings. What if Vanessa was wrong? What if all of this is part of something very, very bad? Maris reaches out to steady me and hands me water in a small crystal cup. I accept it, but I don't drink it.

"Go on," I say, refusing to expose any further emotion. She takes a long breath and studies me before she continues.

"They required two conditions for your soul to be reborn. First, that you be born to a mother who has seen both sides of the veil."

"What veil?" I ask as calmly as I can manage.

"Second," she snaps, holding up a finger. "That the original blood be joined with the original soul for your path to be set in motion. And I can smell it on you. He did it somehow."

"He, who? What blood? What are you talking about?" I sputter.

"Ever since we suspected that Spera's soul was reborn in your body, we have done our best to shield you from their sight. Spared no heartache to keep you hidden," she continues as if she doesn't hear me.

"Wait, hold on. My head is spinning. Shield me from who? Spera? What does Spera want with me?" I demand. In my head, all of the things I know I shouldn't believe in are strung around me like flimsy threads of a spider web: the mark on my chest, the surges of ridiculous strength that come and go whenever they please, Lucas, the little glowing horseshoes I don't see anymore, the black apparition haunting the trees at Wildwood Farm, and the creatures that chased Hopewell through the forest that night. Subconsciously I've been searching for a connection, wondering what could've triggered these things. But I realize that these threads tie back to only one thing: me.

I am the connection. I just don't know how. Or why. Everything hinges on her answer. I can feel it humming under my skin like a swarm of bees. Maris gives me a sad smile.

"No, girl. You *are* Spera. Your soul was born first in her body and returned to us the day you were born again." I rock back on my heels and watch her watch me as I absorb the answer. In my mind, the threads wrap around each other and hold. Piece by piece, the web completes itself at its center. But I still have no idea what it *means.*

"So if I'm Spera, what does that mean exactly?" I lift my chin and stare straight into her eyes, daring her to tie the knot.

"Spera died before making the decision. So that responsibility now falls to you. We suspected early on that it was you. Oh, how I wept with your mother."

I chew on the inside of my cheek, the earlier agitation stoked by her ambiguous response. *Dad, I could really use your help here,* I silently plead. I close my eyes and concentrate on a memory of his face. Out of nowhere, a memory of learning how to jump blossoms in my mind, the horse ducking away from the jump over and over. "What's happening?" I'd asked him, frustrated into tears. "She doesn't believe you, Tee," he'd said. "You have to make her believe you. Take her to the center. Be specific about it. Block her shoulders to send her straight." *Be specific. Make her believe that you believe.*

"My mother," I say the word firmly, as though to mention her doesn't hurt and never has. "You said she could see both sides of the veil. What does that mean?"

"A veil separates the world humans see from another realm, from the Unseen things."

"What are Unseen things? Ghosts?"

"No, child. We are not ghosts," she says, her face softening. "Our world exists with yours, like two plays on one stage, only you can't see through the curtain."

"Wait, 'we'? You're an Unseen thing? Then why can I see you?"

"I am on your side of the veil. When we cross over, we are forced to take forms that Seen things can comprehend."

"What do you look like on your side?"

"I am the hand in the undertow. I am the rainbow in the mist," she repeats, slowly shaking her head.

"You won't tell me," I sigh in defeat, the effort it took to scrap up any usable information heavy on my chest. She gives me the same sad smile, her eyes trained on my mark. I automatically move to cover it, but I catch myself and force my hands to my lap. "Let's say any of this is actually true. What does it have to do with me?"

"There is a way for you to witness your Origin, Spera's first life."

"What if I don't want to see it?"

"That choice is yours to make. But I would suggest you see what you're up against, because it is going to happen either way. Asher has clearly found you. It's only a matter of time before he makes his move, if he hasn't already," she says, plucking a small red bottle from her wooden chest. She holds it out to me but I don't move for it.

"Who is Asher?"

"He wants to open the veil between our worlds."

"Why?"

"He wants something that only this side of the veil can provide."

"What does he want with me?"

"You are the end," she says sorrowfully, and tucks the bottle inside her pocket.

"The end of what?" Heat erupts below my collar and spreads through my chest and down my arms. Instantly, beads of sweat collect on the skin above its scorching path. I know what she's going to say next. I can't explain it. I just do.

"The end of my world, or the end of yours." Her eyes begin to burn with the same fury gnawing at my insides, both demanding that I move somewhere, anywhere. She rocks forward onto her knees, reaching out for me with both hands as her lips pull back. I don't wait long enough to find out whether it's a smile or a snarl forming on her face. My body reacts on pure instinct as I shove her back, leap to my feet, and bolt out of the tent.

"Tanzy? Are you okay?" Vanessa's voice calls out as I rush for the inky cover of the trees that hang over the riverbank. But I don't answer, straining to listen for any evidence that Maris followed me out. My brain is so still and focused that it slices through every sound, discarding each one from my ear as soon as it's recognized. Laughter from the crowd around the fire pit, thousands of crickets chirping a two-note melody, my own steps as they crunch across the sand.

Vanessa finally reaches me and grabs a hold of my elbow. Even though my body demands I keep moving, that I disappear into the black of the forest, I drag my feet to a stop.

"You could have warned me that Maris is completely off her rocker," I say without meeting her gaze. Vanessa's grip goes slack, but she doesn't drop her hand. Her lack of a response is unnerving and my mind fills the void, desperate to convince me that she just made some lucky guesses and I blindly gave her the information she needed to fill in the blanks. I know I'm wrong, but I keep trying.

"What did she say?" Vanessa finally asks.

"Is she?" I search her face for an answer before she speaks. But her green eyes are filled only with worry.

"Is she what?"

"Insane?" My voice breaks on the word, the want, the need for it to be true too heavy to shove from my mouth without stumbling.

"Probably," Vanessa answers with a short laugh. "Why? What's got you so upset?"

"She has this crazy theory about past lives and that some souls come back. And that I'm basically the worst soul in the history of souls, but she wouldn't tell my why. She said I was 'the end.' And when I asked her what she meant she said I had to see for myself in an Origin or something. You could have warned me," I repeat in an angry rush.

But Vanessa doesn't start reassuring me with stories about other wild things Maris has said like I hoped she would. Instead, she bites her lip and stares down at the sand.

"Okay, don't think that I'm crazy, but when it comes to that stuff, the past life stuff, I kind of believe her. I didn't know what all she was going to tell you so I didn't want to say anything beforehand. But I've seen it. My Origin. And I believe her."

I try to respond, but all I can manage are a few sounds. There are no words that begin to describe the hurricane gaining strength inside my ribcage, swirling and rearranging and ripping things from their roots.

"I know how crazy it sounds, I do," Vanessa continues, her eyes pleading with mine. "But when my professor did that research on the drum circle, he interviewed her at length. She *knows* things, Tanzy. Things no one should. She knew about the car accident. She knew about the colors. So when she offered to show me my past life, I couldn't say no."

"Did it work? What did you see?" My deep suspicion is lured into mild curiosity by Vanessa's confession.

"Don't be mad, but I can't tell you," she says, her face twisting with regret.

"What's stopping you?"

"It's … you'll see."

"What do I have to do?"

"Did she give you a bottle?"

"She tried. I wouldn't take it." I glance in the direction of Maris's tent. I half expect her to emerge from her door, but the fabric is still.

"Do you want me to get it for you?" she asks, following my stare to the tent.

"No, it's okay."

"If you want to do this, if you want to see what I'm talking about, it's the only way." A thread of frustration bunches her words together. I stiffen, leaning away from her narrow eyes, and cross my arms in front of my chest. "Sorry, that came out wrong. Seeing my Origin helped me so much. It helped me understand what I can do and why I can do it. It made me feel like … like I'm the normal one and everyone else is defective."

The tension slips away in an instant. *Vanessa's just trying to help. She's always trying to help.*

"Then sure, I do want the bottle to have the option. But I'm not sure I'll do it."

"Don't worry, no one can make you," she teases. "You have to want it for it to work."

"Right. Makes perfect sense." I roll my eyes and Vanessa laughs. As she heads toward Maris's tent, a wind kicks off of the river's surface and whistles through the trees. Its cold fingers claw at my hair and slip beneath my collar. A shudder passes through me and leaves me chilled.

I move toward the glow and warmth of the fire as the rush of air seems to double back, stealing my breath from my mouth. The flames curl along the current, twisting into a spiral and then flattening beneath another rush. I stand as close as I can without putting myself in the reach of the living blaze. But it's not close enough to warm past my skin.

I shove my hands in my pockets, and my knuckles brush against something smooth and cylindrical. The bottle from the tent. When could Maris have slipped it in my pocket? With an inward cringe, I remember the wild expression on her face as she made a move for me. But her hands were open. Empty. I stare down at the red vial, half full of whatever Vanessa and Maris believe can show me everything I need to know. I can't help but wonder what Vanessa saw, and if it's all actually true or if I'm just signing up to drink some kind of backwoods, hallucinogenic moonshine. I frown at the little bottle and tuck it back inside my pocket, half hoping it won't be there the next time I check.

The wind softens and steadies, but the cold within me doesn't leave, instead spreading and solidifying like water to ice. I huddle closer to the fire and reach out over the glow. A flame leaps from the base of the fire, licks around my wrist, and leaves a painless swirl of black ash. In an instant, a lifetime's worth of memories I've never seen before flood my mind. Red liquid drips to a cracked and barren earth. Blood-curdling screams echo inside my skull.

Instantaneously, I know what it feels like when a life ends by my own hands. The moment of impossible pressure just before the embattled release. And then, everything goes white.

17
Here goes nothing

I DON'T REMEMBER FALLING. BUT THERE IS SAND BURIED beneath my fingernails and plastered on the side of my face. Unfamiliar faces lean in toward mine, and I fight the urge to kick them away. A hand clamps down on my shoulder. I recognize who it belongs to just in time to stop myself from yanking it off. *Vanessa.* But her presence only works to drive my heart rate even higher, her fear so strong in the air that it tastes like a penny.

"Are you okay?" she asks and pulls me to my feet. I stumble behind her as she tows me away from the buzzing onlookers and to the cover of the darkest edge of the bank.

"What happened? Are you okay?" Vanessa repeats, dusting me off. I can't respond, my mind still prisoner to the flashes of red and cries of unimaginable pain. "Tanzy? Can you hear me?"

"Vanessa." My ears don't recognize the gritty, thick voice as my own. "Maris is right. I think I can be bad. I think I can be really bad." Vanessa's face goes still and rounds with a look I've never seen before. It's a kind of fear, but whether it's for me or of me or both I can't yet tell.

"Get her out of here," Maris whispers to us.

"I'm sorry," I stammer, clinging to the pieces of my mind as it fractures.

"No need for your apologies, child. It's not safe for you here. You are too visible." *Too visible.* She's right. I can feel it. Eyes. Everywhere. My own eyes dart to the woods. Everything inside of me wants to slip into that hazy black and never come back out.

"What do you mean?" Vanessa says, and moves to shield my back with hers.

"Just go. Take her somewhere safe." My insides hum at the sound of her command, driving fresh blood into my muscles and making me ready for whatever has seen me here.

Vanessa wraps a protective arm around my shoulder and guides me through the crowd. The forest that seemed so alive when we came through only an hour before now seems on guard as we slowly make our way back to Vanessa's car. I don't object as she helps me into my seat and buckles the seatbelt across my trembling body.

"What did she mean when she said I wasn't safe? Who saw me?" I croak.

"I don't know. I just know that she knows. And that's enough for me."

I close my eyes and lean into the side of the car. The cold window feels good against my throbbing head. *I just know that she knows. And that's enough for me.* Vanessa's words echo in my brain. And Maris's musical voice: *I know everything.*

Does she? She seemed to know everything about me. And she knows my mother. At least she says she does. And all those words she bit back. She knows way more than she was willing to tell me. I slip a hand inside my pocket and squeeze the little bottle, grateful it hasn't disappeared. *She said that the rest I have to learn for myself. Is this the way?* I have to try.

"Tonight."

"What?" Vanessa asks, clearly distracted.

"I am going to see my Origin tonight." Saying it out loud slides something into place. Something that soothes and burns at the same time. But I have to see. I have to know.

"I didn't get the bottle. Maris wasn't in the tent when I went back. I didn't see her until she came up to us after you fainted, and at that point I'd forgotten all about it."

"I have it," I say and show her Maris's red bottle. Vanessa's eyes dart from my hand to my face. "Don't ask. I have no idea how it got in my pocket. I just know that somehow she got it to me. Don't you think that's a sign or something?"

"I don't think it's a good idea. Not with what just happened." Vanessa shakes her head, her face lined with worry.

"That's exactly why it has to be tonight. I saw something. Memories. They felt like memories. But I've never seen them before."

"What did you see?"

Those sounds. There's only one word to describe them.

"Death."

"You saw yourself die?" she asks on the heels of a sharp inhale.

"No. I caused death," I answer, keeping my jaw locked.

A heavy note of silence fills the car as I watch Vanessa watch the road. *Does she believe me?* I'm not sure whether or not I want her to. The hard line above her brow relaxes and she flicks her eyes at me.

"Is this about your dad?" she asks.

"No. It doesn't have anything to do with him. These weren't accidents." Vanessa tries to mask her sudden recoil, shifting her legs beneath the dashboard. I look down at my hands. Even now, they itch with the sensation of having just squeezed something to the point of numbness. I ball them into fists and hide them under my thighs. What exactly am I capable of? "I have to know."

She glances at me. "Okay. As long as you think you're ready."

"Yes. I promise I'm fine. What happened to you wanting me to do this? Are you trying to talk me out of it?"

"It's not that. But I know what you're about to go through, and it's not easy."

"Nothing about this has been easy," I say, biting back a bitter laugh.

"Good point." She settles against the back of her seat. Her body appears relaxed, but her eyes tell a different story, staring wide and vacant at the place where the road meets the horizon.

Vanessa whips so hard into the parking lot that the tires screech against the empty street. She hurries to my side of the car and reaches in to help me out but I wave her off and climb out of the car on my own. I don't know what's coming, but I have a feeling it's going to take everything I've got. I need to make sure I can put one foot in front of the other in a world I know before I attempt to travel somewhere I'm not even sure exists.

Vanessa studies my face with the same haunted eyes. They follow my every step as we make our way to the inn and up the stairs. She opens the door for me and insists on helping me out of my boots. I sit cross-legged on the bed and watch her dig through the bag of clothes for a nightgown.

"Here, change into this. It's really soft," she says and hands me a white cotton slip. She busies herself, sorting clothes on top of my dresser as I shrug out of my layers and pull on the little gown. I walk slowly to the mirror, reluctance pulling at my heart and begging me to stay here. To stay me. I can see it in the reflection of my eyes. I am not different, but I am not the same. And I certainly won't be the same after this. *If it works.*

"How does this work?" I ask, still studying myself in the mirror.

"You are absolutely sure you want to?"

"Yes. Please stop asking me if I'm sure." I turn away from the mirror and clench my hands at my sides.

"I'm not questioning you. I'm just asking because you have to be absolutely sure or it won't work." She retrieves the red bottle from my jacket pocket and sits down on my bed.

"I'm sure," I repeat, claiming a spot next to her. "So what do I do now?"

"Once I've left the room and you are absolutely sure, drink what's in the bottle and go to sleep."

"Then what?"

"If it works, you'll know it. A guide will meet you and will walk you through key events in your original life. It should help make sense of ... everything." She motions from the mark on my sternum to my hands, which are tightly clasped in my lap.

"What do I do when I wake up?"

"Well, that's the thing. I don't know when or where you're going to wake up. But I highly doubt it'll be here."

"What do you mean?"

"When I did mine, Maris told me that I would wake up where my life truly began."

"So I'm going to wake up in a hospital somewhere?"

"No. I'm not explaining this right." She pauses, recalling the memory. "She said life seldom begins at birth."

"I will wake up where my life truly began," I repeat slowly, digesting the sentence. What if my mother was telling the truth—that she isn't actually my biological parent? Will I wake up somewhere that I can find people I really belong to? The thought has wings, fluttering beneath my ribs and fanning warmth across my skin. "Where did you wake up?"

"Even if I could tell you, you don't want to know," she says with a grimace. "Let's just say I had to have money wired internationally so I could buy a very expensive plane ticket."

I don't know what to say, but the expression on my face must tell her plenty about the warning bells going off in my head.

"Here, I don't know what the range is on these things, but we're getting pretty good at it. It won't hurt to try," she says and grabs the ring off of my bedside table. "Otherwise, just pray you wake up somewhere with a phone."

This could get so much worse than I thought.

"I don't know your number," I say as I slip on the ring. She reaches across me and pulls a hotel pen out of the drawer.

"Turn your hand over," she instructs. She writes her number on my palm, and then retraces it for good measure.

"I can't believe this is really happening," I whisper, staring down at my hand. But each time I see my hands, my resolve strengthens. I can kill people with these hands. I have to know why. I have to know how to use it for good. "What is it like? Do I see my whole life?"

"I didn't. It was really fragmented. Kind of like watching a bunch of home movies."

"Did you see me? Did we know each other back then?"

"I can't tell you."

"It feels like we did," I whisper. "I don't know what I'd do without you. I don't know what's happening to me, but if I'd never met you I wouldn't have a chance to figure out what it means."

Her eyes gray over with conflict and she bites at the corner of her mouth.

"What is it?" My spine straightens in alarm.

"I'm going to miss you," she says and tucks my hair behind my shoulder.

"Miss me? How long does this take?"

"Only time will tell."

"Well then, let's get this show on the road," I say, willing my voice not to crack. I let her pull me into a tight hug, mentally pocketing what it feels like to have a friend that cares so much. *More than a friend. A sister.*

Sisters, she calls back. When we pull apart, she hastily brings the back of her hand beneath her eye and turns away. I pretend not to notice, and squeeze her free hand.

"Okay, then. I'll check your room in the morning to see if you changed your mind," she says and stands up.

"I won't."

"I know. Good luck." She casts one more apprehensive glance over her shoulder and slips through the door.

"Be seeing you," I whisper to her absence. *I hope.* The red bottle is so small that it doesn't even span the length of my hand. *This little thing helped Vanessa understand what she can do. Who she is.* And although I don't know how, I'm sure it has something, everything to do with Lucas. Will I see him there? Will he look the same? Or would I know him anyway? The way I'm sure I'll know Vanessa no matter what she looks like.

Before I can lose my nerve, I pull out the cork and pour the contents of the bottle into my open mouth. The liquid is cool and sugary and is gone in a single swallow. I brace myself for a spinning room or a wave of nausea, but nothing happens. "Here goes nothing," I whisper as I take a final look around the sparse room and close my eyes.

18
A path to where I first began

"We've been waiting for you," a woman's voice says, shattering the dark numbness. I leap to my feet and whirl to face the sound. She extends a pearly hand, not in greeting, but to ward off any advancement I might make. I take a step backward and drop my fists to my sides. She lowers her own protective stance, staring straight through me with eyes the color of water under ice. They freeze a path from my skin, through my heart, and to my spine, sending chilly warnings to my limbs.

"I'm Tanzy," I say, and then instantly cringe at my coarse reply.

"No, you're not." She gives me a disdainful stare and purses her lips. A long sword is slung across her back. Behind her stretches a graveyard of a forest, its bare limbs twisted by heat and drought. A narrow path divides the dying trees like a scar. Suddenly, I realize who she is: my guide. The one who will show me who I really am. And we're off to a spectacular start.

She eyes me warily. I follow her gaze and examine myself, self-conscious under her hard stare. My cotton night gown has transformed into a simple linen dress and my feet are bare. Unfortunately, so are my hands. No ring. No phone number. *Great.*

"Step forth," she says. I lean away reflexively and then force my feet forward. She brings a flat palm to my mark. I wait for it to burn beneath her touch, but instead her cool skin sends quiet vibrations through my core. "What you hear is sealed within. What you see is sealed within. Agree you not and be cast from here. Walk with me to see your Origin." Without any further introduction or explanation, she turns away from me and starts down the dusty trail.

The moment I take a step in her direction, the vibrations intensify, pushing and pulling at my ribs. I stagger to a stop and clutch my chest. *Is she trying to kill me? Or is this what it feels like to be sent back?* My eyes move briefly to my guide, who is still and watches me with little interest, before they close as I bite against the pain. And then understanding takes hold: I am being sealed. It doesn't lessen the pain, but it makes me more willing to accept it. Embrace it.

"Do you understand the oath of silence you are making by taking another step toward me and your path?" my guide asks, her voice flat and detached.

"Yes," I stammer, caving to my knees, and silently cursing Vanessa for not giving me better warning.

"She is sealed," her airy voice announces, and instantly the pain vanishes. I draw in a deep breath and climb to my feet. The closer I move to the mouth of the path, the more I understand how hard it would've been for Vanessa to describe why she couldn't tell me: I know with absolute resolve that I will uphold the oath. There's no question. No desire to tell anyone. Not out of fear. Not out of anything that I can name. Still, I wonder at the solidity of it, probing my relieved chest with my fingers.

"You must join souls past and present with a touch, or you will be kept from full knowledge," my guide calls from the mouth of the trail.

"What does that mean?" I ask, moving to her side.

"You must acknowledge why you are here. Who you're here for." My mind immediately leaps to Lucas and Vanessa. I tuck the thoughts within my heart and follow her into the twisted, thirsty woods.

The trees thin as we reach the edge of a blistered clearing. My guide pauses and steps aside as if to allow me in front of her. I oblige, but not by much. The rocky, brown earth surrounding us is as vast as the sky, meeting the horizon in a sickly gray line. Boulders mark the expanse like gravestones, and sudden chasms gouge the flat surface.

Several voices cry out from somewhere ahead of us. The words are foreign but they are angry in any language. The unmistakable scuffle of horses' unshod hooves on dirt draws my ear. Piqued adrenaline thickens the air. And something else, too. Something about their smell pulls at me like a magnet, like they're where I belong. I don't have to search for them. I know where they are. My blood knows. It quickens in my veins, demanding to be taken to the herd. A tremor passes through my muscles, begging them to action.

"Let go of your mind and follow your blood," my guide says, her eyes studying my face.

"Are you coming, too?" I ask, aware of the endlessness of my surroundings.

"Yes. Fear not on this matter, for I have no choice in it." Her answer makes me pause, marveling at her polite contempt. But then a new voice calls out, clear and shrill. And deeply afraid. I move toward it without thinking, jogging across the burning sand and stone. More shouts. I follow them around the face of a near vertical cliff. The salty smell of lathered horses makes each breath warmer than the last.

The precipice opens in a crescent. I flatten myself against the sharp surface and carefully step around the stony lip. A girl stands between four men and a small band of nervous horses, which are only a few perilous feet from a canyon ledge. They are boxed in on both sides by the massive rock formation. *If those horses spook they might run right off the cliff.* The moment the thought passes through my mind I realize with horror that it's exactly what these men intend to do.

As if to offer proof, they stretch a thick length of twine between them and take a couple of steps closer, shouting at the girl. She's younger than me, but not by much. The adrenaline pounding through my body roars in my ears, and every part of me wants to plant itself between her and that rope. *I'm behind them. They'll never see me coming.* My guide seems to sense my plan and places an icy hand on my shoulder, rooting me to the spot. I stare up at her, my eyes asking what words can't. She answers me with a slight shake of her head, and then moves her gaze back to the men.

"Why do they want to kill the horses?" I whisper to my guide.

"Those men are farmers here. They believe these wild horses are competing with their cattle for the grass, even though there hasn't been grass here in years. This region is in a terrible draught. Even the idea of grass is precious."

"So they're trying to drive the competition off a cliff," I say.

"They are."

"Will they hurt the girl?"

She doesn't answer. It's answer enough. Instinctively I strain against her hold, determined to offer what little help I can. But my guide squeezes her fingers into my shoulder like a mother stopping a child from running into the road. Her eyes say she hates me. Her touch says something very different. I relax and glance up at her placid face.

"Keep in mind that this has already happened. They can't see you. You can't affect the outcome. That's not why you're here. You must remember why you are here."

I watch them move a step closer. *If she could grab the rope hard enough, she could throw them off balance and maybe make some room for the horses to get out.* Without warning, the girl leaps toward the men, grabbing the rope in both hands and twisting it hard around herself. The farmers grunt in surprise, yanking back on the thick twine. But she leans forward, pulling them toward the center as she makes a full loop around her waist and deliberately collapses to the ground. The men crash toward her, dropping the rope to keep from falling.

"Go, go!" I scream at the horses, even though they can't hear me. But their ears prick forward the moment the rope hits the ground. In a flash, they take off at a dead gallop, disappearing seconds later into the brown stretch of nothing.

The girl glances up and watches their trail of dust, a delirious smile on her face. She doesn't see one of the men reaching a hand back, aiming for her face. Just before he lets his fist fly, a fork of purple lightning streaks down out of the clear sky and strikes the red earth so close to them that they have to shield themselves from the shower of sparks. The force of the blast sends me to the ground. Grit and blood mingle in my mouth. I spit it out and cover my head with my hands as the sky hums with warning. Another bolt of lightning crashes somewhere between us, pelting my back with rocks and embers.

After a few seconds of silence, I lift my head and look around. The men slowly climb to their feet as the girl works to free herself from the tangled rope. My eyes dart back and forth between them, an internal alarm gnawing at my insides. Their faces twist with the kind of frustration that can be lit into rage in an instant. They call out to each other in confusion as they point at her and then up to the sky.

"They think she's controlling the lightning, don't they?" I ask. Before my guide responds, the four men descend on the girl, drag her to the edge of the cliff, and without a moment of hesitation, toss her over the side.

"No!" I cry out and sprint toward the ledge. The farmers run past me and in the other direction as the burning hum builds all around us. But I can't worry about taking cover. I just want to find the girl. I *need* to find her.

The sky crackles with energy and a brilliant bolt of lightning spears down from the heavens. But it doesn't vanish when it strikes the ground somewhere on the floor of the canyon. The glow straightens between the earth and the sky, and the air fractures and groans as the column of energy widens. I stumble to the edge of the cliff and peer down.

The girl is suspended just a few feet above the canyon floor, floating limply in the center of the bolt of lightning. *This can't be real.* I hold my breath and stare unblinking at her body. A spider web of electricity rolls across her skin as she slowly rises from the canyon floor. She finally passes the top of the cliff. The column of light bends over the ledge and gently eases her to the ground only inches from my feet. I stare, mouth open, at her face. She draws in a jagged breath and tears of relief prick the corners of my eyes.

"We are done here." My guide's nimble fingers square my shoulders to hers. I keep my gaze trained on the girl, but my guide brings my face around with a finger on my chin. "Look at me." Her dazzling blue eyes are like a vacuum. Once mine lock into hers it is impossible to see anything else. "I choose what you should see and what you should not see. I control when we move from one memory to the next. Do not fight me. You will not win. I will do you the favor of giving you warning before we move on." Her eyelids meet, and I am plunged into the deepest black I've ever known.

My ears are filled with a murky quiet. Suddenly, the thick void is ripped apart by angry screams. I can't focus yet, but the tension in this new place is tangible, even more eager than the near murder we'd just left. In a single breath, the water-color images sharpen, and I let out a gasp. We are standing in the middle of a huge group of people. They are all staring in the same direction, their faces gaunt and hard. I stand on my tip-toes, straining to see what they're glaring at with such fever, but I can't see over the crowd.

I slip through the crush of people like a ghost, sure my guide will stop me with one of her freezing hands at any moment. But she doesn't, following close behind instead. Simple stone buildings line the sandy courtyard, leaving a narrow path along the edge of the crowd. I inch along the meager space. On instinct, I try my best not to bump into anyone, although I'm not sure whether or not they'd feel it. But I feel them. Not their bodies. Their want, their need, a sea of rage.

Finally, I reach the front of the courtyard. Two cloaked figures huddle over something on the ground. A few feet away, a man and a woman throw themselves against crude restraints. I can't understand the words that they say, but it sounds like they're begging. An urge to touch the woman, to wipe the tears from her face, fills me with such longing that it scares me. *This is not the time or the place to hash out your mother issues, Tanzy. That's definitely not Vanessa or Lucas. Remember why you're here.* I lock my hands around my elbows and look away from her.

Up front, the dusty cloaks flutter with motion as two men stand, each with a vice-like grip around a girl's arm. Dried blood and dirt crust her bare skin. Her knotted hair spills over her slumped shoulders. She won't lift her head. A swell of ferocity burns in my chest, threatening to break through my ribs if I don't release the roar clawing up my throat. I lock my jaw shut, letting the hot air out in a hiss.

The men work to bind her hands with a crude rope, and then cover them with a heavy black cloth. They shove her hard from behind and she falls to her knees. Fists punch into the air as the crowd breaks into a menacing chant. Each person is holding something round and gray. Stones.

"They want to stone her to death?"

"That is their intention," my guide answers. My next question stills on my tongue as the man and woman held captive scream out in pain. But no one is physically harming them. In fact, people closest to them are reaching out to them in sympathy. *This doesn't make any sense. Why would they tie them up and then act sorry about it?* Their agony is inconsolable, as if this is the end of their own lives.

My eyes drift back to the girl. Her chin lifts toward the sounds coming from the two people crying in the corner. *Her parents.* But the obvious tie between them and the sudden stab of pain it brings are washed away in the wave of my own recognition: the girl from the canyon, no doubt about to be hastily tried and executed for surviving her own murder.

That same pull from the open desert is back, drawing me to her like a magnet. One foot in front of the other. We're so close I can see the grains of sand moving in time with her heavy breaths. It wasn't about the horses. It was never about the horses. I'm here for her. *Now if only I knew what that meant.*

The girl's empty gaze falls back to the dirt. Blood might still course through her veins, but her spirit is clearly dead. *She's giving up.* In my mind I am back at Wildwood, watching the water at the bottom of the ravine, sure my father would break the surface at any moment. He could swim. He was strong. He was a fighter. But there was no thrashing in the muddy water. No effort. No fight.

"Don't you give up," I whisper fiercely to her. "You have to fight. At least let them know that you tried. Don't just give up!" She doesn't flinch. "I don't know what to do," I plead with her, automatically reaching my hand for her dirty arm. *Join souls past and present with a touch.* My guide's instructions from the beginning of this journey come back to me, wrapping around my insides like a blanket. Could it be so simple?

I reach a shaking finger closer to her. *Just do it.* In a rush I close the last few inches between us and clamp my hand around her forearm, willing any fight in me to flow into her body. But grabbing her arm feels like holding on to an electric fence. The hard jolt is ice cold as it flows up my arm and straight to my heart. I clench my jaw and try to pull back, but for several seconds we are bound together by something as strong as it is invisible. I stare at Spera's face, expecting to see her writhing in the same pain. Except for a quiet shudder, she doesn't seem to feel a thing.

And then the pain is gone, evaporating in an instant. I open my hand and sit back, staring at her with my mouth wide open. *Did it work? What just happened?* As the ringing in my ears subsides, words filter in. Words I can understand. Whatever language they speak here is now familiar and natural in my frazzled brain.

"Witch! She has brought this famine upon us!" a woman shouts. Her mother lets out a choked plea as another angry chant ripples through the mob, making me regret being able to understand.

"Wait," a new voice commands smoothly. Everyone goes silent at the sound, which is eerily familiar to me. *The psych patient from the hospital. I wouldn't forget that voice in a million years.* The instant recognition makes the hairs prick on the back of my neck. As I turn to look for confirmation, everyone else in the courtyard drops into a deep bow. The only two left standing are him and me. And now I am certain that he is the same person from the hospital.

In the daylight he is breathtaking and horrifying, his eyes the same silvery white. My heart leaps involuntarily at the physical similarities between him and Lucas. The same towering stature. Wide set shoulders. Capable hands. An unwanted shiver slinks down my spine. *He is not Lucas,* I remind myself, reprimanding the unwanted flutter beneath my ribs. *And if Maris is right, he's also a thousand years old.*

He runs one of those capable, pale hands down the length of his black cloak and then draws the hood over his thick black hair before he steps from the shadows and into the unchecked afternoon sun. Panic floods my veins as he glides fluidly toward us, but his white eyes are locked on Spera.

"Who is he?" I whisper.

"They call him Asher. The people here think he is a prophet," my guide says. She raises her chin in a silent salute of defiance. But a fearful tremor claims her shoulders. Her eyes dart to mine, likely assessing whether or not I'd noticed it. Our tense silence feeds off itself, multiplying in the meager space between us.

Asher towers over Spera. His long shadow covers her completely.

"Have mercy, I beg of you! She is just a girl," her mother pleads with him. "At least see if she can be saved."

"I will do as you have asked, good woman, as your spirit is clean of sins against the gods." His deep voice reverberates throughout the courtyard, stilling any movement in the crowd. He closes his eyes and stares at the heavens for several seconds. Bathed in sunlight, his face is white as snow. "Show me what lies within the girl," he commands to the sky.

I draw in a breath as he swoops down to one knee in front of Spera and lifts her dirty chin with his hands. Her black eyes stare straight into his. The fear coiled within my belly now seems to belong to me alone.

"I can save this child," Asher bellows and turns to face the silenced mass. "I can free her from the demons that hold her body hostage. There is no need to end her life this day." The crowd roars in celebration. But a satisfied twitch in Asher's mouth makes me feel sick.

"What did he see?" I whisper to my guide.

"Nothing," she bares her teeth around the word. My eyes move back to Asher, studying everything about him: the marbled smoothness of his skin, the lean muscles that rope his forearms, the way his fingers curl when he speaks. But his eyes, burning and chilling at the same time, command my attention the most. They give nothing away and yet say everything each time he unknowingly fixes them on me: he will have his way.

"Thank you for your mercy," her parents sob, collapsing against their restraints.

"She must come with me so that I may cleanse her spirit, you understand." He bows his head in a show of sympathy.

He saved Spera from certain death, but at what price?

"Whatever it takes, please!"

Spera's eyes silently plead with her parents, but they look only at Asher. I see everything she's trying to tell them. And it boils down to one simple thing: she would rather die. Even though we stand a few feet apart, her contempt for Asher rolls off in waves of heat that brand the side of my arm.

"I must take her this very moment," Asher says, as if he's offering them a choice. *What choice? Watch her die or let him take her away? What choice is that?* Spera's sentiments take root within me as I watch their exchange unfold.

"Anything," her father agrees. "Anything to save her."

"I will send word of her progress. I will keep her safe," Asher says with a sad smile. "But she can never return."

"We know," her mother says, fighting to keep the devastation from her voice. "May we please say goodbye?"

"Of course." Asher gestures to two men standing guard. They pull daggers from their belts and cut Spera's parents unceremoniously from their restraints. The instant the ropes drop from them, they rush to their daughter's side and cover her with their arms and their tears. She stares vacantly over their shoulders, and I wish with everything inside of me that I could beg them to pull back and look at her face, to look in her eyes and see what she can't say to them out loud.

"Take this, dear Spera," her mother says as she fumbles at the back of her neck. She straightens and holds her hand out. A silver horseshoe dangles from a leather cord. She fastens it around Spera's neck and puts a trembling palm over it. "This is my most precious possession. Keep it with you and you will never be alone."

I choke back a sob and clutch at the empty space where the necklace should be. *How could I have left it?* If only I'd known what it really meant. Where it really came from. A flash of anger at Vanessa fans heat across my collar, but I ball my hands into fists and reason it away. *She didn't know what it meant either. She was only trying to keep it safe.*

"It is time to leave," my guide says as we watch them prepare Spera for transport.

The black of transition is there and gone in the same second. I blink and am surrounded by red rock and blue sky, which stretch uncontested to each horizon. My guide stands at the very edge of a steep peak, peering down into the chasm below. I move quickly to her side and follow her gaze. A small caravan tracks westward, the slow procession lead by two men. They're huge. They appear human, but I've never seen someone so tall. *Yes, you have. Lucas.* The thought of him makes my heart leap in my chest. *He must be here. How else did he get that necklace?*

My eyes wander over the rest of the struggling party. Behind the leaders trail twenty people marching in pairs, one gigantic man nearly identical to the first two and one wisp of a girl. From this distance any of the men could be Lucas, and any of the girls could be Spera. The girls are tethered together at their waists and their legs are bound with shackles. As they pass beneath our vantage point, their features become more distinct. Spera is in the last pair. She doesn't look up, but she doesn't have to. I know that it's her. I can feel it.

Is Lucas here? He'll keep her safe. I scan the line again. But the men are harder to tell apart. Metal vests of armor cover their torsos and lengths of belted, burgundy fabric fall halfway to their knees. Copper-colored sword blades are slung over their backs.

"Who are the men?"

"They are Asher's guards."

"They work for him?"

"They live for him," she says with a faint growl. Her answer makes my stomach clench. *Lucas is one of them? He lives for Asher?*

"What are they doing?"

"They are escorting these candidates to Asher's fortress." Escorting seems a wholly inappropriate word for what is happening on the canyon floor.

"How long have they been walking like this?"

"Weeks. There were thirty girls when they started."

"What happened to the rest?" I regret the question as soon as I ask it. Only one answer makes sense.

"He only needs six candidates."

"Candidates for what?"

She answers my question with a withering stare. I press my lips into a firm line and quietly study Spera's every movement. *She and I are really the same?* It had seemed so clear in the courtyard. But maybe it was just my need to protect someone being unfairly attacked. Not that she wanted anyone to protect her. *That's something I can relate to.*

The girl directly ahead of Spera collapses to her side. Dust billows up in a rust-colored cloud as her body falls broadside to the ground. I gasp in disbelief as her guard drags her to her feet by her hair. Spera trips in her shackles as the motion ahead of her yanks at her bony frame. I steel myself for whatever cruel excuse for help Spera's guard is going to offer her. But he quickly shoots out his massive arm and steadies her before she loses her balance. He stares at her for several seconds, as if assessing her condition. As if he cares about her.

"Lucas?"

"There is more for you to see. We are done here," my guide says and takes my hand.

"Was it him?" My words are lost in the transition, still echoing over the endless desert we've left behind.

19
Scars

THIS NEW MEMORY IS SO DARK THAT AT FIRST I THINK we've gotten stuck, suspended in time somewhere. As my eyes adjust to the dreary surroundings, part of me wishes we had; that we'd gone anywhere else instead of this gloomy place. Collecting moisture drips from a gray, rounded ceiling. We must be in some kind of tunnel or cave. But it's obviously manmade. The edges are too smooth, too deliberate. A rotten odor makes me reluctant to inhale the damp air as we walk through shallow mud along a meager stream.

The cylindrical hallway opens ahead, letting in a scant amount of light. We step down into a dank cellar. The floors are still muddy and the stone roof hangs even closer to our heads. It reminds me of the coffin we bought for Dad's memorial service. When no one was watching, I had slipped inside and closed the lid. That kind of darkness is crushing. It's a thief, snuffing out chances and hopes and tomorrows. And this feels the same: not just that there's no way out, but that no one expects you to try.

"What is this place?" I ask, failing to stop the shudder that forces my shoulders to shake beneath its sickly grip.

"Asher carved a holding chamber in the base of a mountain."

"By himself?"

"Certainly not. He has more than enough help in this." *She's not just talking about the chamber.*

The sound of something stirring on the wet floor draws my eye farther down the hall. Just a few feet ahead of us, the solid stone wall recedes. The opening is striped with thick metal bars. A tiger turns tight circles in the small enclosure. It hisses in frustration and wheels again. The next five cages are filled with five more large cats, different only in their species. The rage and confusion flashing in their wild eyes is identical. Part of me wants to walk as close as possible to the opposite wall. The other part is searching for something to pick their locks.

"What is he doing with these animals?"

"He has matched each animal with a candidate." *He only needs six,* her earlier answer echoes in my mind. Six animals. Six candidates. *Did Spera make it?*

"Is Spera—"

"Would you really wish this life for her? For yourself?" She cuts me off, her words like a slap in the face.

"That's not what I meant," I stammer, bringing a hand to my cheek as if they'd actually left a physical mark.

"You would not be here if she wasn't."

I start to offer an apology but she waves me off. "He is transfusing each girl's blood with her match. Human souls are very powerful, more powerful than any other living creature. But human blood is thin and ordinary. For Asher to succeed in his quest, he must find the perfect match between a Vires blood and a Vires soul."

I wait for her to say more, but she presses her lips into a firm line and motions me ahead of her. Human fingers wrap around the next set of bars. They're so thin that the only thing left between the dank air and the bones is a filmy layer of skin. I hold my breath as I step to the front of the cage. A girl's head hangs low between her skeletal arms. She's so still that at first I think she died in this position. But her back rises and falls in shallow quivers that barely disturb the thin fabric of her dress.

"Is he starving them?"

"Yes. He needs to keep them as close to death as possible."

"Why?"

"The body must be truly hungry or it will reject the transformation."

"What kind of transformation?"

"The physical body of the final candidate will be turned into an Unseen. Replacing their blood is the first step. But the transformation is much more than that. Watch; he's about to feed them."

Six guards enter through an arched opening at the other end of the wet aisle. My heart leaps in the hope that Lucas is with them. But as they walk in single file, all I notice is their hands, which are holding different pieces of some kind of deer. Blood drips from the severed ends of the obviously fresh kill. *He can't be here. He wouldn't stand to be a part of this. Would he?* I turn away as they begin heaving body parts into each cage.

The low cellar fills with growls. *What is making that noise?* As if to give me an answer, the first girl pounces on a severed hindquarter and glowers unknowingly at me as she guards her bloody meal. She bares her teeth and snarls a warning before tearing a piece of skin off. My stomach lurches in protest, making me gag on my own spit. The sounds grow louder and more intense as the others begin to gorge themselves. Tearing turns into smacking, and then to crunching, which is by far the worst, as bones crack between their famished jaws.

I push my fingers into my ears, desperate to dull the manic sounds, and stare straight ahead. Most of the guards don't cast as much as a glance at the imprisoned candidates before marching back down the aisle. But the last one lingers. He checks the locks on each iron cage as the others leave. His long black hair falls like a curtain, hiding his profile.

Lucas? I hold my breath and will him to look at me. But he doesn't. In fact he seems so lost in thought that he doesn't seem to notice anything around him. *Not that he could see you anyway, Tanzy,* I chastise myself. He checks the lock on the last cage, and then kneels in front of the crude bars.

"Spera," he whispers and reaches out for her.

It is him! I marvel at the warmth that spreads over me by the sound of that name in his voice. But the recognition comes at a cost; he is no longer just the man who loves Spera. He's also the man who serves Asher. I tiptoe down the muddy aisle and find a vantage point just behind Lucas's shoulder. As soon as I put eyes on Spera, I wish I'd stayed where I was. She is weaker than the rest, as close to death as I've ever seen any living thing. Her black eyes barely flicker at him as she raises her head from her knees.

"I brought you something," Lucas says so quietly that I can barely hear him. Slowly, she lowers herself on all fours and crawls across the wet floor of the low slung cage without acknowledging the untouched deer leg in the corner. Although the thought comes as a shock, I can't help but wish that she would eat it.

Exhausted from moving the short distance, Spera leans forward and rests the side of her face in his big, open palm. All of the doubts I had about Lucas disappear as he gently strokes her cheek with his other hand. The desperation in his eyes pinches my throat and makes it hard for me to swallow.

He reaches inside his belt and retrieves a tuft of bread. "Do you want this?" Without a word, she plucks it quickly from his hand and devours it. "I'm sorry it's not more."

Every time he speaks he draws me a little closer to him. I can't help but wonder if he can feel my breath on his bare shoulder. But now that he's so close, something about him looks wrong. With a start I realize that the side of his face is perfectly smooth. *What gave him those scars?*

"Are you thirsty?" he asks. She dips her chin lower to her chest. His jaw sets with worry as he turns from her and cups water from the underground stream. Taking care not to spill a drop, he brings his hands to her dirty face and holds them perfectly still as she laps up every bit of water. Up close, she looks much older than she did in the village courtyard.

"How long has she been here?" I ask my guide.

"Only a year. Asher's process is very hard on the body."

"What happened to the others?"

"Asher has brought them to the brink of death over and over. Sometimes the body will continue to fight back. Sometimes it won't. He's weeding out the weaker ones." Horrified, my eyes move back to Spera, who is clearly the weakest of the six remaining girls. *Is she next?*

"Did that bring you any strength?" Lucas whispers. She nods, her eyes already a little brighter. "Could you run? If I give you a way, do you think you have enough strength to run from here?"

"Perhaps, but Lucas—" She stares at him with wide eyes.

"No," he cuts her off. "When I tell you to, you run as fast and as far as you can and don't worry for me. I will find you somehow. You have my word. But I can't see you in here for one more moment." Her chin trembles and her eyes drop to the soil. "Promise me."

"I promise," she rasps.

I promise, I catch myself mentally calling out to them both. I don't yet know what my promise is for, but I know what it's made of. Hightowers don't go back on our word. The spell is broken as the other guards lumber back through the archway. Quick as lightning, Lucas leaps to his feet and smashes his open palm into the cold bars. Spera screeches like she's been burned.

"Having a little fun, huh?" one guard smirks at Lucas.

"You know how she is, Calen. She was being difficult."

"That one doesn't like to follow the rules. But I bet she's all talk," Calen gives Lucas a nudge with his elbow.

"She'll be the first to die once the battles begin," another guard chimes in. Their exchange makes me bristle. I cross my arms in front of my chest, tempted to test just how invisible I am by socking them both. In a cage a little farther down, a candidate giggles to herself as she licks a bone clean.

"Spera," she calls in a sing-song voice and drags the bone along the bars of her cage. "Spera. Can you hear me? I'm coming for you." A delirious grin cuts her face in half. She narrows her almond eyes to slits and lets out a challenging hiss. Her black hair falls across her gaunt face, leaving only her teeth exposed. The shape of them draws my eye, her incisors longer, sharper than a person's should be.

"Are we ready to begin?" The sound of Asher's voice makes everyone go silent, the girl taunting Spera forgotten. He glides toward us, and for a brief, horrifying second I forget that he can't see me. I scan for a place to hide, but his white eyes root me to the mud. He casts a smirk at the line of cages, and the dizzying fear leaves me. *He can't see you. He can't see you.*

"Are you all right?" my guide asks. Her voice does not have a hint of concern, but for the first time since we met it isn't laced with disdain either. I nod without taking my eyes off Asher. Five pairs of hands reach out for him as he strides past his candidates. But Spera glowers at him from the back corner of her cell. A low growl rumbles in her throat. I resist the instinct to do the same.

"Won't you be a willing recipient this time, Spera?" Asher says, genuine concern in his voice. "I told your mother I'd take good care of you. But you're making it difficult."

Her dark stare does not waver. His face twists in frustration and he slaps a hand against the front of her cage. "Are the blood transfusions prepared?" he snaps as he moves away from Spera. I force my lungs to slow their pace, only allowing air in and out in measured, steady breaths.

"Almost, Asher," Calen says with a bow of his chin.

"What's taking you so long?" Asher barks.

"My deepest apologies—"

"Your apology is of no value to me. Just get it done."

"We will need your help with Spera. She's difficult," one of the guards adds, which makes the others wince. Asher lets out a bark of a laugh.

"She's a girl. She hasn't accepted a drop of her match's blood, and she hasn't eaten in weeks. She shouldn't be alive, much less stronger than you, and she has no access to her precious sky. Figure it out," Asher snarls without turning around as he storms back through the stone archway. The guards look hesitantly at each other. The fact that Spera can make six giant men this nervous makes me flush with pride.

"I'll see if the transfusions are done," Calen says and then steps into another room. I study Lucas's profile while they wait. As if sensing my gaze, he turns to me. But the sight of his face snatches the measured breath right out of my mouth; his eyes blaze pure white as they wander the dank hall.

"But?" I gasp and stare at my guide. Her eyes soften as she gazes down at me, but she doesn't offer an explanation. I want to shake her. To shake him. But mostly, I just want to wake up.

"It's ready. We'll dose the first five and then help you with your brat. Or we could do ourselves a favor and just let her die," Calen jokes from the side room. Lucas manages a short laugh, ducking away so they can't see the pain on his face. But I can see it, and for the first time in this life, he looks like I remember. *Like my Lucas.* He moves to stand guard by Spera's cage as the others file into the side room.

"Why are his eyes like that?" I ask as we wait for whatever happens next. "They're not like that now. Does that mean he's like them?"

"Lucas is an Unseen, as are the rest of them. And as am I."

"Are all Unseens … evil?" I have to ask, even if it means upsetting her.

"No, we're not all evil," she reassures me. "But Asher and his guards, they are what we call the Tenix because it's how they draw their power. And yes, the Tenix mean harm to all they encounter. Particularly in your world." She lowers her eyes at them. "And your Lucas used to be one of the worst of all, one of the most savage creatures on both sides of the veil. His atrocities are how he found favor with Asher."

My throat constricts as I absorb her words. Lucas, a savage. Atrocities. Harm to all they encounter. "What changed?" I whisper, watching Lucas watch Spera.

"Spera," she says. "He put eyes on Spera and something inside of him changed. It came as a shock to us all, most of all Lucas. No one knows why it happened, or how it is possible. But he hasn't fed on live Tenix since."

A sudden commotion in the side room draws our attention, ending the conversation before I can ask her more about Lucas or Tenix. The guards come back out one by one, each carefully holding a leather pouch. One container is so full of blood that the liquid sloshes over the narrow lip and dribbles down the side. It's ruby red in color, and so hot that it literally glows in the musty dark.

"How does it work?" I ask as my eyes follow the rivet of red that makes a break for the meager creek.

"Asher has discovered a way to cure the blood so that the human body accepts it orally. In fact, the body prefers it to its own blood. As the transfusions are absorbed through the lining of the stomach, they use the body's own red blood cells to replicate themselves over and over. Since the body prefers animal blood, it begins to filter out its own blood to make room for the thicker and stronger transfusions," she explains as she glances at a large metal bowl barely visible through the doorway.

A new round of snarls builds in the tunnel. Spera curls herself into a ball in the far corner as the other five candidates lunge at their cage doors.

"Are they trying to scare off the guards?" I ask, my eyes again finding the candidate who called out for Spera. She reaches between the front bars and makes a swipe at the girl next to her. For the first time since seeing the cages, I'm glad the walls between the girls are solid stone. They'd certainly tear each other to pieces given the chance.

"That's not resistance you're seeing. It's impatience. The strength of the new blood is like a high for them. They become addicted to it." A dark thought brews in my mind, a wish I can't admit out loud. I want Spera to drink every last drop. I need her to be strong.

"Why doesn't Spera want it?" I ask as casually as I can.

"Because nothing comes without a cost. As the blood takes over, so does its nature. Asher is not only trying to rid the candidates of their weaker blood, he's trying to rid them of their humanity."

"And she knows that?" I ask, guilt seeping out of my skin in a sudden sweat.

"No one knows why she refuses the transfusions. In the centuries that Asher has done this, she has been the only one to refuse." The cavern becomes eerily quiet as the other candidates receive their transfusions.

"Then why doesn't he just let her go?"

"Her choice to refuse him has had the opposite effect. It makes her all the more special to him."

"But he's still willing to let her die?"

"Of course he is. Asher has existed since the very beginning of this world, as have all Unseen things. When you live as long as we have, you have no choice but to see a bigger picture. If he can't convince her in this life, he will let her die, which will release her soul for reentry in another form. Asher will take the gamble that her soul will return with a more cooperative personality in the future."

"Me?" I whisper, the pieces sliding into place.

"You."

20
Run

EACH GUARD WATCHES OVER HIS CANDIDATE AS SHE drinks her transfusion. They study every movement and wince at each grumble of discomfort. One guard even pets his candidate on the crown of her head as she finishes her transfusion. But the girls hardly notice them. They only acknowledge the blood.

"Why are they staring at the girls like that?" I whisper, unwilling to create a louder sound in the uneasy quiet.

"Each guard hopes that his candidate will succeed. Her guard is certain to find favor with Asher."

"How do they succeed? What happens?"

"Asher is searching for a queen to rule at his side."

"That's what this is about? Asher wants a wife?"

"That will be her title, but it is much more than that. Countless queens have sat by his side, but he has yet to discover the one who can open the veil."

"Why does he care so much about opening the veil? You guys come and go whenever you want, right?"

"We cannot cross in our true forms. Opening the veil will allow us to cross over exactly as we are. If the Tenix can ever cross over in full form, your world would not survive," she explains, her face clouding over with a thought she doesn't share. She firmly grips my arm and points at Spera's cage front. "Watch, now. See for yourself how much Lucas has changed. Keep this memory with you in the days to come."

Calen and four of the other guards move back toward the main archway, but Lucas does not leave Spera's door. He leans with his back to the bars of her cage and carefully slides his thumb across the face of the lock. As he watches the guards file through the wide door, my eyes move to the lock. A tiny sliver of air is visible between the body of the lock and the latch. I turn my gaze to Spera, willing her eyes to follow mine to the little gap—to what's probably her best, her only chance to get out of here.

She peers at the door from her tangle of black hair and then creeps silently across the wet straw floor. She rocks back on her heels. She is so close to the bars that her breath leaves a film of vapor when she exhales. Lucas gives her a faint nod over his shoulder as he slips his heel between the edge of the door and the barred wall. The opening is impossibly narrow, but she is bone thin. It is enough.

She slides through without making a sound. Suddenly, Calen's voice returns to the cavernous chamber as he ambles toward them. Spera freezes, her body rigid with indecision, but Lucas grabs her hand, curls his fingers around hers and slashes them across his own face before shoving her down the hall. He stumbles, blood gushing through his fingers, as he bellows in pain.

"Calen!" Lucas shouts as he moves his body to block their view of her escape.

"Brother! What happened?" Calen snarls as he lunges for Lucas.

"Spera. She took me by surprise," he seethes, pulling his hand away from his face. I gasp in horror, his teeth visible through the tears in his cheek. Even Calen seems distracted by the extent of Lucas's injury.

"She asked for her transfusion. I thought at last my luck had turned. But when I opened her door, she struck me through the bars and then slipped out," Lucas grimaces, retrieving a piece of cloth from his thick leather belt and pressing it to his face. It is completely saturated within seconds. With a start, I realize what I've just seen: how Lucas got those scars. He'd done them to himself. He'd done them for me.

"Good riddance, if you ask me. She's been the most difficult by far. But Asher thinks she could be the one. You know he'll have your head for this, Lucas," Calen says.

"Then we must give chase," Lucas says in a low growl. "I owe him every effort."

The others roar in agreement and they take off after her. But a sudden chill floods the cavern. Even before I turn around I know exactly what could make the air change like this. *Asher.* His taunt face twists in fury as he assesses the open cage door and the frantic guards.

"What has happened here?" The guards stop mid-stride and turn to face him. Their instant fear and shame make the air hot. "How could you have let Spera escape? Do you have any idea how important she is? In thousands of years we have never seen a candidate like her. Find her. Your lives depend on it," he snarls, and his guards move to the armory room in a charged silence.

"Do their lives really depend on it? You said that Unseens have been around since the beginning. Can you actually die?"

"We can only perish on your side of the veil. On our side of the veil there is no beginning and no ending. No death, no birth."

"So why do their lives depend on it?"

"This is still your side of the veil. Extreme physical force can kill the guards. And as their leader, Asher can demand that a guard forfeits his life."

"What happens then? Do Unseen souls reenter, too?"

"No. We are immortal, but we are only immortal once. We are given everlasting life or we are given no life at all." *So if Lucas dies, it's forever.*

⬭ 205

"Are you as slow as you are foolish? Must I do this myself?" Asher's voice splits the thick air like thunder. Fissures glow across his broad body. I flatten myself against Spera's cage as his flesh rips apart. He springs forward and lands on all fours. Standing just a few feet from me is the creature that chased me through the pasture at Wildwood. *Run,* my mind begs. But I will my body to stay in place.

Asher's new form takes off downstream, swinging his yellow-eyed, saber head from side to side to pick up any traces of her scent. The only thing that scares me more than Asher is the horror on Lucas's face. *Spera doesn't stand a chance.* No sooner has the thought echoed across my brain than the underground cellar instantaneously falls away.

The void of transition is over quickly. Wherever we are now is so bright that I instinctively close my eyes against the burn. The dry air that fills my lungs leaves familiar grit in my throat. We're back in the desert.

"Where's Spera?" I ask as I shield my eyes with my hand. My guide points in the opposite direction. The instant I see her, I wish she'd died in the cellar. Then she'd be at peace, resting. Free. But instead, she drags herself across the sand, her movements so weak that no dust rises from what little progress she's making. The memory of questioning her will to live burns in my mind like a branding iron. She crawls a few feet more and then collapses.

I move hesitantly closer. Her lips are cracked and bleeding. She brings a clenched fist to her face. Her fingers shake as she opens them. The silver horseshoe gleams in her dirty palm. She squeezes her hand shut as a cry of pure desperation sounds from her peeling mouth. I close the distance between us, reaching out for her skeletal shoulder when I hear the sudden muffled crunch of paws on sand.

Spera barely stirs as Asher's panther-like form approaches. His lips pull back in a victorious grin as he stalks closer. I take a defiant, futile step between them. *You might not be able to see me, but you're going to have to go through me first.*

Without warning, the ground quakes beneath my feet, and I brace myself for the transition. But the barren surroundings do not fall away. A familiar rhythm in the rumble makes my heart pound in my chest: one-two three, one-two three. *Horses.* And from the incredible sound of it, there must be hundreds. Their approaching forms shimmer on the horizon, distorting in the heat that radiates from the ground. Asher pauses, baring his teeth at the coming herd. He flattens his black body against the ground and waits, his long tail swishing in agitation.

"Is Asher afraid?" I whisper as I watch his body language.

"As afraid as an Unseen can be," she says, clearly amused.

"Why?"

"Horses are unconquerable by any power, Seen or Unseen. You of all people should understand that. And they are the only mortal creatures that can cross to our side of the veil," she says, entirely unaffected as they roar toward us without a hint of slowing down.

This feels familiar. They gallop in tight formation and make an impenetrable circle around us. As soon as the circle is sealed, they slow to a walk and then turn in to face the center.

A black horse steps out from the solid wall and takes a guarding position between Asher and Spera's failing body. He unknowingly stands so close to me that I can hear his heartbeat. A dry wind whips his wild mane across my face. He smells like the ocean: salty and powerful. I've seen thousands of horses in my lifetime, and none compare to the majesty of this creature.

His deep eyes lock on Asher. His muscled body quivers with readiness, and he issues a shrill challenge. Asher's saber disguise dissolves and he climbs to his human feet. As if testing the horse's commitment, he takes a quick step toward Spera. But the horse strikes his perfect head like a snake at Asher. To my surprise, Asher jumps back. The horse moves toward Spera and lowers his muzzle to the ground, pawing at the sand by her face.

"What does that mean?" I ask, filled with dread by the utter satisfaction the horse's actions bring to Asher's face.

"The leader of the herd is giving his life for Spera. He is presenting himself to Asher for capture." My eyes move back to the black horse in disbelief, certain I'll still see the earlier fight in his movement. But she's right. His eyes still smolder with freedom, but his tail has dropped from its arched, defiant display and his weight is evenly distributed between his four legs, no longer coiled in his hindquarters like a loaded gun.

"How does that help Spera?" I spit out the words, bitter and sharp. The thought of watching Asher kill the horse is almost as gut-wrenching as the idea of Spera's inevitable death.

"Only a horse's blood is strong enough to save her now. It is the strongest kind of mortal blood. And he is willing to let Asher use it to save Spera."

"But why would the horse offer his life to save Spera?" I ask, glancing at her ethereal face.

"Have you already forgotten? Spera laid down her life for him and some of his herd when the farmers tried to drive them off a cliff. There is only one way to repay that kind of gift." A life for a life—a cycle that can't possibly save anyone at all. Spera wouldn't have wanted this. I wave my arms and jump up and down in hopes to scare the black horse away. But he stands like a stone.

Like a statue.

The thought makes the desert fall away as my mind races a thousand years into the future—into Vanessa's monstrous home, where the statue of a black horse stands in her office, his mane still blowing in the desert wind. How is that possible? But if it is true, if that's really him, then he's safe and protected. *Vanessa adores that statue. She'd never let anyone take it. She wouldn't even let me touch it.*

"This I did not expect," Asher muses, derailing my train of thought. He plucks a long black feather from a leather pouch strung to his belt. Spera doesn't flinch as he drives the sharp end of the feather straight into her arm. Her eyes roll back in her head as her body relaxes.

Asher sweeps Spera off of the ground in a single, effortless motion and places her limp body across the horse's broad back. The black horse makes one last trumpeting call to his herd. My heart stills as the entire herd drops their heads to the ground simultaneously, both honoring and mourning their parting leader.

"Is that it? Am I done?" A tear of exhaustion rolls down my cheek. I don't bother to wipe it away.

"Spera's journey has just begun," my guide says, her eyes drifting skyward. "Can you see this through?"

"Do I have a choice?"

"You always have a choice, child. Always."

But there isn't really a choice at all. I have to see what happens to Spera if I have any chance to save myself from whatever choice she never made. That much I know for sure.

"Let's go," I tell my guide, and the desert falls away.

21
To the death

THE NEW SURROUNDINGS ARE NOT YET VISIBLE, BUT THE urge to run skitters through me and leaves an electrified trail. The air is too still, too quiet. A muted rustle makes me jump as the darkness dissipates.

Spera paces a small room. The high walls are made of coarse black rock, which glitters despite its unfinished surface. She isn't afforded any windows, but a column of translucent stone stripes the back wall and allows a bit of dusk's weak orange light to filter through from outside.

A heavy blanket lies rumpled in one corner. The rest of the room is bare. But the energy radiating from Spera fills the space, pushing me against a rough wall. I stay as still and quiet as I can, regarding her with the same fearful care one might give a wild animal: startling her may result in the loss of a hand. She wrings hers as she walks, picking at something dark crusted in her fingernails. A sudden pain draws my eye, and I look down to find I've drawn blood from my own cuticle. I stick it in my mouth to dull the sting.

Spera unknowingly faces me, and I smother a gasp. She stares through me, the same eyes revealing none of the forfeit I'd last seen. Her face is harder and more angular, and her black hair gleams with health.

"She's so different." I find myself running my hands through my own hair, darker and longer than even yesterday. And with a start I finally realize why: it's hers. The thought sets my insides buzzing with both recognition and denial. It's impossible, but it makes sense. Before the roar drowns out the world around me, I twist my hair behind my shoulders and force myself to ignore it altogether. *That's not why you're here, Tanzy.*

"While she was sedated Asher replaced all of her blood with blood from the horse. Myths have existed about the power of a horse's blood but until Spera there was never proof. Clearly the myths were born in truth."

"And the horse?"

"He will remain Asher's prisoner indefinitely," she answers.

I already know what she won't say: Asher turned him into a statue. But I have no idea how to set him free. *At least I know he's safe.*

My eyes move back to Spera. She drops her hands to her sides. A single ring leaps from the skin above her torn dress, swollen and red.

"How did she get that circle?" There's just one, but it's identical in shape and size to mine. At the sight of it, mine begin to burn, radiating heat across my skin.

"Asher makes them fight for their lives. If a girl is victorious, he honors the kill with a mark."

"She killed something?"

"Yes." Her succinct answer is too big to fit inside of me, pressing down on my stomach.

What if he had her kill a horse? I bring my hand to the marks on my chest. If my hair is hers, these marks are no doubt hers also, and Spera will kill three things before this is all said and done. The memory of John's blood pooling on the asphalt in the alley snatches the air out of my lungs and replaces it with something so thick it makes me choke. I close my eyes and force my brain into a stormy quiet, the threat of more memories still rumbling on its edges.

Someone knocks so softly on the other side of the door that for a second I think I imagined it. Spera rushes the short distance to the door. It silently cracks open and Lucas slips through. My heart leaps at the sight of him, and the darkness in my mind scatters, replaced with dizzying relief. I automatically step in his direction, needing the reassurance a simple touch would bring. Spera beats me to him and wraps her arms around him. I let my hand drop and step back as she buries her face in his bare chest. He cradles her head to him and runs his hands through her raven hair. I back away until I bump against the wall, trying to convince my heart to remember that this is just a memory, that he doesn't belong to her anymore. I'm losing.

Spera lets out a jagged sob, which shakes a finger at my self-inflicted wounds. *Get a grip, Tanzy. You're here because of Spera, and Lucas found you because of her. Not in spite of her.* Still, I feel an unbidden stab of jealousy as my eyes take note of every place his skin touches hers. He pulls back from her and looks her over.

"Are you hurt?"

"No. She only got close a couple of times."

"But you are wounded." He runs his hand carefully down the length of a cut that spans the width of her back. The skin is flayed open, a mess of deep red beneath.

"Only surface. It will heal."

"And your spirit?"

"I made it as quick as I could." Her face falls to the stone floor.

"It was not by choice. Her blood may be on your hands, but the fault lies squarely with Asher. He branded you in the front? The others are branded on their backs."

"I will not submit my back to him. I will not offer him that kind of control."

"Is it painful?"

"Only in my heart," she reassures him. He takes a damp cloth from his belt and wipes her hands. *Blood. That was dried blood in her nails.* My eyes drop to my own hands, the torn cuticle scabbing over. I don't know what kind of blood that is, but I know what it feels like to be covered in it. To never be able to feel clean enough.

"You will have to do this twice more."

"I know." She steps away from him, still unable to meet his gaze.

"I don't judge you, Spera. You must know that. I've done things ... horrible things. I want you to win," he adds. But the words of encouragement make her wince.

"So that I can be at his beck and call? So that I suffer the touch of his hand each day and night? So I can one day be a Vessel for him?" Her voice cracks. Lucas wraps his strong arms around her shuddering frame.

"Once you rule at his side we can run away from here," he murmurs into her hair.

"We've tried that before."

"You are stronger now."

"He will find me. And if you are with me he will kill you. But he won't do me the favor of taking my life as well, and I will have to live beside him without you. Anything is better than that," she says. I catch myself moving closer to them and take a step back.

"Tell me what to do and I will do it."

"Just be with me. You are the only light in this wretched place," she says bitterly. Her words bring a smile to his scarred face.

"No one has ever called me a light." He strokes her cheek as she nestles into the crook of his neck. "Look what I found." He plucks a leather cord from his pocket. The dangling horseshoe shines even in the dim cell.

"Where did you get this? I thought I dropped it in the desert," she gasps as he places the necklace in her hands.

"Asher brought it back. He said you wouldn't open your hand, even tranquilized. He had to pry your fingers apart once you were completely unconscious." He presses it into her open palm. I close my empty fist and take a step back. I feel wholly undeserving of that necklace, to breathe in the air that may have cycled from her lungs only moments before. Of her blood. *She wouldn't let go of the necklace even in the face of death, and I left it on a bedside table.*

"Why did he give it to you?" Spera asks

"I am to make a crown. For his queen. He wants the horseshoe to be part of the center piece. If you don't succeed…" He stops and looks away from her. The agony in their eyes cuts me to the quick. Two seconds ago, I was certain there was no part of my heart left intact. But there was. And it just shattered like a fist to a mirror. Spera and I are not the same. We are not alike. Not in the least bit.

"You don't want anyone else to wear it," Spera whispers.

"I can't bear the thought."

"I can't risk wearing it. He'll see it. He'll know that you gave it to me."

"Hide it in your blanket. That way I'll feel like I'm watching over you when you sleep. Now get some rest. Tomorrow you must fight twice." He scoops her into his arms and gently places her on the ragged blanket. "I cannot lose you."

She smiles without making any promises. Her silence is not lost on Lucas. He glances back at her once more before reluctantly slipping from her cell. I look from the closed door to Spera, drained into speechlessness. It's not just her I've lost; I've lost Lucas, too. He just doesn't know it yet, because he has no idea how little of Spera made it into me.

"I will return for you in the morning," my guide says solemnly, breaking the spell.

"You're going to leave me here all night?" I whisper without taking my eyes off Spera. When my guide doesn't answer I turn to her, but she's already gone.

The sun finally sets outside, washing the room in a milky blue. And for an instant I can pretend that I'm alone. That I'm anywhere else. But just when I think I'm going to be granted a moment of peace, a tiny flame light flickers at the base of the translucent stripe, and then creeps up the inside of the stone like a burning vine of ivy.

Spera turns her back to the light. She seems as desperate to escape into the dark as I am. Her breathing slows, but even sleep does not loosen her tight hold on the horseshoe. She tosses in her sleep every few minutes, and cries out more often than that. I slump against the hard wall and watch helpless; a worthless guard over her through the longest night of my life.

The strangled silence picks at the lock on my mind and rifles through things tucked deep within. What my father said right before Teague took off. It haunts me because I can't remember it. Only the half smile he gave me over his shoulder right before he said it.

That I resented Dana when she stepped up to fill his position and his desk. She'd been with the farm for years, but the first day she sat in his chair and rearranged his files she became a stranger. I loved her before that day. But afterward I had to learn how to accept her all over again. And now I miss her, and I can't help thinking that all I'll be able to do from here on out is miss her, that there's no place for her in this, whatever this is. There's no place for who I used to be, either. She's a stranger now. But most troubling of all, she's no more familiar than the thoughts and hopes and power presently lurking within my skin.

The white glow of my guide returning to the dark cell is the only thing that finally makes these truths retreat, still too skittish to reveal themselves in the light.

"It is morning," she says, her words tinged with bitterness. I rest my head on my knees and hug my legs against my chest.

"What is he going to make her fight? I mean kill." The last word stumbles on its exit. *Or does she kill it? Is this how she dies?*

"He makes the candidates fight each other," she says, studying my face for a reaction. I'd thought of more possibilities than I cared to count: the animals kept with them in the cellar, the guards, Asher himself—although admittedly that doesn't make any sense. The idea of them killing each other never crossed my mind.

"How does he make them do that? Couldn't the candidates just refuse?"

"They want to survive. Wouldn't you? It's an instinct he uses to his advantage."

"Still," I start to argue.

"Would you be immortal, if you could?" she interjects.

"Immortal? What does that have to do with it?" My spinning brain can barely keep up, my own realities blurring in and out of what I've seen here, the gnawing truth that I still don't understand.

"Asher's queen will be given the choice to make herself immortal. Truly immortal, if the legend is correct."

"But why doesn't he just pick the one he likes the most? Why make them kill each other?" I need the pieces to fit, for a path to appear.

"This process is not just about the body, but also about the soul. He needs them to forsake their own humanity of their own free will, and killing each other is the most effective way. There were two battles yesterday. Spera was victorious in the first, and another candidate called Lenya triumphed in the second. They must now prove themselves by fighting twice today. If they each succeed in their first battles, they will face each other at sundown." My eyes wander over Spera's clutched fists, aware of what they're capable of doing.

Spera bolts upright on her makeshift bed and stares at the heavy door. It jerks open and two guards duck under the narrow frame. Spera's nimble fingers tuck the necklace under the coarse blanket before she gracefully stands and strides across the cell floor.

"I will not make your task difficult today," she says, presenting her wrists. The guards' eyes are wary with distrust, but they take utmost care not to harm her as they bind her hands together.

"Why are they being so nice to her now?" I whisper to my guide. "She is considered the strongest candidate, which means she is likely to become queen. The new queen will rule the guards as well. She could demand their lives if she chose to. Any mistreatment on their part could be a death sentence."

I flush with unwanted curiosity at the promise of such power, and then flinch as I consider the cost. To become Asher's queen is synonymous with becoming a killer.

We follow Spera and her guards out of the cell. Five more doors identical to hers line the stark wall. Two of them are swung all the way open. I peek inside the cells as we walk by, but they are both empty. There isn't even a burlap blanket. Wild shrieks draw my attention further down the dimly lit hall. The last door shakes on its frame as whatever is behind it throws itself against the solid barrier.

"Sounds like she's getting ready for you, Spera," one of the guards muses.

"That's a girl in there?" I ask my guard.

"Do you remember the candidate who called out to Spera in the underground chamber? They call her Cavilla. Spera will face her next."

Of course I remember. How could I forget the sight of the dark-haired girl raking a bloody bone across the metal bars like she was playing an instrument? I watch Spera for any reaction, but she doesn't acknowledge the guard's words or the snarls coming from the closed door.

The hallway widens, and descends gradually to a sandy floor. Once we reach the bottom, the tunnel forks around a huge cylindrical structure. An acrid, burning stench slaps me across the face. I cover my nose and force a breath through the crook of my arm.

"What's that smell?" My words muffle against my clammy skin.

"Asher believes that a spirit is only released whole if the body is burned." *The girls who died yesterday.*

"That's how I, how Spera, came back? He released her soul?"

"Yes," she says and gives me a sideways glance.

So she dies today. I die today.

"Asher has learned how to mark a Seen soul, how to ensure that it comes back. We doubted him at first. But the souls of his candidates did reappear. It was undeniable. That's when the Powers put conditions on your return."

"Why me?"

"Because the match was perfect. That had never happened before. A Vessel…" She stares at something only she can see as she considers what to tell me next.

"Asher's impatience has caused many false starts. But this time, with these six, he was correct, and he can feel it. We all can. Your match is a crucial part, but it is only a piece of the puzzle. Each of these six candidates has a role to play. He will do anything to make sure that these six souls are reborn in the future in case something goes wrong. All of you had to be reborn within the same mortal life span. Asher has waited for you for almost a thousand years. The souls of the other five have returned many times, but not you. We've all dreaded your return since the day Spera died."

"What do I do? How do I stop whatever this is from happening?" I plead. Time is running out. I can feel it. And I'm no closer to learning how to stop Asher.

"You don't. You are the end. There's no stopping it. And there's no time to have this discussion."

As if on cue, the ground beneath my feet vibrates and horns blare through the cylindrical wall. The rolling tremors bait something inside of me, something I don't want, but can't refuse: I need Spera to win.

"Now let's go. They're about to start." She takes me by the wrist and moves quickly to an archway. We make our way up a narrow ramp, which opens on the stained floor of an arena. Thousands of guards are on their feet. They roar louder and louder, the calls for battle blending into one ominous sound. As the cries organize into a chant, they raise their spears in the air in some kind of salute and stare toward one end of the stadium.

"Asher! Asher!"

The hair on the back of my neck stands on end as Asher glides across a balconied ledge.

"There are so many of them," I say, my eyes scanning the length of the dome.

"These few soldiers are but a piece of Asher's army."

"What does this have to do with me?"

"Lucas has requested that he alone answers that question for you. I do not enjoy honoring his requests, but the Powers have bid it so. Now watch. This is what you're here for." She faces ahead and nods at me to do the same, but I can only think of Lucas. And that he wants to be the one to tell me. For the first time since beginning my Origin, I feel like I still matter to him in this form. That he might care about me like he did about Spera.

The metal gates on the long end of the arena swing open and Spera and Cavilla are led by guards into the center of the arena. Their limbs are bound and shackled. Cavilla's skin is lined in places, darkened in a pattern that is all at once familiar and completely foreign. With a start I realize the effect on her skin, just like Spera's hair: the blood from the match is manifesting physically. Cavilla is obviously matched with the tiger, and Spera is no doubt the weaker of the two. Without warning, she lunges at Spera, nearly toppling the two guards holding her chains. A primal hiss escapes her bared teeth.

"Be still!" Asher calls smoothly to Cavilla. "Soon you will have nothing holding you back."

Their eyes lock on each other's as mine dart back and forth between the two. The guards remove their restraints and the floor begins to tilt, the stale air held captive in my lungs burning a path up my throat. I let it out and draw in a new breath, the arena refocusing in my wide eyes. *This has already happened. This has already happened.*

"Now. Fight for me. Fight for us all. And fight for my love!" Asher cries and raises his hands. "Let it begin!" A roar grows so quick and so loud inside the rocky chamber that I ready myself to run, sure the walls will come tumbling down at any moment. But the stone holds, even as the sound intensifies and Asher's army pounds their spears against their shields in a horrific, hypnotic rhythm.

The two girls circle one another. Even though every eye in the arena is trained on them, my eyes feel drawn to Asher's throne. He leans forward on his marbled chair, staring hungrily at Spera. He hasn't glanced once at Cavilla. Another girl sits to his left, but she isn't watching the fight. Her gray eyes gaze unwaveringly at his cold face. She runs a hand through her long blond hair. Even from one hundred feet away, I recognize the shape of the ring on her finger.

"Vanessa," I whisper, astounded.

"That is Lenya," my guide says and motions to the girl at Asher's side. "She was the other girl to gain favor with Asher. She fought this morning and was victorious. She and the victor here will face each other at sundown."

I am besieged by a wave of familiarity and an earthquake of grief. Best case scenario, one of us lives. Worst case scenario: both Spera and Lenya are burned in a pile of other candidates' ashes.

Cavilla lets out a roar that sounds so much like a tiger that it makes me crash out of my head just in time to watch her lunge for Spera's throat. Spera drops her shoulder and Cavilla rolls across her narrow back, dragging two clawed hands across her spine. Spera closes her eyes against the pain, her jaw setting as the carnal need to survive ripples in every visible muscle. She squares her shoulders and lowers her body to a crouch as Cavilla springs to her feet, the delirious grin from the underground cellar reappearing on her face.

"Are you ready, Spera?" she sings, weaving her head back and forth. Spera waits, her stance unchanging, as Cavilla circles to her left. "Don't you know better than to leave your back unguarded?"

she hisses from directly behind her. Cavilla waits, no doubt expecting Spera to move or turn or run. Just like I am. Like we all are, watching the standoff in eerie quiet. Cavilla sinks down on the balls of her feet and then springs forward. She closes the distance between them inside of a single heartbeat, Spera still unmoving.

Cavilla punches the final step off the ground, soaring toward Spera's torn back. Spera turns and lifts her hands toward Cavilla's head as Cavilla reaches for her throat, claws outstretched. But Spera is faster, planting her palms on either side of Cavilla's face. The crack of her neck is swift and loud. Cavilla goes limp in her hands, life leaving her body instantaneously. Spera lays her fallen competitor down on the sandy floor.

The audience erupts in a thunderous roar and pumps their spears into the air. Spera does not acknowledge their cheers. Instead, she kneels beside her enemy's still body and closes her eyelids with her fingers. Her lips move quickly in a silent prayer. Without a single glance at the audience, she stands and walks quickly to the towering gates. Asher's stare never leaves her back.

My eyes move from Spera to Cavilla. To my hands. And then to my mark. *Three circles. Three deaths.*

"Spera kills Lenya," I whisper. "It's the only reason I have three. I can't watch her die."

"Then I suggest that when the time comes you close your eyes," my guide responds. I move away from her. She catches me by the hand. "The reason you're here has yet to be revealed. You must understand where you've been to recognize what lies ahead. The three kills are every bit as important as the new blood. The process cannot truly begin without them."

I open my mouth in protest, but before I can utter a sound the wretched arena falls away.

22
The worst kind of choice

THE TRANSITION IS MERCIFULLY FAST, AND GIVES THE whirling in my mind a new distraction. *Just make it through this. There can't be much more. And if Asher is after me, then he's after Vanessa, too. The more I see here, the better I'll be able to defend us both.*

We stand in the corner of a large banquet room, which is filled with soldiers from the arena. The high walls are made of translucent quartz. Flames dance behind the clear stone from floor to ceiling. Silver platters stacked high with meat blanket a long marble table. Asher sits at the center, posing regally on an onyx throne. Lenya and Spera are chained on either side of him. Their shackles are only long enough for them to reach from the table to Asher's mouth; Lenya feeds him each time he sets his eyes on her.

Spera stares straight ahead, holding her chin high in defiance. I catch myself mimicking her. It's the first thing that's made me smile since first putting eyes on Lucas in the dungeon.

"Are you not hungry, my dear?" Asher's smooth voice makes me dizzy with resentment. I clench and flex my hands at my sides.

"No, thank you," Spera answers without facing him.

"But you must have worked up such an appetite."

"You eat although you do not hunger," she counters. His pale eyes glower at her.

"Lenya, you are certainly the more enjoyable company. I do wish you well this evening," Asher says without taking his menacing eyes off of Spera's stony profile. Lenya's gray eyes flicker briefly to Spera. Suddenly, a moan escapes her lips and her body begins to seize.

Spera jumps to her feet but her chained arm yanks her sideways and she falls into the side of Asher's throne. She grits her teeth and stares across the lofty room. I follow her gaze to Lucas's face. His body tenses with helplessness.

Lenya whimpers face down on the marble table. Asher pets her head and watches her rolling eyes.

"What's happening?" I whisper to my guide.

"Lenya can see visions of the future."

Vanessa can do that, too. Lenya blinks rapidly as she regains consciousness.

"Lenya, darling. Tell me what you see. What does the future hold?" Lenya collapses across Asher's lap, and he nuzzles her face against his broad thigh like a cat. He strokes her hair with his hand.

"Of my victory, my beloved. And of the new life that follows."

Spera's amber eyes are hard and fast on Lenya's face. As are mine. What if Lenya kills Spera? Fear and guilt crawl up my back; Spera's defeat at the hands of Lenya is a possibility I haven't considered. *And why not? Maris herself said no other Seen thing is stronger than me. And if I get my strength from Spera, then she should win no problem.* Before I can stop it, my mind begins to create how the fight might play out.

"I have waited so long for this day," Asher says. He casts his eyes from Lenya to Spera and traces their jaws with his thumb. Lenya moves into his touch. Spera pretends that she doesn't feel it. A moment of conflict creases his face and then vanishes.

"Come now, so that I may reward you for your efforts," he says with a growl. Spera shudders at his words, the same shiver finding my back as well. We both keep our eyes trained on Lucas as he steps to her side with a second guard and shackles her arms and legs. Calen and another guard fit Lenya with her restraints.

Asher leads the way across the great hall to a pair of double doors made of solid iron. My guide and I blend into the small processional and follow them into the next room. It's not like anything I've ever seen before, ethereal and impossible. The round wall is made of a blue-black stone that glitters like a clear night. The circular ceiling and floor are mirrored, reflecting the tiny sparkles over and over.

The guards usher Lenya and Spera into the center of the round room and then step away. Asher walks a menacing circle around the two, leaving a wake of black flames behind him. As he closes the ring, the fire seals the three of them inside. I watch, horrified and spellbound, as Lenya bows in front of him. He smirks at her show of submission and brings a finger to her bare back. Her skin sizzles under his touch as he draws a second perfect circle beside the brand from yesterday's battle, which has already begun to scar over. She does not wince, even as smoke and blood trickle from her skin.

"Vanessa said she'd never seen a mark like mine. Why doesn't she know that she's marked?"

"I am not to speak of the Origin of another," my guide offers in monotone words. "But if you can each call out the other's original name, you will be able to speak about what transpired here."

Immediately, I begin to catalog what I need to relay to her—starting with the most important thing: keeping our eyes out for Asher. If Lucas can shape-shift into other people, I have no doubt that Asher can, too. Is it possible that he's already in our lives somehow? He's shown this face to me, so I doubt he's hiding as anyone in my life. But what about Vanessa? Could he have already found her?

I watch Lenya thank Asher as she stands. He moves in front of Spera, who stares unwaveringly at his face.

"I have come to rather enjoy your resistance in this. True, you will not bow to me, but this also brings your face so delightfully close to mine," he says as he brings a finger to her sternum. Spera is a statue under his touch. My gaze falls to the identical symbol burned into my chest. A new pain throbs from the mark. Three circles. Three wins. Three deaths. Vanessa's death.

"I can't watch Lenya die. I won't."

"We are moving on," my guide says, ignoring me. I watch Spera and Lenya standing together in a ring of black flames until they have completely faded from view.

A dimly lit room with a dirt floor solidifies around us. Spera and Lenya sit side by side in separate cages, each dressed in identical, white linen shifts. Lenya leans against the wall between them, her gray eyes trained on Spera.

"Where are we?" I ask, keeping my voice as low as possible.

"Beneath the arena. This is the final holding chamber. Asher makes the last candidates spend time together before they fight."

"Why?"

"If they learn about each other or bond at all it will be a more complete betrayal of humanity for the victorious one. Asher is closer to his goal now than he has ever been before. He will not leave anything to chance."

"I have something for you," Lenya whispers. Spera doesn't move a muscle. "Spera, please. I come in peace."

"Is that so?" she scoffs.

Please, Spera, I silently beg. *Just give her a chance.* But on the heels of that thought, reluctance crawls across my skin as survival lays claim to my nervous system.

"It is. I promise you," Lenya pleads.

Spera glances at her over her bare shoulder. "I'm listening," she snarls.

A guard I hadn't yet noticed shifts his weight in the shadowed far corner. As he repositions, Lucas's face is revealed in the glow of the closest lantern. I close my eyes against the idea of running to him, seeing if he would be solid beneath my fingers.

"I know about Lucas," Lenya whispers quietly. Spera's eyes go wide with panic as mine fly open and search Lenya's face. "No, I don't mean you any malice," she adds quickly. "I only mean to live. You want your life with Lucas, and I want mine however I can keep it."

"I do not believe you. I have seen the way you behave with Asher. You love him," Spera argues, visibly shaken.

"We do what we have to in order to protect our interests, don't we?" Lenya says and glances in Lucas's direction. "I wish to live, and that would not be possible in this next battle. You will kill me easily. But I do not want to die, and you do not want your secret revealed. I can protect your interest if you can protect mine."

"I will not let you kill me."

"That's not what I am asking. I think there's a way that we can both survive this night." Lenya twists a ring off her finger and hands it to Spera. "Take this. I have another one. If we each wear them, we can speak without sounds." She shows Spera the identical ring on her other hand. "Do as I tell you once the battle begins and I will do my best to make sure we both survive."

"How do you know this will work?" Spera asks as she slips on the ring.

"Because this is what I saw during the banquet," she confesses. "What I told Asher was a lie."

Spera studies her face with skepticism.

Do you hear me? Lenya's mind calls out. Spera's lips crack with disbelief. The sound of Lenya's voice in my head brings me to my knees, the connection to her too heavy a thing to square with the thoughts I've had about Spera's victory. Never had I considered they might both come through this alive. Of course Lenya would think of something. Vanessa always does. I crawl beside them and press my own hands against the front of their cages.

Can you hear me? I call out to them, but nothing comes. I rein in my disappointment and wrap my fingers around the bars, so close to them that I could reach out and touch them.

"What else have your visions revealed to you?" Spera presses, edging toward her with new interest.

"I have seen Asher's greed. He fantasizes about having us both. And I think we can use that to our advantage." The grinding sounds of moving metal screech from somewhere above the holding chamber. "It's almost time," Lenya says, flitting her eyes to the ceiling. "You must trust me, Spera. Follow my lead once we're in there. We can both survive this, and then I will help you and Lucas escape."

"Why would you help us?" Spera asks, her eyes narrowing in suspicion.

"I have done some dark things here," Lenya answers softly. "My soul is desperate for a way to set something right."

"If you truly think you can help us escape, why not leave with us?"

"He made me slaughter my own parents in their sleep the night he took me. My first battle was against my sister. I have nothing to go back to."

"Asher's cruelty is not a reason to stay. I won't leave you here," Spera insists through clenched teeth. I have to forcibly stop my own hand from snaking through the bars and grabbing hold of Lenya's arm. The sound of marching footsteps grows louder as guards approach the little room.

"Focus, Spera. We must both live first, and we will only have one chance," Lenya hisses back. "Let us get through this day first and then we will find a way out of here."

Spera turns a tense eye to the main door as it swings open. Calen leads two fellow guards into the holding chamber. Lenya growls and lunges at Spera, swiping at her face through the gaps in the bars. She bares her teeth, shrieking angrily.

Follow my lead. Lenya's silent words echo in my mind. Spera glowers at Lenya and throws her lean body against the metal bars.

"This is going to be something to see; your Spera versus my Lenya." Calen says and claps Lucas on the back. "Everyone is whispering that Asher has truly succeeded this time. The whole Unseen realm has its ear turned to us this day. We're almost free, brother."

"Finally free? What does that mean?" I ask my guide in a hushed voice.

"Their true forms will be set free to roam your world and to feed on the Tenix until your world is just like ours." Her face sets like a stone as she glares at the guards.

"What is Tenix?"

"It is that which binds," she says. My face falls at her answer, my mind too exhausted and too full to decipher another one of her cryptic explanations.

"Binds what?"

"Everything."

"Hands," Lucas orders gruffly, drawing my gaze and ending our conversation.

Spera dutifully slides her forearms between the metal bars and Lenya does the same for Calen. Their hands are shackled with thick metal cuffs before they are allowed from their cages. As soon as she steps through the cage door, Lenya makes a show of throwing herself once more at Spera.

"Yes, this will be something to see," Lucas says, mustering up a cruel laugh as they lock another set of restraints around their ankles.

Spera looks unsettled as we follow them into the arena and onto the battlefield. Asher's plan has worked: Spera knew what she had to do before she sat side by side with Lenya. But uncertainty is now plain in her hard face. If Spera wants to win, she will. There is no question. Even Lenya seems resigned to that fact. But I doubt Asher imagined how quickly they would bond.

Could she live with Lenya's blood on her hands? *Could I?* But there's one question I can answer: I trust Lenya with Spera's life. I've sent that thought out to Spera but it isn't getting to her, echo-ing in my own brain like a voice across a canyon: *Trust her, trust her, trust her.*

The soldiers chant and raise their spears as Lenya and Spera are led to separate ends of the ring. Even Lucas seems lost in the finality of the moment at hand. He absently runs his hand across Spera's in a subconscious offer of comfort.

Careless! Lucas is drawing Asher's eye, Spera, Lenya's frantic voice calls out in my mind. I throw a worried glance at Asher's throne. Lenya is right. Asher narrows his eyes as he stares hard at the pair. Spera reacts instantaneously and lunges at Lucas as he kneels to remove the cuffs around her slender legs. Surprise twists his scarred face, but understanding quickly follows, setting his mouth in a grim line. He draws his spear and presses the sharp end against her throat.

"Behave, candidate," he orders.

"Enough," Asher bellows from his high throne. "Lucas, you might pay for that little exchange if she becomes your queen. And my dear Spera, save your strength for the battle at hand. This is, after all, the beginning or end of your life. Treat this moment with respect."

Prickly relief washes over my skin as a thunderclap of cheering begins again, distracting Asher from Lucas and Spera.

Thank you, Lenya. I will trust you in this, Spera's mind whispers. Lenya locks eyes with her for a fraction of a second. My insides release and then knot again. Spera chose as I would have; there's no way I could kill Vanessa to save myself. But now both of their fates are uncertain.

"And so finally this day has come, this splendid moment," Asher announces as the soldiers quiet down. "We have waited long enough, my brothers. Let it begin," he growls and eases back onto his black throne.

As soon as Asher's words have left his mouth, Lenya charges across the sandy pit and leaps for Spera's crouched body. Spera knocks her off easily and spins to face her, ready for another attack. Lenya again closes the distance between them. They claw at each other's throats, feigning a desperate fight for a fatal hold. Lenya suddenly cries out and stumbles. Her palms clamp on either side of her head as she drops to her knees.

Come for me, Spera. Make it look good, Lenya's voice echoes in my mind. Spera rushes for Lenya's seizing body.

"Stop! Spera, I command you to stop!" Asher shouts as he leaps to his feet. Lenya collapses, lying face down in the shallow sand. Spera circles her limp opponent, lunging and snapping as she inches closer. "Lucas, restrain her!"

Spera bares her teeth at Lucas as he moves to her with faked caution. He cuffs her arms and holds the head of the spear to her back. Lenya moans as she rolls to her side.

"Asher," Lenya whimpers and climbs weakly to her knees.

"What did you see? What must have been so important that the stars decided to reveal it to you at this most crucial moment?"

"My love, please do not make me repeat what I have seen."

"But you must, my dear one," he croons, his curiosity blatant in the way his fingers tense over the arms of his throne.

"But I do not want it to be so. I want you all to myself! Please tell me there's another way."

"Lenya, love. Tell me what you have seen!" Asher commands. "What upsets you so? Name it, and I will destroy it," he baits her.

I glower at him and his silvery tongue from my invisible post along the arena wall.

"I have seen that neither of us are enough power on our own. I cannot command the fire of the skies and she cannot see what is to come. The resistance we will face is great. If you are to be successful, I must share you with that wretched girl," she cries, spitting her last words in Spera's direction.

Command the fire in the skies? Spera really can do that? I think back to the terrible moment she was thrown over the canyon ledge; the steady streak of lightning that lifted her from certain death. *She did that?*

Voices murmur uneasily as Asher silently considers Lenya's message. A devious smile slices his perfect face in half. "Do you see now, my brothers? Do you see how blessed our goal has become?" Asher shouts.

Every soldier punches his spear into the air and shouts in celebration. Spera stares at the roaring crowd, shock rounding her haggard face.

We've done it, Spera, Lenya's voice rejoices in my head. If Spera answers her I don't hear it. I cry out to them anyway, joy like a songbird in my mind.

"Guards, prepare two rooms fit for my queens," Asher calls down to the arena floor. "Keep my prizes separate until they learn to tolerate one another."

I let out the breath I didn't know I've been holding as Calen and Lucas carefully guide their new queens from the arena.

"We are done here," my guide says in my hot ear. "It's time to move on."

"What could possibly kill Spera if she survived that?" I ask her. Even though she doesn't answer me, the darkness brewing deep within her frigid eyes says enough. However it happens is far worse than the end she could have met here.

23
Chains and crowns

MY EYES STING TO THE POINT OF BLURRING, AND AS the new memory settles around us I'm sure I'm hallucinating, my mind no longer willing to accept the pain and darkness that chase Spera down like a rabbit. Because beauty like this can't possibly be real. The round room is made of translucent crystal, which glows the softest gold as sunlight saturates the smooth stone. Four circular windows are carved into the cylindrical wall like the points of a compass.

Asher sits high on a throne made from the same crystal, a guard at each side. Several more guards arm an arched doorway on the opposite side of the grand room. I spot Lucas among them and follow his gaze across the room. Spera stares vacantly out of the window pointing to the afternoon sun. A breeze whistles by the opening and her silky white dress ripples in the free air.

She hugs her arms to her chest. A golden snake cuffs each wrist. Spera's long black hair is pulled back in a single thick braid. Precious stones glitter in each ear. Coils of gilded metal adorn her slender throat. *Is she wearing the ring?* I step beside her to get a closer look. Her hands are bare. I swallow my disappointment and follow her gaze across the vast nothingness.

Red flat earth stretches for miles. A darker blue streak acts as a border between the desert and the sapphire sky. The faintest scent of salty surf rides the current of air that blows steadily past the opening. *The ocean.* Instinctively, I glance through each of the other three windows. The same navy barrier divides the land from the sky all the way around the tower. *We're on an island. How in the world are they going to escape?* A feeling of utter helplessness settles within my core as I study her motionless profile. Even though she drips in gold and jewels she wears the face of a prisoner.

"How long has it been since the battle between Lenya and Spera?" I ask my guide.

"Nearly a year," she answers vacantly, her mind as far away as my own. I shudder at the thought of a year in this horrible, stunning place.

"Spera, darling," Asher calls smoothly from his throne. She turns to face him. The third circle has been burned across the others, completing her mark.

"She has the third mark," I whisper. "Did he make them fight after all? Is Lenya dead?" As if on cue, Lenya glides into the room before my guide opens her mouth to answer. Her long dress is a black replica of Spera's. She gingerly carries a silver tray to Asher's throne, offering him an assortment of food. As she passes me I glance at her back. She has three rings now, too. *What did he make them do for the last ring? And why didn't I see it?*

"You are so caring, sweet Lenya," he croons without taking his eyes off Spera's bare back. "Might you offer your services to me as well, Spera?"

"What is it that you require, Asher?" Spera's voice is hollow and flat. My eyes dart to Lucas. He flexes his hands at his post.

"Don't be so cold, my queen. Haven't I provided you with much? Could you have imagined a life filled with such riches?" Her gaze moves to the window again. "I find you most ungrateful."

"And how might I demonstrate my gratitude?" she asks curtly. I blanch at the possibilities.

"All I want you to do is put on a good show for the men. They caught something just for you," he says casually.

"What did they bring?" Lenya's voice is high with eagerness.

"An alpha lion, and a big one. They are in awe of your strength and are thrilled each time they see it tested," he says. Lenya claps her dainty hands with enthusiasm. They both stare impatiently at Spera's back.

"I am delighted to do what pleases my king," Spera concedes without facing him. I am certain she can feel his triumphant stare on the nape of her neck.

"And I am glad to hear it," he says and rises from his throne. "My vizier is on his way. He has sent word that he may have found the door to the veil and that the journey ahead will be long and difficult. Our armies need a morale boost before we mobilize. And I think watching their beautiful queen dismember such a formidable opponent should do the trick."

Lenya giggles and brings a hand to Asher's arm, but he absently brushes it off. Her whole face falls in response. She seems genuinely hurt. I study her clouded eyes, watching for any familiar defiance to shine through. But she remains completely in character, obviously determined to secure her position in Asher's deadly palm.

"I must depart for my own chambers. My vizier should arrive at any moment." No sooner have the words left Asher's mouth, the heavy doors swing open and a willowy being enters the round room. He is nearly identical to my own guide and moves with the same otherworldly grace. But where my guide looks like she was carved from a pearl, this Unseen is the color of gunmetal and seems every bit as hard and capable as the barrel of gun.

"And so here he is," Asher eagerly greets the new arrival. "Raffin, punctual as always." They exchange a dark, knowing look as they clasp their hands around each other's forearms. My eyes move from Raffin to my guide.

"Do you know him?" I whisper.

"I do," she says, her resentment of him too fierce a thing to come from anger alone. Whoever he is to her now, I can tell he used to be something much different. She fixes her icy stare on his charcoal face. "We are done here," she says flatly as Asher and Raffin stride to the open doors.

The last thing I see before the scene dissolves is Spera leaning ever so slightly out the window, closing her eyes as the wind catches her hair and angrily snaps it free from its braid like the crack of a whip.

24
An offer

THIS NEW MEMORY COULD BE A TROPICAL PARADISE,
unless you factor in the armed guards and the pair of locked doors
fit for a maximum security prison. The walls and ceiling are the
same incredible, bewildering crystal as the high tower we just
left. Sunset makes the clear stone glow blood red and casts deep
shadows over the two guards standing at attention by the side of a
circular pool. I immediately recognize Lucas's backlit outline and
assume that the other guard is Calen.

Spera sits opposite Lenya, submerged to her bare shoulders in
water hazy with heat. This is the most relaxed I've seen her yet. But
she still won't close her eyes. Lenya plucks an orange blossom from
the rainbow of flowering lily pads adrift in the pool and pulls the
petals off one at a time. Spera reaches absently toward water tumbling freely down a cascade of unfinished white rocks and stares
blankly at her hand. *The ring! She has the ring on.* My eyes dart to
Lenya. I press my lips together in anticipation as I catch sight of
Lenya's ring.

I am thoroughly enjoying Asher's absence, Spera calls out silently
to Lenya. A little smile tugs at the corners of Lenya's mouth as she
pretends to glower at her fellow queen. *Do you know how long he
and Raffin will be gone?*

At least a couple of days more. He said that the journey is very far. He once told me that he has tried opening the veil in nearly ten thousand places but none of his attempts have made a dent, she snickers. I can't help but smile at their playful exchange, grateful to see some of Lenya's true self make a return appearance. She reminds me so much of Vanessa when she's not fawning all over Asher.

Do you think he's right this time? Do you think we will be asked to open the veil? Spera asks.

Who knows. Calen seems to think so, but I overheard him talking to another guard this afternoon. Some of them have their doubts. I don't think Asher ever believes himself to be wrong. But there are whispers that Raffin located an important piece of the ritual scroll. Something about the elements.

I only wish there was a way to be certain. Spera lets out a frustrated sigh and drags her fingers across the milky surface.

"Are you weary, my queen? Shall I escort you to your quarters?" Lucas calls out, keeping his voice distant and reverent.

"Not yet, Lucas," Spera answers without turning her face. "A few minutes more."

Have you had any visions? Seen any way for us to escape yet? Spera asks tentatively.

No. Asher has doubled the guards surrounding the exterior of the fortress. Unless you plan on tunneling to the sea, there's no way to get out undetected. Vanessa's eyes flit to Lucas. *But perhaps you could have a little escape of your own.*

What do you mean?

You and Lucas should spend some time alone while Asher is gone. You don't get very many chances to touch each other, do you?

No. She bites down on her lip and stares at the water. *What if he comes back early and catches us together? He'll kill us for sure.*

Would that be such a sorry fate?

Not if he killed us both.

My eyes move to Lucas's stoic face as he forces himself to stare straight ahead. The only thing keeping me from losing my mind at this point is the knowledge that he survives whatever Spera doesn't. She must not know that Lucas would never come back if he was to die. Not in this form or any other.

Use the garden off my room. If Asher does come home early, I will make myself visible in the main area of the compound. He won't look for you in my quarters. I should be able to buy you a little time together.

And what of the others? Might they get suspicious if Lucas and I are absent?

If anyone asks too many questions I'll demand that his life be forfeited to me, Lenya says.

I have to hold back a laugh. That sounds exactly like something Vanessa would say. Except I can tell that Lenya is dead serious. I can't help but think of the man in the alley that night. The way Vanessa nudged him with her bare toes. The way she didn't mind his blood pooling onto the street.

The two queens lock low eyes over the top of the swirling water. *Calen is a lazy fool with Asher away. He leaves his post by my door soon after he escorts me from bathing and doesn't come back again until well after sunrise. Spend the night with me tonight. Tell Lucas to come just before dawn as the guards' shifts are changing. You two can spend the whole day in my courtyard if you like. I will make sure that you are undisturbed.*

I am grateful for you, Lenya.

And I as well for you, my friend, Lenya agrees. Even though this dangerous favor happened nearly a thousand years ago, I feel even more in debt to Vanessa than I did upon discovering she'd paid my hospital bill. Her generosity is transcendental.

"I am finished here, Calen," Lenya says, making her voice flat and bored. He opens a length of plush, ivory fabric and she wraps it around herself as she emerges from the steamy water. "Asher really ought to see that this pool is made bigger. I found it too crowded today," she jeers.

Calen casts an amused glance at Lucas over Lenya's nimble frame and then follows her out of the iron gates. Spera watches them leave and then steps into the middle part of the pool. Lucas's eyes follow her as she reaches for a white blossom and plucks it from its floating pad. His hard face melts into adoration as she sweeps the flower behind her ear.

"They're alone now. Why are they still being so careful?" I whisper to my guide as quietly as I can. Even though I know they can't hear me, it feels like a crime to disrupt the silent spell between Spera and Lucas. My guide nods at the crystal walls, which are as clear as glass now that the sun has set. Guards pass by on two sides in fifteen second intervals. Their heads don't turn as they march down the hall on the other side of the translucent divide, but nothing out of the ordinary is happening to draw their eyes.

"You seem in good spirits, my queen," Lucas calls out softly to her.

"I am, Lucas," Spera replies without taking her eyes off the water. She turns her back to him so that her face is shielded from the guards rounding the hall outside. "Lenya has an idea, a way for us to be together if only for a day. And I think it will work." Spera tells Lucas about Lenya's offer with her back still turned. Her hands absently skim the water's surface as she talks.

I can't take my eyes off Lucas, mesmerized by the storm of want and fear that clouds over his face. His chin begins to tremble so slightly that at first I think I'm imagining it. But then a single tear drops from his eye and rolls down his scarred cheek.

"It is time," my guide says. Her voice seems so out of place in this most tender moment. I forcibly resist the overwhelming impulse to argue with her and instead let out a hard breath as conflicting emotions fill my chest to bursting.

I long to be a part of what they have, to believe that I am connected to the devotion I see on Lucas's face. But as I watch them together, the only thing I feel is distance. I know I'm invisible here. But each time he turns his eyes to Spera instead of me, it widens the gap between us. My grasp on where I belong in this is disintegrating to dust. One swipe across its surface and it scatters in the wind.

25
Burned

I'M NOT SURE WHAT I EXPECTED LENYA'S ENCLOSED GAR-
den would look like, but I'd underestimated it by a long shot. Every
inch of the two acre yard is covered with something blooming. For
just a moment I can't imagine why anyone would ever want to leave.

Is this even real? I reach for the closest thing to me: an arbor
made out of thousands of braided morning glory vines nearly ready
to open their petals to the new day. Shimmering flower dust leaves
a silver streak on the tip of my finger.

Asher's tendency to cage everything has only added more surfaces for plants to climb. Blossoming white vines stretch skyward
along the crystal walls, giving the effect of a flowering spider web.
The first light of dawn filters through the uncovered spaces of the
crystal barrier and makes the mossy ground shimmer with a blanket of faint rainbows. I stretch my arms in front of me and marvel
at the same effect the refracted light has on my bare skin.

The sound of moving water draws my ear. A cluster of weeping
willows leans toward a pond nestled in the far corner of the garden. In impossibly artistic fashion, the crystal wall behind the pool
appears to melt like ice into a steady stream of water that tumbles
down the face of a white stone and into the pond. I draw a deep

breath, anticipating the cool, lingering scent of wild water to fill me with a sense of freedom, no matter how false.

Suddenly, just loud enough to be audible over the easy cadence of the little waterfall, comes a sound I've never heard before: Spera's laughter. And then a familiar chuckle. Lucas. I am torn between giving them a moment alone and wanting to be a part of it. In a matter of seconds I'm halfway down the length of the garden, just in time to see Spera throw her head back in a genuine smile, her hand covered by Lucas's.

They sit together on the far side of the pond, shielded by a dense grove of lilies and irises. Lucas says something that makes her laugh again. She reaches her other hand to her neck and plays with the silver horseshoe charm as she contentedly watches his happy face.

He lights up with animation as he enjoys the company of his beloved Spera. The sight of it is bittersweet, because it belongs to them and only them. There have been moments during this journey that I have felt so one with Spera that there was no question we were and are the same being. But in this special moment, I have never felt so separate.

"I have never seen a more stunning creature," he marvels as he stares at her face with eyes full of wonder. She blushes under his attention and spreads the white fabric of her dress across her folded legs.

"Lenya helped me get ready. I wanted to look like myself for our short time together. Not like Asher's queen," she whispers, rubbing her bare wrists where her serpent bracelets should be.

"May I ask you something?" Lucas brings a thumb to her ear and traces the curve of her jaw line.

"Of course." She leans into his open palm.

"Is it true what they say? That you can control the fire in the sky. Make lightning strike at your bidding?" I wait for her to tell him about the horses she defended, my own heart quickening at the memory of her body rising from the canyon floor in a beam of lavender light. But her eyes narrow to angry slits as she springs to her feet.

"Is that where your interest in me began? Does it tempt you? Are you so much like Asher after all?" she spits. Her devastated accusation hangs between them like a guillotine. *It can't be true. Can it?* The hair on the back of my neck stands on end as I consider the awful possibility.

"No, no. Spera. You misunderstood." Lucas reaches out for her, but she ignores his hand.

"Then explain yourself. I would be safer if I had even one reason to stop loving you. What I feel for you is truly my gravest threat, the most unbearable torture of all," she says.

"I promise I am not interested in exploiting your gift," he pleads with wide eyes.

"Gift?" she scoffs. "You think that would be a gift? To be declared possessed by a demon? To have drawn the attention of Asher, and to be cast from my home and family?"

We stand so close together now that I can feel the slight increase in her temperature as her pulse quickens under her bronze skin. The angry rhythm pounds visibly along her slender neck. I am hypnotized by the rise and fall of it. And all at once I know her deepest, darkest places, for they are mine. Her wounded heart is beating in time to the hot blood coursing through my own veins. *Two bodies. One soul.*

"Asher, no. Wait, darling!" Lenya's tight voice fractures the peace of morning and makes all of us spin toward the top of the garden. "Don't go out there. I am keeping a surprise for you in the garden. Please don't ruin it."

"He's here," Spera whispers, guarding her throat with her hand.

"We have to find a way out of here." Lucas moves between Spera and the sounds of Asher and Lenya arguing inside.

"How? We will have to pass him to get out," Spera argues, panic rising in her voice.

"We'll have a better chance if I can get you out in the open where you can have access to the sky," Lucas says and takes Spera by the wrist.

"Asher is wrong. It doesn't work like he thinks it does." Her words freeze Lucas in his tracks. His jaw tightens as he tucks Spera behind his broad frame. She wraps a nervous hand around his arm and peers toward the blooming arbor.

Something too familiar about the way she's dressed makes me pause for a split second, paralyzed by the sensations of déjà vu. My eyes scan the full length of Spera and then down myself. We are wearing exactly the same thing, each of us standing barefoot in a simple white dress, loose black hair falling wild against our backs. To my horror, I realize there is no difference between us but the horseshoe charm resting above her mark—both of our hands are bare. Spera is not wearing her ring. Lenya couldn't send early warning. *How could Spera have forgotten to put it on?*

"She is here, I know she is. And I could smell Lucas the moment I set foot in your chambers. What are they doing here?" Asher snarls as a loud crash sounds from the entrance to Lenya's room.

"They're helping me with the surprise, that is all," Lenya pleads. Their voices are too close. He'll see them for sure. But what would he see, exactly? One of his queens enjoying Lenya's garden in the required company of her guard? What would be suspicious about that?

"You are friends with Spera now?" Asher's voice is saturated with malice.

"We have had time to speak freely to each other in your absence. We have come to an understanding of one another," Lenya says in a rush.

"Is that so?" The three words boom unhindered across the enclosed courtyard as Asher steps through the delicate arbor and storms down the sloped garden. Lenya hangs back, watching his descent from the top of the hill.

"Asher, I am glad to see that your travels were safe," Spera calls as she steps from behind Lucas.

"That would be a first," Asher growls without slowing down. "What are you doing here?"

"Lenya wanted to prove to me how superior her garden is to mine. I decided to come see for myself. And I am reluctant to admit that she is right," Spera says as she creates more physical distance between herself and Lucas.

Lenya cautiously makes her way toward the tense exchange.

"This place is beautiful," Spera adds. "I would be pleased to have one such as this."

"This place is worthless," Asher counters. But his rage has simmered to an angry pout. "I could create something truly spectacular for you, something equivalent to your beauty. This is no match."

"You still find her so much more beautiful than me? Even in commoner's attire?" Lenya interjects and crosses her jeweled arms in front of her chest. Asher's eyes flit to Lenya, distracted by her presence.

"I did not know you would be home or I would have made myself presentable," Spera says, following Lenya's diversion. "When you are gone there is no one to impress."

"You taking a sincere interest in impressing me would also be a first," Asher muses as he narrows his white eyes.

"When you are pleased I find you more tolerable," Spera backtracks. But Asher's face twists with rage. He moves within a hair's width of Spera in a single stride, snaps the leather cord from around her neck and squeezes the silver charm in his big pale hand.

"There's only one way you came to possess this necklace again," he says, turning his cruel stare to Lucas. "The necklace that you said broke, you worthless thief. You know the punishment for stealing from me. How could you be so foolish? What would possess you to steal from—"

Asher stops midsentence, his white eyes moving from Lucas to Spera. Disbelief flashes across his face, followed quickly by the twisting anguish of rage as the back of his hand makes contact with the side of Lucas's face. "Are you courting my queen?" he spits, barely able to speak.

Before Lucas can right himself, Asher clamps a pale hand around his neck and lifts him from the ground. Lucas sputters as he claws at Asher's vice-like grip.

"Asher, please! Don't hurt him," Spera begs and bows in front of Asher.

Call down the lightning! What are you waiting for?

"Do not bow before me now, you adulterous girl. It only serves as another lie. And you will not lie to me again," Asher snarls. Lucas's eyes roll back into his head.

"You want the truth, Asher? Are you so sure that you wish to hear it?" Spera asks, deflated and bitter. He snarls an impatient answer, his hand trembling with the force he's using against Lucas.

"The life you hold in your hand is the only thing of value to me in this entire world. If you kill him, you kill me, whether you physically end my life or not. But death will not change how I feel about him." Spera says, her words even and unapologetic.

"Do not speak of death as if you understand it. As if you control it. Death purifies. It changes everything," Asher says. "The only thing it saves is the only thing I need. Don't you see? Death and I are on the same side."

"I can't watch this," I whisper to myself and start to turn away.

"You must. This is why you are here," my guide insists. She takes me by the shoulders and gives me a strong shake. "You must see this through. You are too close now to surrender to fear. We will need you to be brave in the days ahead."

246   ◯◯   *Jadie Jones*

I draw in a broken breath and face whatever end is coming.

"Asher, leave these two alone in their poor judgment," Lenya says, stepping to his side. "I can be enough for you. I want nothing more than to be the one true queen. If Spera is truly necessary to open the veil then demand that she give you at least that measure of loyalty. Make her swear an oath that if she can open the veil, that she will be your Vessel. It is in her best interest to deliver the gift, is it not? Then we all get what we want." She runs her hand down Asher's clenched forearm. Her close proximity to his lethal hands makes my heart race with panic.

"You do as I say or you will watch me gut him," Asher says evenly, narrowing his eyes at Spera.

Is he really considering Lenya's offer? Will he let Lucas and Spera be together? In my heart I know it's not true, but I hold on to the possibility like my life depends on it.

"Anything," Spera says, closing her eyes as a single tear slips out.

Asher tosses Lucas's limp body to the ground and draws a small dagger from his leather belt. He holds the handle of the weapon out for Spera.

"Make an oath to me, a blood vow that you will spill your blood on the door of the veil and should it open, that you will be my Vessel. Make this vow and I will allow Lucas to live despite the atrocities he has committed against me."

"I have your word?"

"You have my word," he says without wavering his fiery stare on her face.

"Then you have mine." Spera plants her left hand into his open palm and shoves the dagger hard and fast through both of their hands. Her eyes shine with pain and relief as their intermingled blood drips to the mossy ground.

Lucas begins to stir, moaning as he rolls to his side. My heart leaps when he opens his eyes. But the look on Lucas's bewildered face turns to agony and shreds my fragile hope that Spera might make it through this after all.

"Seal your oath with a kiss, a last taste of your lips, and I will consider Lucas's debt repaid," Asher wagers.

Spera closes her eyes and takes a measured breath before leaning into Asher's waiting face. Watching them kiss is like seeing an explosion. I can hardly stomach it but can't turn away. I can practically feel Asher's hot touch on my own skin as his hand moves from her jaw to her collarbone. Spera winces under his palm as he presses it flat against her mark.

"Don't!" Lucas rasps as he pushes up to his knees.

Suddenly, Spera throws her head back as a horrific scream rips from her throat. Asher pulls the knife from their hands and watches her stumble backward, her mark glowing blood red. Before I can ask my guide what he's done to her, the three circles burst into black flames. Her charred skin peels back, curling against the heat as the exposed flesh smolders beneath.

"Asher," she manages to cry out, pain and disbelief making her voice crack.

"It's for your own good," he states, his face emotionless.

She flings herself face down into the tranquil pond. A scream of pure agony sounds from somewhere behind me as Spera meets the water and the surface erupts with fire. I stop breathing; shock and grief and terror making me too still to draw in air. The luminous walls melting into the stream. The sour smell in the air. Whatever accelerant Asher uses to fuel the flames inside the fortress walls is cycled into the pool of water, and Spera's burning body just detonated it like a bomb.

26
Ashes to ashes

WHATEVER IS LEFT OF SPERA NEVER RESURFACES. Lucas crawls to the fiery edge, and for a second I think he might reach through the flames to try to find her. But a small flash of silver sails past his face and drops to the ground by his outstretched hand. Spera's necklace. He turns empty eyes toward the last piece of her.

"What happened to you, Lucas? Betraying me for a mortal girl," Asher growls.

Lucas doesn't acknowledge him, his wet eyes locked on the horseshoe charm. He plucks it from the earth and cradles it in his giant hands.

"Be grateful for my generosity. At least now you'll have something to remember her by while you wander this earth alone."

Lucas doesn't seem to hear him, but he slowly rises to his feet and staggers away from Spera's grave.

"He won't try to kill him?" I ask through jagged breaths.

"No. It is far greater a punishment to let him live without his reason to live."

But he does have a reason to live. Me. I rush to his side, determined to let him know that Spera will return to him one day, even if in a different form. If there's any way that I can give him any peace, I have to try. Just as I reach a hand for his trembling arm, he stands still and lifts his grieving face to the rising sun. Dawn casts a single beam of light through the crystal ceiling and washes Lucas in the pale glow.

"I swear to you," he whispers through clenched teeth. "I swear that if you let her return, I will guard her with my life. I will protect her from any threat. He will never possess her again. I ask that you make me her Contego, her Shield. Please. I am begging you. Let me cross so that I may take the oath." His voice cracks as he pleads with the sky.

I swallow the lump in my throat and step closer. Every inch of him shimmers. And then he's gone, his entire being dissolved into the beam of light. Frantically, I scan the ground for Spera's necklace, but it's gone too.

"At last, it is just you and I," Lenya says with a quivering voice as she wraps an arm around Asher's bare back and reaches to tilt his face to hers.

She's just trying to protect herself. But her affection for him feels deeply wrong, with Spera's charred remains still smoldering only a few feet from them.

"I told you I could be enough on my own." Her words make his face twist and he slings her to the ground in a single motion.

"You are not enough!" he barks. "Your blood cannot open the veil. You and I both know that. Spera is the only one that I need, the only rightful queen. She is the only piece. Do not fool yourself into believing that you are equal to her. I only let you live because you amuse me." He glares down at her stunned face before turning away from the burning lake and starting up the hill. Lenya slowly climbs to her feet, the color drained from her porcelain skin.

"Asher, please! You are wrong!" she screams at his back. But he doesn't turn around. "And so you shall have neither of us," she whispers as she backs toward the fire, opens her arms wide, and lets herself fall.

"No!" I scream, rushing to the edge of the pond. *Maybe she's still alive. Maybe I can help her out somehow.* But the bright flames consume the pond and I can't see through them to the water beneath. "No," I repeat, barely a whimper, as I sit back on my heels and stare into the orange glow.

My burning eyes sweep up the length of the garden and lock onto Asher's retreating form. "Asher!" I cry out, rage like I've never felt flooding through my veins.

"Tanzy, no," my guide pleads as she pulls on my elbow, but I shake her off. I spring to my feet and race for my enemy, closing the distance in seconds.

"Tanzy, you are finished! You have seen your Origin through. We must leave!" My guide's words barely register as I steel myself for whatever might happen once I touch him.

"Asher," I call out as I clamp my hand around Asher's thick forearm, both horrified and delirious to feel his solid form under my grip.

Shock passes through his eyes as he spins toward the sensation of my touch. I reach my free hand back, ready to let it fly, when an awful grin spreads across his colorless face.

"I know you," he rumbles.

"He sees you! What have you done?" My guide gasps beside me and grabs my hand. I shove her to the ground, the instinct to fight back coursing unbridled through my body.

"Temper, temper. You difficult girl," he says as my guide scrambles away from us.

"You destroy everything you touch!" I scream at him.

"No, my dear girl. You destroy everything you touch. I created you to end every ending," he croons and reaches for my face. "And now I know that you will return to me. And I know exactly what you will look like." His words force me back like a slap in the face. "Yes, don't you see? You have given me everything I need to know. Perhaps you and I are on the same side, after all."

"That's not what I meant to do," I whisper.

He swaggers toward me. "Yes it is," he counters, his silvery white eyes rooting me to the ground. His hand whips around my head and his fingers tangle in my hair. With a low growl, he pulls my face to his and presses his lips hard against mine. Heat from his mouth takes over my body like a riptide. Spera's entire life flashes before my mind's eye as the current intensifies. I can't bear another moment. I don't want it to stop. I let out a frantic gasp as he pulls my head back by my hair.

A purple streak of lightning blazes down from the clear morning sky and crashes against the crystal ceiling, sending up a shower of sparks. The clear barrier begins to fracture in places as another bolt of lightning strikes the stone.

"I know you. I alone know your heart." His hand slides through my hair and claims my throat. He traces my pulse to the hollow above his mark. The rings beg him closer, a warmth spreading along my collar. His eyes close with pleasure the moment the heat reaches his fingers. He flexes his palm above the brand, releasing me from his touch. The places left behind shiver with exposure and relief.

Surges of want crash down from all sides. The want to wrap my hands around his arm and snap it from his body. To wrap them around his wrist instead and beg him to reach inside the void beneath my ribs and fill it. To feel the sizzle of his skin on mine again. To twist his neck until it breaks.

A splintering crescendo blows the thoughts away like wind to smoke, their scent still lingering in my brain. My hands instinctively lift to protect my head as a chunk of the crystal ceiling tumbles to the soft earth. The wall feeding into the pond collapses, and fire erupts from the rubble. My eyes dart back to Asher. Even though the world around us crumbles, his gaze on my face is steady and calm.

252   *Jadie Jones*

"I will always find you." His promise cuts through the deafening roar as the garden dissolves into an empty black, my Origin finally, horribly complete.

✑

I can feel this new place before I can see it, bitterly cold and thick. My skin feels like its waking back up after going numb. All at once my lungs begin to burn, begging for oxygen. Instinctively, I draw in a breath, but icy water shoots down my nose and floods into my open mouth. Frantic, I try to right myself but I can't tell which way is up. I kick out blindly. My toes scrape against a sandy bottom. I draw my legs underneath me and burst through the surface.

The air is so cold that each breath feels like swallowing a knife. Freezing rain pelts my face. Walls of earth and rock climb up each side of the river. Runoff pours over the high ledges, which tower at least forty feet above me. *I have to get out of here.* Dizzy and bewildered, I swim to the closest side.

"This feels familiar," I whisper, hazarding another glance up as soon as I can plant a hand on the muddy wall. The hardwood trees. The reddish clay. I swear I smell manure. Everything about my environment reminds me of Wildwood, but I don't recognize this place and I've been over every inch of that pasture.

Is this real or is it still part of the Origin? I strain for any sign of my guide but the driving rain makes focusing impossible. I begin to shake as a deep chill sets in. A scream of frustration escapes my clenched teeth. *I have to find a way up.*

"Think, Tanzy!" I berate myself.

Don't think. Just listen. Spera's raspy voice resonates within my reeling brain.

"Listen to what?" I call out. But she doesn't respond. I will her to come back, but all I can hear is the steady hammer of my heart.

One-two, one-two, one-two. Everything else falls away as I lock into the rhythm. Fear and indecision evaporate, leaving pure instinct.

Climb.

I move one hand at a time up the slippery cliff. And finally, my hand reaches forward instead of up. I dig my fingers into the solid ground and heave myself over the lip of the ravine. The rain pelting my bare skin is an afterthought to the hard-won ascent. I am nearly delirious with exhaustion and relief. The prickly sensation of unwanted familiarity skitters across my skin like a spider.

I do know this place. I sit up, closing and opening my eyes over and over in hopes that the picture will change. *You will wake up where this life began.* Maris's words echo in my frozen, disbelieving mind. The bottom of the ravine, my father's true grave. My life began when his ended.

"Spera." Lucas's voice spins me around. He emerges from the trees a little ways down the overgrown trail. I look back down the ravine and then to his beautiful, scarred face. I let out a grief-stricken sob and drop to my knees.

"Spera," he repeats and sprints in my direction.

I must still be in the Origin.

I close my eyes against the sight of him. *I can't take any more. I want to go back home.* But I blindly reach out for him; perhaps by some miracle I might feel him as he runs past me in search of Spera. My heart weighs too much. What I've lost weighs too much. Together, they blot out Lucas's face as I collapse to the rain-soaked earth.

27
The calm before the storm

STALE SMOKE TAINTS THE AIR AND MAKES ME WINCE. The smell triggers a memory like an electric shock and suddenly Spera's face, twisted in agony, writhes in my groggy mind. I bolt upright and gasp for air. The soft something I'm sitting on shifts beneath my movement. A solid hand steadies my body and prevents me from toppling over. But the world around me keeps spinning. *Where am I? Who's here with me? Why am I all wet?*

My dimly lit surroundings come into focus a little at a time. Pressed pine walls. Rakes and pitchforks. Loose hay on the floor. A glowing safety lantern on a nail hook. Stacks of alfalfa in the far corner. *Wildwood.*

"You're shaking, Spera," Lucas's smooth voice says from behind me. I jump at the sound and quickly scan the room for Spera. But his eyes are on me.

"Is this real?" I whisper, wrapping my arms tightly around myself. The dress from my Origin is soaked through with rain water and sticks to my skin.

"It is," he says and kneels beside the hay bales serving as my bed.

"Was that real? What I saw. My Origin." I drop my eyes and shudder. The memories are foggy and distant. Each time I reach for one it slides further back into the depths. But the feeling of terrible loss lingers heavily in my chest. Without warning, flashes from Spera's life explode in my battered mind. I press my palms onto either side of my head and grit my teeth against the onslaught of violence. The screams. The grief.

"Spera?" Lucas asks, his voice heavy with concern.

"I'm Tanzy. I'm not Spera."

"You are both," he offers.

"No, I'm not. She was brave and strong. She wasn't afraid of anything. I'm—I—I don't know what I am."

Lucas sits beside me and offers the support of his arm. I lean into the warmth of him. The jagged scars that mar the side of his face are visible even in the dim light. The jealousy I'd felt in Lenya's garden fills me with guilt. I wanted to have Lucas for myself. But now I'd do anything to give him back what he lost.

"Did you really love her?" I whisper, their last conversation playing in my mind. "Or was she right? Did you just want her for the same reason Asher did? Is that why you want me? You think I can do the same thing? I can't."

"I have regretted asking you that question for a thousand years," he says and moves away from me. "That you died unsure of my feelings for you."

"Stop saying that."

"What?"

"Acting like Spera and I are the same. I thought we were. I wish we were. But I'm not anything like her."

"You may not share every attribute, but her soul is reborn in your body. Of that we are all sure. I will protect you from anything and everything, including myself. I failed you before. That won't happen again."

His eyes drop from mine, and instantly I see how much guilt

he has carried with him. He stares into the driving rain, no doubt reliving the moment he watched his beloved Spera die. He thinks it's his fault. That she died never knowing if he truly loved her.

He did, Spera. If you can hear me somehow. If you and I are really the same, Lucas loves you. And then, in her unmistakable voice, I hear within my own being: *I know.*

"She knew," I whisper to the floor, feeling at once a part of their love and yet further from it than ever before.

"Don't say that to me unless you're certain."

"I think she just told me," I say, the admission both comforting and unnerving. His powerful hands clutch my back and draw me to him.

"I never stopped loving you. I never stopped searching for you," Lucas whispers in my ear as his hands cradle my face. His hot skin presses against mine and I move into it, any distance between us too much. "I'm sorry," he says, pulling away.

I reach out to stop him. "Why are you sorry?" I ask, completely lost in the feeling of his skin on mine.

"I know that you aren't Spera. You are, but you aren't. I know your heart. But you do not know mine."

"I think I do. I saw everything. How you helped her. You tried to save her more than once."

"And a great shield I turned out to be then." He turns away, unable to meet my eyes.

"You found me. I don't know where we were during my Origin, but it definitely didn't feel like Virginia."

"Near Egypt. An island off the east coast," he whispers. His dark eyes go blank as his mind takes him somewhere else, undoubtedly back to that barren place. *His eyes. They were white before. Like Asher's.*

"Why aren't your eyes white?" I ask, tempted to touch them.

The corners of his lips pull back a little at my question. "A Contego is considered dangerous because we hold a Seen creature's safety above our own. They color our eyes like yours as a warning," he says and locks his gaze with mine. I watch his scarred face, spellbound into silence.

"You are shaking again," he says and moves to my side. He shrugs out of his jacket and slips it around my shoulders.

I rest against his chest and tuck my head under his chin. The sudden heat and the droning rain on the roof act as an elixir to my jumbled brain. I relax into his firm hold and slip a hand around his waist. He presses his cheek against the top of my head. For the first time in years, I fall asleep feeling like I'm right where I belong.

28
Red in the morning

THE HAY SHED IS LESS MAGICAL IN THE GRAY LIGHT OF dawn than it was in the moonlight. But Lucas is breathtaking as he stands guard at the slanted doorway. He watches steadfastly through the crooked gap. I silently push up from the bale of hay, reluctant to break the spell.

"You didn't sleep?" I ask softly, trying not to startle him.

His eyes find me and a smile warms his tense face. "No. I couldn't leave you unprotected."

Words both amazing and terrifying. That he wants to protect me. And that I need it. I climb to my feet and inspect myself. My dress is wrinkled but dry. And so is my hair, which is coal black and as unruly as a yearling colt. I reach up to pluck a few strands of hay from the dark tangles. Vanessa's ring gleams on my finger. I'm glad to have it back. To have her back.

I can't wait to tell her what I saw. My eyes move back to Lucas. *Well, maybe I can wait a little while.* I twist the ring upside down and push her from my mind. Vanessa, of all people, would understand.

"It's a beautiful morning. Come see," Lucas says. I tiptoe across the blanket of hay and take his hand in mine. Surprise softens the lines on his face.

"It is beautiful." Above us, the early sky is streaked with burgundy. "Storm sky." I point to the horizon.

"Another one is coming."

"Is Asher?" The question slips out before I can stop it.

"I don't sense him," he begins, his voice grave. "But that doesn't mean he's not coming. I can't predict him the way I once could. We have not come face to face in hundreds of years."

I shudder at the last memory of my Origin.

"He saw me. In the Origin, he saw me. He talked to me. He said I would destroy everything, that I was the end of all endings. What did he mean?" I stammer.

Lucas's eyes turn away from my face and wander aimlessly over the pasture. "Are you sure you're ready?" he asks without turning back to me.

"Yes! I have to know. It's my fault that he found me. If I hadn't been so stupid—"

Lucas lets out a little chuckle.

"What's so funny?"

"That decision you made in the garden, that was Spera through and through," he says, his eyes softening at the memory.

"You saw that? But you disappeared. What happened to you?"

"I went behind the veil one last time to take the Contego oath. Since then I have searched for you."

"The whole time?"

"The whole time," he repeats. "You see, you showed your face to Asher, but you also showed me."

"So you were on the other side of the veil but you could still see what was happening in the garden?"

"Yes. The veil works like a one-sided mirror. We can see through, but you can't. Mortals can't," he corrects.

"I can?" I ask, quickly pouncing on what he didn't say.

"Soon," he answers gravely. "Things will soon be set in motion that can't be undone."

He steps out of the shed and moves toward the empty pasture. I follow silently beside him as we walk deep into the barren field. His stony face does not change with each glance that I steal of him. He reaches the edge of the tree line where the winter grass is still high in tufts and sits down cross-legged. I sit next to him and watch him pluck a couple of brittle strands from the ground. He starts to braid them together and I let out a gasp.

"This is the first place I ever saw you," he admits. "You'd just moved here. Your mother showed you how to make bracelets out of grass." I stare on, speechless, as he finishes the bracelet and fastens it around my wrist. "I've made thousands of these since then."

"So why now? If you've been around all this time, why did you wait so long?"

"If I had been successful and kept you hidden, you never would've had to see me. But I failed. And they found you."

"Asher?"

"Yes. And those he holds close."

"What do they want with me? Besides the fact that they think that…" I pause. *Am I willing to say this out loud?* "Besides the fact that my soul is Spera's, and they think I can open the veil," I finish deliberately.

His eyes regard me with surprise. But his face goes from light to dark inside of a single breath. "Have you felt it? The process?"

The strength. The rage. The man I nearly killed in the alley.

"You were there, weren't you? In Kentucky." Shame burns a path from my throat to my ears.

"No, why? What happened in Kentucky?"

"I, I hurt someone. A man. He tried to … so I hurt him. I didn't mean to. I was strong. Really strong."

"The strength you feel now is only the beginning."

"You aren't going to ask me about it?"

"About what?"

"The man I hurt."

"I know your heart Spe—Tanzy. I know you wouldn't hurt someone unless your life depended on it. But I have not always been able to say the same for myself."

"My guide said … she seemed to think you used to be a lot different."

"She is right. Our true forms, what we are behind the veil, are powerful beyond anything you could imagine. Humans have made guesses as to what we might look like. They write about us in stories and fables with very little accuracy. But they do have one thing right. When humans describe monsters that can end your world, they're talking about us," he explains, studying my face for a reaction.

"And that's what you really are?"

"That's what I am."

"And this body?" I ask, motioning to him.

"It's like a uniform we take on your side of the veil."

"And Ryan?" I ask, feeling a little silly for even calling him by that name.

"Ryan is how I hide on this side. We can recognize each other in these forms," he says, gesturing to himself. "But any other form we take is like a mask. Unless one Unseen sees another Unseen make the transition into that form, they would just assume it was a human. But it's very dangerous for us to take a human mask. We are the most vulnerable when we use one."

Immediately I think of Dr. Andrews, of his abuse of Vanessa. Could Asher be hiding as Dr. Andrews? Tying himself to Lenya's new body, having Lucas work beneath him as Ryan. And the statue of the horse, the one I was sure was safe in Vanessa's unwitting possession. It can't possibly be a coincidence. There's no way Asher's going to have access to either Vanessa or Lucas anymore. Not if I can help it.

"What about Asher? Does he have a human mask?" I venture, feeling out whether or not Lucas suspects the same thing about Dr. Andrews.

"I highly doubt it. He prefers his true form to anything, but is willing to assume a uniform." Lucas sounds so certain that my plan to storm Vanessa's house and set her free dissolves and is blown into the morning wind like a dandelion seed. I fiddle with the hem of my dress.

"I think I've seen his true form," I start nervously. "Something like a black, shimmery shadow." That thing in the pasture. It had to be him. *Which means Asher killed my father.*

"We can all do that," he answers, trying to hide his amusement. "It's the fastest way to travel on your side of the veil. Those forms are invisible to mortals. You can only see them because of your Origin."

"Oh." I frown at the dead end, my mind filled with puzzle pieces that fit a hundred different ways.

"Are you all right?"

"I'm getting there. I just still don't see what this has to do with me. Why Asher thinks I can open the veil, when I don't even know what it is. Or how to open it."

"You are in good company there. No one is absolutely certain how to open it. The Powers hid the ritual to open the veil in six different riddles and cast them all around the world. Asher has been hunting for pieces of the ritual for thousands of years."

"Raffin," I say, recalling the gray cloaked figure. Lucas nods.

"Raffin is still translating a couple of lines of text even now," he explains. "Asher still doesn't know everything about how to destroy the veil, but he may know enough."

"What does he know?"

"The decision must come from a human soul, but the blood that feeds the soul must be more than human."

"How is that even poss—" I stop midsentence and cringe as the memory of the dark cellar springs to my mind.

"Asher figured out how to test different kinds of blood in the human body. He's been searching for the right combination for centuries. His process creates an Unseen Being with a Seen soul. The Vessel," Lucas says.

"What does that mean?"

"A human soul protected within an immortal body."

I won't admit it out loud, but my heart leaps a little at the idea of it, of being able to live forever like Lucas. With Lucas. *What would be so bad about that?*

"What makes him so sure that Spera was the right soul?" I ask instead.

"Because her soul resisted him. She's the only one during the whole process that never asked for immortality."

"What does immortality have to do with it?"

"That's the choice she would have had to make." He pauses and gives me a hard look. "The prophecy reads that she who opens a door to the veil will rule forever at the right hand of Asher. That she will provide the gift of life, and death will be taken away from her. Eternally."

"The gift of life?"

"A child."

I can't move. Can't breathe. *A child? With Asher?* Lucas's face clouds over at whatever he sees in my eyes.

"Birth and death do not exist in our world. The prophecy reads that there will only be one Unseen birth in all of time. They call it the Novus. We don't know much, but we do know that it must be conceived in the Unseen Realm by the Vessel, and that the mother must cross to the Seen realm and deliver the Novus while in her true Unseen form.

"If the Vessel chooses to open the veil and deliver the Novus, she will conceive by injecting a drop of Asher's blood into her own heart. But he can't force her to do it. The decision must be made in the heart of the Vessel, the heart of the queen. It is her choice to make."

"What's the other option?" I whisper.

"To seal it forever, which will deny Asher and all other Unseens birth and death. It also seals the veil against Unseens crossing over in any form. Permanently."

"Well that's a no-brainer. I choose that. You can stay on this side, right?"

A sad smile creases Lucas's scarred face. "Securing the veil eternally will cost you your life. Your eternal life," he adds.

My breath stills in my throat. He makes himself hold my gaze for a second longer before dropping his eyes.

"Okay, so Asher wants a kid. What's the big deal," I mumble, steeling myself against the thought of what it will take to do such a thing. My lips tingle at the memory of Asher's fevered kiss. I shake off the unwanted reaction as fast as possible.

"When he opens the veil, it will create a permanent door."

"Is that bad?" I ask.

"It would be catastrophic. The kind of Unseen that I am absorbs Tenix to gain power over other Unseens."

"I thought you couldn't die over there?" My back stiffens with alarm. I find comfort in knowing there is a place Lucas can go and be safe no matter what.

"Power isn't about strength, necessarily. In our world it's more political in nature. We can bend other Unseens to our own will using Tenix."

"So what is Tenix, exactly?" I ask, trying hard not to think about Lucas's past atrocities and what kind of will he might have exerted over other Unseens.

"Your world is made up of four primary elements: earth, air, water, and fire. Tenix is like the glue. It's what binds the elements together to create life. If you take the binding away, what is left behind dissolves into its elemental form."

"I'm not sure I follow you."

"When a human body dies, what does it turn into?"

"Dirt, I guess," I answer, making a face.

"Earth. The element earth. Unseen beings like me will strip mortal creatures of their Tenix and reduce them to their elemental breakdown. And in our true forms, we are very, very effective at absorbing Tenix."

"But what about the baby? Wouldn't it be a target, too?" I will away the unbidden protectiveness over a child I could never possibly want.

"The child would be an Unseen being, an immortal. The Novus must draw first breath in the Seen world, and then will require breath no longer. Then Asher's need for your world is over."

"What if I refuse to make a decision at all? What if I pretend I didn't ever know any of this?"

"I would give my own life if it meant you were spared this choice. That's why I tried to keep you hidden. But I realize now that you were created to make this choice. In this lifetime or the next," Lucas says, "Asher will find you. And it will begin again. This choice lies in your hands. In your blood."

I can't move. I can hardly breathe. *Maybe this is all just a bad dream.*

"But my blood isn't even mine," I start in a rush. "They had to replace all of it after the accident—" I freeze, realizing that what had given me a bit of hope is instead the exact reason that the final piece falls into undeniable place: a man from another country replaced every drop of my blood with something no one had ever heard of. It could only be one thing. Spera's blood. And there's not a doubt in my mind that Asher was in that operating room. But did he hide as Dr. Metcher or Dr. Andrews?

"It won't be long now," Lucas says, staring up at the charcoal clouds.

"What won't?" *Please be talking about the weather.*

"Now that you know. Asher felt it the moment the knowledge of your choice reached your heart." His words are tinged with venom. Suddenly, Vanessa's frantic voice splinters through the thoughts in my whirling mind. *Don't! Please, David, don't do this.* I gasp, clamping my hands on my ears as my head fills with her screams. *Tanzy, help me! If you can hear me. He knows. The affair. He knows! He'll kill me. Tanzy!*

"Vanessa!" I cry out.

"What's wrong with Vanessa?" Lucas asks. As Ryan he would know her, but I don't have time to explain.

"Something's happening. Something bad." I press my hands into my eyes to try to relieve the waves of pain. "I think he's trying to hurt her. I have to—"

"This ring. Where did you get it?" Lucas asks, snatching my hand. The dome swirls blood red, undoubtedly Vanessa's pain brewing beneath its surface. I jerk it away from him, stunned by the roughness in his touch.

"Lucas, I have to go. I don't think I have much time."

"It's imperative that you tell me who gave you that ring."

"Vanessa. I have to go to her."

"Just say the name," he pleads, not realizing I already did. Impatience begins to hum under my skin.

"It's Vanessa! Now I have to go," I say and turn east toward the rising sun and Keswick.

"Tanzy, please wait," Lucas says as he races to catch up with me.

"I'm sorry. I have to do this. She's in trouble. I've already watched her die once. I can't see it again. I know you understand that."

He stops in his tracks. His expression is like nothing I've ever seen before. It almost makes me wait, but I can't let anything happen to Vanessa. I'd never forgive myself if I got there too late.

"Meet me there," I call over my shoulder and start running as fast as I can.

29
Love and lies

MY FEET POUND INTO THE GRASS, PROPELLING ME forward in giant strides. Oxygen fills and exits my lungs to a rhythm I recognize—the same tempo that drummed against the dark night when Asher chased down Hopewell and me. And now he has Vanessa cornered, all doubts that he is hiding as Dr. Andrews vanished the moment she cried out in fear. But he won't win this time. The black horse's blood that saved Spera now flows through my veins and feeds my muscles. His speed. His strength. His heart.

I'm coming for you, Asher.

I close my eyes and allow the wild around me to guide me in the right direction. The currents of air act like a road map. I shift a few degrees north and push myself faster. Wildwood's acreage is behind me in less than a minute.

Hang on, Vanessa.

She answers me immediately, calling out for me again in terror. A snarl escapes my lips as I leap forward, demanding even more of my burning legs.

Time and distance blur. The terrain becomes steeper as I finally reach Keswick. Rain falls and makes the ground slick. I can smell her house. The wet stones give off a warm earthiness and I use the scent like a beacon to guide me the rest of the way. *Vanessa?* I call out to her. But nothing comes back.

I crest a near vertical hill and almost collide with a logging truck that makes its way down a familiar road. I throw myself into the wet grass to keep from being struck. *Vanessa's road.* I pause long enough to spot her stone pillars peeping out from a bend a quarter of a mile to the west. Relief washes cool over my sweaty skin. But the hardest part is still ahead. Am I strong enough to kill Asher? Am I willing to end a life?

The crush of indecision I felt beneath Asher's touch warms my mark. I fight against the tingling memory, and force my mind to fill itself with Spera's brutal final moments. Lenya's suicide. The torture Lucas still carries in his eyes. A new resolve condenses my thoughts into one goal: changing history. *I will do whatever it takes to keep Vanessa alive.* I leap across the street, glide over the black board fencing, and race blindly for the summit of Vanessa's property.

The face of the gigantic house is completely still behind a thick curtain of rain. Neither life nor light peeks from its long windows. But the statue in the fire fountain is whirling faster than I remember, liquid flames spilling over the edge and leaving trails of steam on the driveway. It feels like a warning, but I can't figure out what it means.

The driver's side door of David's car hangs open, dinging in ominous protest. That message is loud and clear: he was in a hurry to get his hands on her. I swallow the dread that makes my throat tight and silently move to the French doors. They're flung wide and reckless to each side. Tiny, sparkling shards of glass litter the foyer. They're under my feet too, but there's no pain. The only thing I can feel is a gut-wrenching need to get between Vanessa and Dr. Andrews. Asher. But I have no idea what to do.

I step further into the hushed entryway, waiting for a sign. My breath echoes off each polished surface and my mind creates silhouettes in every towering shadow. *Where are you Vanessa?*

I close my eyes and let my other senses take over. The unmistakable scent of blood stains the air. And I know exactly where it's coming from. My room. My bare feet meet the jade stairs without making a sound. I pause at the top and flatten my back against the marbled wall. No one speaks. Or screams. Or breathes. An anguished moan shatters the thick quiet and I am outside the door to my room within a single heartbeat.

I wrap my fingers around the curved handle and feel the hint of resistance by the engaged lock. A sudden ferocity fills me with such rage that I snap the handle from the door and shove the thick wood completely out of its frame. And as it falls to the ground, I close my hands into ready fists and prepare to defend Vanessa. No matter the cost.

Dr. Andrews's eyes snap to the broken door as it crashes to the ground. Fresh tears streak his face. His hands shake, hovering over Vanessa's still form.

"What did you do?" I cry out, moving toward Vanessa. Dr. Andrews rise and blocks her body from my view. "Vanessa!"

She lets out a low whimper and rolls on to her back, helpless and exposed. My pulse roars within me, drowning out the piercing silence in the dark room. Every movement slows down. But this feeling is familiar: the adrenaline rush in the alley, my blood responding to the worst kind of threats. He opens his mouth to speak, but I've seen enough. And I know too much. I know exactly what it feels like to watch her die.

He stiffens as I move toward him. His jaw tenses, the sound of his teeth grinding together nearly as loud as the thunder outside.

"I am going to give you one chance to get away from her," I order, my voice low and level. Surprise ripples across his face, and then fury replaces it, hardening the corners of his eyes.

"Over my dead body," he snarls and draws a fist back in warning. It's all the permission I need. I close the distance between us in a single stride and pause for a fraction of a second, letting his punch pass by the left side of my face. He stumbles forward, thrown off balance. My first strike lands squarely on his chin, throwing him backward. He slams against the blue stone wall and the air leaves his lungs in a hard rush. Vanessa stirs on the floor, drawing my gaze. Her nose is bleeding badly. The side of her face is already darkening with bruises.

"One chance," I reiterate, my eyes moving from her to Dr. Andrews as he staggers to his feet.

"I am not leaving her with you," he says.

"Then you're not leaving," I warn.

He lets out a grunt of painful effort and charges again. I drop back as my leg coils at my hip and then explodes forward. His sternum gives way under the force of my bare foot. He cries out in agony and drops to the ground, clutching his chest.

"Why are you doing this?" he asks through ragged breaths.

"She's my friend. More than that. A sister. And you aren't going to hurt her anymore."

His bewildered stare moves to Vanessa as he crawls toward her. He closes his fist around a piece of paper by her side. Before he can get any closer, I snatch the collar of his shirt and fling him away from her. He lands on his back in a heap.

"Last chance," I growl. But he doesn't move for the door. *A human would have run. A human should be dead.*

"I found her like this," he mumbles, his eyes rolling in their sockets as he tries to focus.

"Liar!" The memories of Spera and Lenya's horrible deaths flood my mind as I race forward and pin him to the ground. "Show me! Show me your true face, Asher. I know you're in there," I demand, my hands tightening around his throat.

Instead, he slowly brings his hand to my face, still clenched around the piece of paper. I read the first sentence, and my world goes still.

"Darling, Tanzy Hightower is very dangerous, and I have reason to believe that she wants me dead."

The rest of Vanessa's perfect script blurs on the page. My wide eyes move to Dr. Andrews's desperate face as my hands fly open. He tries to force a word out of his mouth, but blood trickles out instead. His wet fingers wrap around my forearm as the light fades from his frantic stare. His hand and his head drop back together as a weak, last breath leaves his lips.

A wild giggle fractures the still air. Vanessa sits up and wipes the blood from her face, a smug grin slicing her porcelain face in half.

"Vanessa?"

"Tanzy!" Lucas's voice spins me around, but he's not there. The air begins to crackle and distort. A living shadow darkens the broken doorway and then solidifies, arms and legs materializing from the quivering mass. His scarred face finally emerges. My eyes follow his shocked gaze to the blood soaking my hands.

"What have you done?"

Neither my mind nor my mouth can form a response.

"Don't act so surprised, Brother," a smooth voice answers from the hallway. We both jump at the familiar sound. Asher brushes past Lucas and moves into the room. "We made her for this, after all. She was born for this. My queen. My Vessel." He traces a perfect circle in the air between us, leaving a smoky ring in its wake. "One down. Two to go."

30
Surrounded

"CORRECTION," A TOO FAMILIAR VOICE PURRS FROM THE doorway. And with that one word, the last eight years of my life collapses.

The first day she introduced herself to me. The way my insides warmed at the fact that she didn't talk to me like I was a kid. She shook my hand and looked me square in the eye. The first time she called me Tee instead of Tanzy. The surprise birthday party she threw me in the indoor arena when I turned thirteen. That she held my hand at Dad's memorial service. That she wept for him. That she'd spent the last three years working tirelessly to do right by him. By me. The mental cloud of debris billows back over the memories, covering them with corrosive ash.

"Dana?" I have to say her name to see if she reacts, praying to whatever watches from above that she won't respond, won't recognize the name. But she does, once again staring me straight in the face. Her dark eyes dare mine to hold her gaze for a full second before she breezes past me and pulls Vanessa to her feet.

"Two down," she says.

"Dana," I repeat, barely a whisper. Lucas makes a move toward me but Asher stops him with a single hand and backs him against the wall.

"Do tell," Vanessa instructs, her voice like velvet as she strokes an ivory finger down Dana's hollow cheek.

Lucas's voice is yelling words like "run" and "get out," but they blur into the buzzing noise that fills my ears. *This can't be happening. This isn't real. Wake up, Tanzy. Wake up!*

"My queen, they pulled dear John off life support this morning. Two down, one to go."

"My queen?" I mumble. And then Dana's words reaches my brain, searing a path to its center: John. The man from the alley. Dead. No, killed. By me. *Two down.* My stomach empties its acid on the white carpet.

"Spera's efficiency is clearly transcendental. As is her surly temper. Turns out it can be put to good use though," Asher muses, smiling at the body of Vanessa's husband. "Who knew?"

"I knew," Vanessa smirks. Her ivory face twists with such fierce resentment that I hardly recognize her. I expect the new distance to be another stab of pain, but there's nothing solid left to cut. The void quakes, something hot and capable shouldering its way through the dark.

"You set me up," I say and spit the sour taste from my mouth. A first round of tears burns the backs of my eyes but I will them back.

"The good doctor had served his purpose," Asher answers before Vanessa has a chance.

"What purpose?" My voice cracks, the question coming out like a demand.

"He's the chief of surgery. Well, was," Asher says. "He was the only one who could grant me permission to save your life that terrible, terrible night."

And then he lists every piece put in motion, every trick and trap they'd set along the way. How Vanessa spotted me on the playground at my preschool in Vermont. How Dana introduced herself to my father at a horse show and told him she was looking for work.

How Asher volunteered at a local fire department and calculated the average time it would take the truck to get from the station to the barn.

The room spins, and I catch myself on the bed post.

"God, you're pathetic. This, Asher? This is what you've waited a thousand years for? You've got to be kidding me. Vanessa," I plead. "He's a monster. He's just using you."

"Right. I'm just the stand-in. The runner-up. Your substitute. Maybe the first time around, but not anymore."

"Listen to yourself! You don't even know what you're talking about. He killed Spera. He will kill me, and he'll kill you, too," I argue, practically yelling.

Her eyes darken as they move to Asher. I follow her gaze, my throat constricting as I take in the sight of Lucas trapped in Asher's hand. His mouth is still, but his eyes beg me to run. To leave him behind. *That's not going to happen.*

"Don't you dare look at Asher! He's mine, selfish girl. But your selfishness worked to our advantage. All your poor mother asked of you was to stop riding. But you couldn't give her even that, could you?" Vanessa rants, pacing back and forth. "You made it so easy." She stops and turns to face me. Her eyes lower with malice. "Didn't anyone ever tell you not to ride alone?"

She lets out a wild cackle like she's made some kind of joke. Something in her laugh triggers the memory of being chased through the woods that last night at Wildwood. Part of me already knew Asher had everything to do with that night, but I can't accept that Vanessa was there. That she had anything to do with it.

"Have you put it together yet or do I get to tell you about the fun we had chasing you through the woods that night? Although I have to hand it to you, you put up one hell of a fight. That horse has quite a kick in him. Well, had."

The memory of her leaning over me to tie my hair back in the hospital the first time we met is crystal clear in my mind. The bruises along her collar bone, the marks she'd blamed on her husband. They made a perfect horseshoe.

My eyes leap to Dana's face. *She killed Hopewell. She killed him. And she burned my father's farm to the ground.*

"Don't you just love surprises?" Vanessa smirks.

"No. You're lying. You wouldn't do that." But even as the words whisper from my lips I know they're not true.

"Still think there's hope for me? Still think you can save me, Tanzy?" she mocks and takes an angry step for me.

Dana folds her arms and watches me with an ugly expression.

"Shh." Vanessa brings a finger to her lips and closes her eyes. "Somebody still has a secret." She saunters toward Lucas.

"You touch him and I will end you." I cling to this truth, the only thing I know for sure. The only thing I've got left.

"I have no intention of harming this poor, confused creature." She reaches up and pets his scarred cheek twice before giving him a sharp slap. "But you might."

"You have lost your mind."

"Is that so?" she says more to Lucas than to me. "Because I see a secret locked inside."

Lucas's eyes plead with me over the top of her head. *What are you trying to tell me?*

"Tsk, tsk Tanzy. That's cheating. And he can't hear you anyway. He's not a mind reader. He's not much of anything really. But I bet we could still have some fun together. Don't you think so, Lucas?" She nuzzles her cheek against his bare chest and then runs a nail from his sternum to his navel, leaving a line of blood. I mask a flinch and level my glare at her green eyes.

"Just tell me, Vanessa. Go ahead. There's nothing you can say that would make me want to hurt him." Lucas is not like Asher, and never will be. I know that in my soul. And she won't be able to convince me otherwise.

"Are you so sure about that?" Dana interjects.

"Of course I'm sure." I look to Lucas's face. I want him to see what smolders within me for him. That I am sure. That I know his heart. But he won't meet my eyes. *What's wrong, Lucas?*

"Why don't you see for yourself?" Vanessa sings and grabs my hand. Instantly we are on the seldom traveled trail at Wildwood Farm, moving along the lip of the ravine.

"You don't have to show me this. I relive it every day," I say. But the girl who watched the river for hours waiting for her father to surface also believes Vanessa might still be on my side, might be trying to show me a way to save us all in this very moment. I grip my fingers around hers and stare her in the face, watching closely for any sign.

"This is how I remember that day. The first day. The beginning of everything. See it through my eyes." The view shifts down the trail forty or fifty feet, staring head on at Teague and my father as they lead the way through the overgrowth. My fifteen-year-old self follows close behind on Moonlit. She stares into the trees to her left, searching for the black apparition.

The view begins to zoom in as Vanessa slinks closer. The shapeless static jumps to the ground in front of Teague. He rears to his full height and then bolts forward. The sound of Teague gathering a stride before the lip of the ravine makes me instinctively close my eyes, but the memory plays on. He jumps, straining for the other side that he'll never reach.

My younger self tumbles from Moonlit's galloping retreat and runs toward the place they went over. Vanessa's perspective lowers as she crouches lower in the underbrush. But she's not watching my younger self. She's watching the quivering dark still visible on the trail. A human form begins to take shape in the shadow. Legs, arms, and a head emerge and solidify. The features sharpen and color fills in the void. As his face turns down the trail to Vanessa, my body goes still. *Lucas.* He takes one more step toward my grieving, fifteen-year-old self before slipping back into the cover of the trees.

I stagger away from Vanessa. Lucas's eyes search my face as my knees surrender to the crushing weight of this betrayal.

"You killed my father." It comes out in a whisper, but the words echo in my brain, banging from side to side like a battering ram.

"What are you going to do about it?" Vanessa asks in feigned sweetness.

"You can do whatever you want to him, love. I'll be happy to hold him for you. It would be so fitting for Lucas to serve as your third kill," Asher says.

His words fade as the pieces from that horrible day at last slide together. *My guide thinks Lucas changed. Even Asher thinks he changed. But they're all wrong. Lucas is still a killer. He wasn't protecting me. He was hunting. And he fed on my father. That's why they never found his body. Whatever Lucas left behind turned into earth.*

The sound of someone sobbing works its way through my thoughts and pulls me to the surface. It's me. I'm crying.

"Asher, we don't need her. I have enough of what we need from her. We have hundreds of horses to match. Tanzy even hand-picked a few, so we'll start there."

The horses ... Moonlit. I hand-delivered my beloved horse for slaughter. What have I done?

Vanessa pauses, no doubt anticipating a reaction. But I can't lift my eyes from the floor, each second heavier with deceit and failure than the last.

"Raffin is wrong. She can't possibly be the true Vessel. The Vessel is a fighter, a warrior. She will have to guard your child against every attack. Do you see her defending your child any time soon? There's not an ounce of fight left in her. She's worthless to us. To anyone." Vanessa's words deliver a pain more overwhelming than betrayal; they deliver the truth.

She's right. I don't have anything left to fight for.

Yes you do, a familiar voice skirts the farthest regions of my mind, drowning out whatever Vanessa is saying. *Fight for me. Fight for yourself.*

Spera?

We are one.

But I'm not ready. It's too much. And I don't know what to do.

I know. And you don't have to. Today is not important. But you must live to fight. Because they need you. They all do. You are the final piece. You are the only piece.

I'm not sure yet what Spera means, but I know she's right. All of these lies and tricks and effort—they are for me. A thousand years of waiting and scheming. Incredible, impossible measures taken on both sides to keep me hidden and to draw me out. They need me. And only me. No matter the cost of the past, no matter the price of what lies ahead, I am the only piece.

Vanessa says something to Asher, her perfect face now little more than that of a stranger. But I don't hear her words. I only hear the steady lub-lub of her pulse, see it rising and falling along her ivory neck. Blood courses through her veins like that of a mortal. I don't know what she is. But she can die.

In a single motion I spring to my feet, snatch her by the throat and slam her against the wall. Dana instinctively moves toward us, but I stop her with a look. And I know Asher won't attack, Lucas still captive in his hand. No one can help Vanessa now. And no one will. But if there's one thing my Origin taught me well, there is suffering far worse than the peace of death.

I bring my mouth so close to her ear that it feathers across her skin. These words are for her alone: "You're wrong, Vanessa. Asher doesn't need you. He doesn't want you. He doesn't think about you. He thinks about me. Only about me. Your blood won't open the veil. You are not the Vessel. You are not the true queen. I am. We both know that. Asher knows that. The only thing that he really needs is me. I am the final piece. I am the only piece."

I run a steady finger down her ivory cheek and pull back to look her dead in the eyes. Their jade centers are fractured with doubt and coated in glistening pain. And then, loud enough for all of them to hear, I deliver the words that Spera announces in me. A promise. A warning. The last truth either of us has left. "You're wrong about one more thing, Vanessa. This is the beginning of everything. This day, this moment, is only the beginning."

And then, I leap across the room and crash through the closest window pane. The shattering glass announces the final break as I leave them all behind.

Epilogue

LANDING IN A PUDDLE OF BROKEN GLASS AND RAIN water doesn't hurt. I thought it would. Even hoped for it. Maybe then I could assign a word to this feeling that has taken hold of me. *Dana. Vanessa ... God, Vanessa ... And...*

I can't even bring myself to think his name. I force thoughts of him aside and race across the open lawn to the cover of the trees. I glance back to the dark house, but no one has followed me out.

"You sure do know how to make one hell of an entrance. Well, exit, I guess," a voice I've never heard says from behind me. I whirl to face the sound. The adrenaline still coursing through my veins instantly makes me ready to defend myself.

"Whoa, no need. You can put those fists away," the girl says and steps from a cloak of dark shadows.

Her pale skin and white-blonde hair make her look like a ghost in the misty gray fog. The weak light filtering through the canopy of limbs stripes her face. As she steps closer she nervously tugs at a piece of her chin length hair, dyed hot pink on the ends. Her other hand clutches the faded strap of a well-worn messenger bag slung across the front of her black sweatshirt.

"Who are you? And don't even think about answering me with some kind of question or riddle. I'm all done with those."

"Jayce," she says, hands in the air. "My name is Jayce."

"That's a name. That has nothing to do with who you are."

"I'm on your side," she insists, working to keep her nervousness out of her voice. It only shakes a little.

"I'm on no one's side." I pass her to move deeper into the forest. *I am the only piece. Only. From here on out I am doing this alone.*

"But you do have a side. And we need you," she says, following close behind. I ignore her and start to run ahead. Her footsteps stop. "Fine! Make a go of it on your own. They'll find you one way or another. And if it were me, I'd want to bring just as many people to that fight as they will."

I pause and glance at her over my shoulder. I'd be foolish not to see what she knows before I take off.

"There are others like us? How many?" I ask, turning back to her.

"Probably hundreds. There's no way to know for sure." She jumps at a sound of something rustling in the trees. "Where's your Shield? I saw Lucas go in the house. Asher didn't kill him, did he?"

"No."

"He's still alive? You left him in there?"

"He's just as bad as Asher. Maybe worse. He killed my father."

"He's your Shield, Tanzy. A Contego."

"I don't care what he is. All I know is he's the reason my dad is dead," I counter.

"A Contego takes an oath of protection. It's wordy, but the gist of it is that they'll defend your life at any cost, theirs or anyone else's," she says, taking a few steps in my direction. "That day on the trail, Vanessa was waiting for you. Lucas tried to stop you guys from going any farther. He didn't know your dad would die because of it, but that's not his concern. He can only care about you."

"How do you know about that?"

"We all do. It was the beginning. For all of us. Don't you get it yet?" Her words sink in like heavy stones.

The beginning. The place my life truly began. The beginning that

Lucas had been so desperate to prevent no matter the cost. He tried to stop all of this.

"I have to go back," I whisper, tugging gently at the braided grass bracelet he had tied around my wrist. *Was that really just a few hours ago?*

"No way, chica," Jayce says and shakes her head. "Not now, anyway. We have to have the element of surprise on our side to get all of us in and out of there in one piece."

"But what if they kill him?" I can barely get the words out.

"They won't."

"What makes you so sure?"

"He's the perfect bait," she answers with a shrug. "They'll keep him alive as long as you're alive."

I can't stomach the idea of leaving Lucas with Asher, but Jayce is right. There's no way I could get him out right now.

I'm so sorry. I understand why you did what you did. I will make it up to you, Lucas. I will come back for you. I send the message to him with everything I've got, tucking my hands under my chin in prayer as I refuse to accept the staggering odds that it will never reach him.

"Don't bother, Tee. Whatever's up there isn't listening. And we don't have time to waste."

"Don't call me that like you know me. You don't know me. And this is not a 'we,'" I snap, gesturing between us.

"Oh, I know you. I know the heart of you," she says, her voice thick. Her fingers shake as she reaches toward the middle circle of my mark. "You made it quick. You didn't have to." She lets her hand drop and steps ahead of me.

Cavilla. The girl I watched Spera kill in the Origin. The girl she prayed for. With a start, I realize that the faint stripes across her face and hands don't change with the light as she moves. Cavilla's blood, the tiger's blood, has found a new home in Jayce. It takes a couple of seconds for the shock to wear off before I can follow her.

"It's Tanzy," I say and fall in step beside her. "Just Tanzy now. Please don't call me anything else."

"You got it," she says.

"How do you know all of this?"

"Because I know what it is to be Asher's queen. I know the power. And I know the price." She levels her blue eyes at mine.

"How were you his queen? You died." I almost regret the question, but the time for tact has long since passed.

"Don't you mean you killed me?" She delivers the news like a punch line, but she's the only one of us who manages to smile. "Your Origin wasn't my first rodeo. And it wasn't Vanessa's, either. She played Spera like a fiddle. And from the sounds of it, she played you, too."

"So what's to say you're not playing me now?" I fight the instinct to create distance, instead stepping closer to Jayce's lithe frame. She clearly knows what I'm capable of, and I'm going to use it to my advantage.

"I guess you're just going to have to trust me. The way I see it, you're running low on options and information. I can give you both."

"What else do you know?" I press, giving her one shot to give me something I can use.

"That no one is strong enough to stop him on her own," she says.

The worthlessness of her answer has more of an effect on me than the sudden tremble that flutters across her shoulders.

"And you really think the two of us are enough?" Agitation snips the end off each word.

"Of course not. But it's not just us. We have Hope on our side."

"That's beautiful. Really. Maybe if the world doesn't end you can go into business making warm and fuzzy cards for warm and fuzzy people," I bristle. *Hope? She thinks having hope can stop Asher?*

"I'm not talking about warm and fuzzy feelings of hope, Tanzy. I'm talking about the name Hope. That doesn't ring a bell for you?"

284 ⟨⟨⟩⟩ *Jadie Jones*

"I only know one person by that name, and trust me, that's not who you're talking about." I slam the door closed on the subject of my mother as fast as I can. I'm barely holding it together as it is, what's left of me bound together by rage and fueled with the guilt of leaving Lucas with Asher.

"You really don't know anything, do you?" she snaps, balling her fists at her sides. Part of me wishes she'd throw a punch, that she'd give me a place to release the adrenaline pouring unchecked into my veins. But a bigger part of me has already left her behind. I turn away from her and start down the hillside.

"No. I never wanted her to have to know about any of this. I had to give her a chance at a normal life." A new, haunting voice answers Jayce from the cover of the woods and stops me in my tracks.

That can't possibly be who it sounds like.

As she steps out of the trees, there's no denying it. Her features are the same. I could still trace them with my eyes closed. But she's not the same. Not at all. Her eyes are clear and bright. The lines of grief are gone, her pale skin as smooth as marble.

Jayce drops to the wet ground in a deep bow.

It takes everything I have left to summon the courage to speak that single word.

"Mom?"

Acknowledgements

Writing sometimes feels like an island, but it takes an army to get here. I am truly grateful and humbled by everyone who touched this story in some way.

First, to my husband, without whom this book would never have been possible, and to my daughter, who makes me want to push myself a little harder every day. To my parents, who instilled the values of hard work and a love of books from an early age. And to my grandparents, who have always believed that any dream is within reach.

To those who have been champions of this dream of mine—Carrie, who first made me believe I might be able to pull this off. Stephanie, who has rallied me up every hill and made me confident enough to aim for the stars. My fantastic team and fellow coaches for your support and flexibility, and the IEA organization at large for your tremendous response. Elizabeth, Jenny and Jen, who read this story a year and a hundred drafts ago, and still understood exactly what I was trying to do. And my soul sisters—Lori, Ashley, Linda, Katherine, Rachael, and Hettie.

To the incredible team at WiDō Publishing. Summer—I don't know how to thank you for everything you did for my story and for my craft. I owe you a lifetime of gratitude. You are amazing. Allie—thank you for loving Tanzy's story as much as I do, and for sending me the acceptance email that made this dream come true. Karen—your encouragement and guidance have been immeasurably helpful during this process. I am lucky to have a managing editor who is so dedicated to the satisfaction of her writers. Steven Novak, who designed one of the best covers I've ever seen—I'm so lucky to call it mine. And to each of you at WiDō who worked on *Moonlit*—summary gurus, copy editors, marketing personel, and more—I am so thankful for each and every one of you, and feel so blessed to count myself among a group of such talented people.

To the fantastic online network of writers that have offered me support and advice at every turn. Even though I have never had the honor of meeting you face to face, you all jump to help each time I ask. I am astounded by the support that I have found among this international family of writers.

And last, but certainly not least, thank you to every person who reads this book. I wrote this for you. As a child, my grandfather would sit me in his lap and weave tales about the Cherokee nation, and a girl who belonged with horses. His words painted a whole new world, and my mind would take flight. I hope that this story has done the same for you.

About the Author

GEORGIA NATIVE JADIE JONES FIRST BEGAN WORKING for a horse farm at twelve years old, her love of horses matched only by her love of books. She went on to acquire a B.A. in equine business management and worked for competitive horse farms along the east coast. The need to write followed wherever she went.

She currently coaches a hunt seat equitation team that competes in the Interscholastic Equestrian Association, and lives with her family in the foothills of north Georgia. When she's not working on the next installment of the *Moonlit* series, she's either in the saddle or exploring the great outdoors with her daughter. *Moonlit* is her first book.

CPSIA information can be obtained at www.ICGtesting.com
Printed in the USA
LVOW081253270313

326307LV00001B/82/P

9 781937 178338